D0393750

Also by Patrizia Chen

Rosemary and Bitter Oranges

It Takes Two

A Novel

Patrizia Chen

Scribner
New York London Toronto Sydney

Scribner
A Division of Simon & Schuster, Inc.
1230 Avenue of the Americas
New York, NY 10020

First Scribner hardcover edition November 2009

SCRIBNER and design are registered trademarks of
The Gale Group, Inc., used under license by
Simon & Schuster, Inc., the publisher of this work.

For information about special discounts for bulk purchases,
please contact Simon & Schuster Special Sales at 1-866-506-1949
or business@simonandschuster.com.

The Simon & Schuster Speakers Bureau can bring authors to your
live event. For more information or to book an event contact the
Simon & Schuster Speakers Bureau at 866-248-3049 or
visit our website at www.simonspeakers.com.

Book design by Ellen R. Sasahara

Manufactured in the United States of America

1 3 5 7 9 10 8 6 4 2

Library of Congress Control Number: 2009002301

ISBN 978-1-4165-7061-5
ISBN 978-1-4165-7070-7 (eBook)

To Kimball

my husband, my friend

"How vain it is to sit down to write when you have not stood up to live."

—Henry David Thoreau

It Takes Two

Volver

(To Come Around)

"Would you like to dance?"

I look at him, surprised. "Tango? I can't dance tango . . ."

He smiles, and holds out his hand to lead me to the dance floor.

I follow him.

"What should I do?"

"Let yourself go. Trust me."

"Isn't it hot in here?" I ask in an effort to cover up my feelings of inadequacy. I take in the dark room, dangling stars over my head, lights flickering. Couples slowly circling us. His arms surround me, shielding me from the others; his lips brush my cheeks; the fire of his eyes burns my skin.

Oh! He can move! and how . . .

I can't see his body but I can sense it: tall, solidly built. My hands rest on his back, touching, exploring, savoring each of his muscles.

He's incredibly musical. I look at him and move as if hypnotized. He smiles. I like him; he's friendly, not aggressive. I dance. I follow his lead.

"Wait, it's too hot . . ." he says, unhurriedly peeling off his red sweater and letting it fall to the floor near a column. I like that he's not in a rush.

"Francesca?"

"Yes?"

"Francesca . . ." He whispers again.

He takes me back into his embrace and folds me against his body. We move. The pleading sound of a *bandoneón* fills my soul and a sudden gush of notes surrounds me. I press against him, we move in unison.

We find our rhythm, forging ahead into the fierce maelstrom of tango notes, but without urgency. His mouth caresses my hair, playing with it, almost kissing, brushing my right temple. It's sweet, it's dreamy, it's slow. It's impossibly hot.

It's like the gentle rising of the tide in the Mediterranean. I begin to abandon all resistance. Maybe I am just imagining the rhythmic intensity between us. "It's a dance, just a dance," I remind myself.

But I need it so much. I need to be in a man's arms, my body yearns to follow a music I heard long ago and have forgotten for too long.

His hard-on is forced against my thigh. I stop his arm with my hand and search for his face. We don't need words. I ask myself again, is this really happening?

"You are beautiful. You are making my night . . ." he murmurs, looking at me seriously.

Who am I to stop this magic moment? I need to let myself go.

Why is my brain constantly at work? I must learn to forget all my worries, to relinquish all thought. Like a drug this dance slowly pervades my body. I reclaim my place in a man's embrace, snuggling against his chest, accepting the power of the warm circle of his arms. I want more.

I'm all liquidity—a stirring of desires. The music has become more insistent. My hips rotate, looking for his, trying to reach him, willing to submit to its sweetness. The unbearable force of this moment overwhelms me as his hands skim my back, following its curve down to the beginning of my buttocks, teasing. Something is happening, rapidly; it's beyond my control.

I let go. I abandon every restraint and surrender to unexpected waves of warmth. My body comes alive. I listen to the vibrations invading me, surging, crashing down over me like huge waves over a long-deserted island.

Adelante

(Forward)

I open my eyes and in that brief moment between sleep and wakefulness, I can't remember where I am. I scan the small room so unlike my Manhattan apartment—it's cluttered with blond wood furniture and that kind of soothing floral upholstery you'd see in the home of an old aunt—and it all comes back to me in a rush. I landed in Buenos Aires only hours ago after an overnight flight from New York. When my editor at *The Travel Magazine* had called with a desperate, last-minute plea for me to fly to Argentina to write a feature article, I thought only briefly of my life—my stale relationship with my husband, George, my grown children, all those charity luncheons and business dinners—and decided it was time for me to do something for myself, by myself. Eight hours later I was on a plane.

I yawn and stretch my arms out above my head on the large king sized bed. I slowly bring down my legs and stand up, grateful for the quick power nap that has brought me back to life. From my tall windows I can see the busy Avenida de Mayo and those stunning buildings every travel article has always promised me: elegant weather-scarred façades graced by tall, Parisian-looking windows, imposing gray shutters, turreted roofs, and heavy doors made of old wood and polished brass. The newsstand brims with

4

colorful magazines and papers from all over the world. Even from the fourth floor I can see stacks of *Il Corriere della Sera,* the Italian newspaper I'm addicted to. But of course! Didn't I read that Argentina has the biggest concentration of Italians outside of my homeland? *Fifty percent of the population* was the staggering count of the guidebook I read on the plane.

A quick glance at the clock and I realize I had better get up and get going; in an hour I'm supposed to be at Confitería Ideal, a famous tango hall and pastry shop, to meet Analia, the guide assigned to me by the magazine. I shed my cashmere sweatpants and start the shower, examining myself in the mirror as the water heats up. I may be fifty but I know I'm beautiful, in my typical Italian way: dark, wavy hair à la Sofia Loren and yes, abundant curves. My olive skin and green eyes have always been a winning combination. My Neapolitan ancestors weren't joking when they delivered me with their DNA. "When you look at me it's like I'm diving into the Mediterranean Sea," George told me years ago. Now his enthusiasm is solely dedicated to the meals I prepare for him, and those years seem like another lifetime, another's life.

How did our marriage become what it has? When was it that we stopped having sex? Where did the love go?

As I dress, I think about George and the lie our marriage has become. We had been so in love, so passionate, such great friends. What happened? How did running away to work in Buenos Aires become the answer? Our life in New York now seems like a parody of companionship; George and I, together, under the same roof, with nothing to share but our love of food, always one of our shared passions. It was George who, at the beginning of our marriage, had suggested I leap from the rarefied world of fashion to the passionate one of culinary excellence. The guests we entertained were always fascinated by the home-cooked meals I served. "You should have a weekly column in *The New York Times,*" they would exclaim, tasting a simple pasta or even a humble min-estrone. "Share your recipes with the world."

It started as a joke, nearly six years ago. A silly game that, when I look back on it now, I find neither funny nor enjoyable.

"*Spaghetti alla Matriciana,*" I had whispered over the phone when he called me from some distant European city. I was at home, in our New York apartment, and George had sounded so tired, so lonely.

"Slice an onion—a lush, fleshy onion—by slowly peeling off its gossamer, rubescent skin . . ." As soon as I heard his measured breathing at the other end of the line, I paused. I felt empowered, tickled that my words could elicit such a reaction.

Then it became a routine, each time a different recipe, my playful descriptions filling the wavelengths, crossing the ocean and reaching my husband's heart. In the still moment that pre-ceded his laughter, aroused and full of lust he would whisper: "You are something! More, more!"

How often in the past years have I longed for him to beg for me that way? I'm a mad case of mingled feelings, my thoughts and emotions are jumbled and confused, as if they were a mess of threads, tangled and knotted by some crazed kitten. I consider George's preference for this kind of gourmet seduction: food cravings have long substituted for his hunger for me.

Today, in Buenos Aires, I look out the hotel window and onto the busy street and I realize how predictable my life has become. I feel like the old *funicolare* that used to go up and down Vesuvio, carrying tourists to the top of the volcano. The monotony of that one track and that lonely red car: the same schedule, travel time, and destination—days in and days out. And one of these days I, too, might explode.

I gather my things—the necessary tools of the journalist: good shoes, a capacious backpack, pens, my camera, and lots of paper—and take the tiny elevator down to the lobby of the hotel, emerging into what seems like a crowded airport scene.

I step out into the busy streets of the city center. Turning right on Avenida de Mayo, I run into the immense Avenida 9 de Julio. Traffic is intense and the babel is staggering. Cars honk wildly at slow pedestrians, young Gypsies juggle bottles, balls, and multicolored ninepins in the middle of the street, in front of red lights. I have never seen anything like this. There is even a young man swallowing fire! The avenue is his stage and he's performing for pedestrians and drivers alike. Everyone here is on a short fuse, and the moment the light turns green the cars spring, sending him to the safety of the sidewalk. How will I ever cross this street?

It feels alive, it feels real. It somehow reminds me of places in the south of Italy—Palermo, Catania—yet the architecture seems to have been plucked straight from Paris. Glancing at the map provided by the concierge, I walk across Plaza de la República, delighted at its harmonious elegance and classic beauty. It's exactly what I expected Buenos Aires to be, but unfortunately gigantic garish billboards are plastered on the façade of most of the buildings, concealing the sophisticated ironwork and details. A striking white obelisk in the middle of the square stands out against the background of a cloudless Buenos Aires sky, like an arrow piercing the heart of the city.

My stomach tightens as an unsettling sense of déjà vu assails me; it's as if I've been here before. I'm suddenly filled with a vague presentiment, a strange fear of something I can't quite describe. I remember another day in Italy, long ago, when I felt like this. I had gone to the house of a fortune-teller. As soon as I entered the crowded, suffocating apartment in Centocelle—one of Rome's poorest quarters—the acrid smell of garlic and olive oil attacked my nostrils. A woman sat at a table with a large bowl of water in front of her. Over the water she held a thread with a pendulum; her entire body was still. She looked up and met my eyes.

"What are you doing here?" Her voice was dusty. "You are one of ours. Go away. You already know too much." The pendulum started to swing with a life of its own, rotating slowly above the water as the large drop of olive oil floating on the surface changed shape, reacting to the pendulum's hypnotic swaying. It was as disturbing as seeing a snake dance.

"What do you mean?" I answered, entranced.

"Didn't anyone tell you about your powers? You have them. You are one of ours, but you choose not to use them. Go away. You don't need me." And with that, the old woman returned her gaze to the bowl. "You'll dance. It will change your life . . . First it will rob you but then it will give back," she mumbled.

I felt as if the entire room were crisscrossed with wires; thin, transparent wires that held and paralyzed me, shutting out reason. It was the strangest sensation I had ever experienced. Trembling, I turned on my heels and left, walking shakily downstairs and then nearly running out of the building.

Sweat seeped through my blouse; I shivered. Her words meant nothing and yet they whirled through my head, aimed directly at my soul. No matter how bright, the sun couldn't take away the chill from my bones.

It was the last time I went to consult a fortune-teller. The next day I flew to Milan for a fashion shoot and then I met George. Dancing . . .

Sometimes it terrifies me when I think about how prescient the fortune-teller's words were. I first met George when I was merely eighteen and it was at La Caccia, that exclusive enclave of the Roman aristocracy. He had volunteered for a United Nations program in Italy, and his French mother had asked my parents to

introduce him to people his own age. My father invited his friends
and their children to a welcome dinner.

It was my first time at the club, in Piazza Fontanella Borghese,
smack in the center of Rome. Waiters in livery tiptoed around
the tables, silently serving impeccable food, in complete control
of the ordered chaos of the busy dining room. "Snobbiest waiters
in Rome," my mother whispered, amused, after Franco, the maître d'—his eyes as bright as his gold buttons—casually informed
her about an impending scandal. "They have worked here for
decades and know the gossip of the entire city."

Sitting up straight in my chair, I looked around at the solemn
heirs to Rome's so-called Black Nobility. Conservative dress was
the evening uniform—perfectly tailored silk suits, pleated gowns
and silk blouses, dazzling cascades of diamonds and pearls, and
hair piled up in elegant, if theatrical, chignons. My curls kept
in place by a velvet band, I wore a simple blue dress and my
grandmother's single strand of pearls: I played my part of a well-
behaved girl from a good family.

"His mother—Hélène de la Varrière—is one of my best
friends from boarding school." I heard Mamma tell our guests
about George before dinner. "She married into an old family from
Boston. You know, one of those names you find attached to the
wings of some of the greatest museums on the East Coast? New
England Brahmins!"

Flabbergasted, I looked at George, silently begging forgiveness for my mother's inappropriate remarks. He smiled back at
me, mischievously, his solemn demeanor shifting for a fraction of
a second to amusement. I blushed, averting my eyes. He was so
cute.

Six years later I met him again in Milan, when a mutual friend
thought it would be fun to see me (an assistant fashion editor) and
George (by then an aggressive banker) hit it off—or maybe hate

each other. As my friends predicted, sparks had flared all over the Nepenta, a club just around the corner from the Duomo, where our friends had convened for a night out.

"Did I hear right? You stopped working for the UN? You left behind the orphans of Burkina Faso in order to become one of the many rich, successful men of New York?" I attacked him as soon as we were reintroduced. "You were so enthusiastic about helping others . . ." I might have been giving him a hard time but I hadn't failed to notice his unconventional good looks and his quick reaction to my playful criticism.

He brushed a lock of auburn hair out of his piercing blue eyes. "It's not like you are helping humanity either . . ." He fingered the embroidered hem of my white jacket.

Silence fell between us as we danced. I let the music flow through my body, pressing my hips against George's and slowly moving to accommodate his beat. For a second he looked at me—surprised—then he, too, slipped into my world, following the rhythm, his hand holding me at the waist, gently studying each curve of my body. With him, for the first time in my life, I felt as if we were floating, riding the same wavelength of sweet notes: no one else but us, two people alone in a crowded disco.

I was wearing a pair of huge gold hoop earrings, which were supposed to enhance my Mediterranean colors. My motto has always been: Over the top; the more the merrier! That night was not an exception. Gold gives a vibrant glow to the skin, and I've always made good use of it. A Chinese top—bought at a street stand in Kowloon during a fashion assignment—completed my exotic outfit. I knew I looked cool.

"I'm going to marry you," said George, whose hand was by now familiar with every inch of my back; he had the skills of a good masseur. I laughed, of course, and burrowed into his arms, touching him, feeling his heart beat. His muscles could have inspired Donatello!

"Really?" I replied with a smile. "First prove to me that you are as interesting in bed as you are on the dance floor."

George was horrified. "Those are men's words; you can't talk like that!" In his tidy world of waspy masculinity, women seldom took the initiative. He loosened his embrace and looked at me, frowning.

But almost as suddenly, his brow smoothed again. "Will you give me children?" George's hand again pressed deeper, slowly walking down my spine to my waist, and across the fabric of my embroidered top, tantalizingly close to my breast. A delicious, warm sensation surged through me unexpectedly. He definitely knew what he was doing.

"Too many vodkas, George. Ask me again when you are sober. For the moment I don't need any promises; let's just go to your hotel and let time decide." I laughed, once again relishing the pleasure of shocking him with my sexual directness. "You behave like a boy" had always been my male friends' outraged reaction to my openness. I discovered early in the game that my confidence was an effective weapon in the difficult field of love and relationships.

Leaving behind the Nepenta and its music, we walked hand in hand through the deserted streets of sleepy Milan to his hotel, admiring squares and *palazzi,* stopping to look at La Scala, reading *le locandine,* the old-style programs hanging outside that venerable institution.

Once inside his luxurious wood-paneled suite, it was only a second before my top was unfastened and sent flying to the couch. My jeans followed, feverishly slipped down by George's impatient hands. My golden hoops got stuck in his shirt, almost tearing it, while I clumsily unfastened the tiny buttons. We both laughed, our hands greedily exploring each other's bodies.

I bent over, kissing his chest, caressing his nipples, delicately biting them, happy to watch him get harder. I surrendered to his body—lean, muscular, tanned—I wanted to give him pleasure. Even then I considered sex an art, as well as an instinct. When it comes to expressing my sexuality and satisfying my desires, I've never known barriers and I have no qualms about reminding my partner about my needs.

And so it happened. What should have been just a one-night stand transformed both of our lives, taking us by surprise, dragging us into days and weeks of passionate frenzy. Friends and family witnessed the rapid evolution of our story and its culmination—two months later—in a small wedding ceremony in Cortina d'Ampezzo, at my grandmother's house. Over the course of merely eight weeks I went from being a carefree assistant fashion editor at a major magazine to a serious wife. George's great American name weighed heavily on my shoulders, forcing me to adopt a new lifestyle.

I moved to New York and exchanged jeans for skirts, T-shirts for proper silk blouses. His impeccable mother wanted to dress me in her image: narrow Ferragamo pumps in practical colors were diplomatically handed out to me in their smart packages. No-nonsense Land's End beige chinos mysteriously found their way into my closet. But my high-fashion friends, all the designers I'd worked with, were delighted. As an accepted member of New York society, I would be their ambassador, wearing their outfits and causing a sensation at all the parties George and I attended.

And that's how I turned into a perfect housewife: I cared for the apartment, the dogs; I attended benefits; I volunteered for the best causes. I joined the Young Members Boards of several venerable institutions; and when the three children George and I had within five years grew old enough, I chaperoned them and their classmates on endless field trips.

After twenty-five years, *What are we having for dinner?* is George's daily refrain. And my cooking skills eclipse my sex appeal: food cravings have long substituted his hunger for me.

Long ago I vowed I'd never again probe the future but, from time to time, the sensation of being trapped by those invisible wires washes over me, always heralding important changes, always accurate.

As I stand at the stoplight in Buenos Aires, a knot in my stomach—that same invisible cobweb—has flooded me with the memory of the fortune-teller's premonition. I take a deep breath and banish the thought from my mind. I cross the street and continue on my way, swearing inside, trying to sweep away any lingering uneasiness.

I turn into Suipacha, a narrow and somber street in the heart of Buenos Aires. The brilliant day has abruptly receded behind the dilapidated buildings and a gray shadow has fallen over the city.

There! Confitería Ideal. The letters emblazoned on the two medallions at the side of the entrance reassure me; I made it. Standing on Suipacha, I admire the corner building graced by an ornate marble framework and walk through the imposing wooden door, straight into a classic turn-of-the-century patisserie: dark wood furniture, an uneven floor, and elaborate chandeliers. I inspect the famous Argentinean specialties—*dulce de leche, almendrado,* and *flan*—arrayed behind a long window. From behind the glass counter, bored waitresses look at me with uninterested expressions on their faces. A skylight outlined in intricate wrought iron casts a dusky, melancholy light on an immense dance hall. Floor-to-ceiling pillars interrupt the open space, creating the impression of different areas; elaborate mirrors and an ornate boiserie decorate the walls. It all speaks of sadness and past splendor. "*Sombra y nada más* . . . Shadow and nothing more . . ." Poignant notes float down a spiral staircase. The voice of a woman with the typical nasal twang of 1920s love songs envelops us. There couldn't be a better place to sit down and celebrate my first day in Argentina.

"La Señora Rivabuona?" Hearing my family name—and professional byline—I turn around. An attractive young girl, thin as a rail, looks at me expectantly; she holds a blue paper file in her hands. Long dark hair, almond-shaped eyes, and a strong nose give character to her narrow, lively face.

"*Sí,* it's me. And you must be Analia?"

What a smile! It lights up her face; her large, sensuous lips curl up playfully to reveal the whitest of teeth. If she were taller, she could be a model. A tight black sweater, dark gray slacks, and a funky pair of purple suede boots give her the look of a cool elf.

"Great! This is going to be good. I can already tell. Come, let's sit down and plan our days." I'm relieved that my Argentinean contact is such a lovely girl.

Analia crushes down on a chair, tucking her legs underneath her, like a child. Her slacks fold in creases around her ankles, emphasizing the fragility of her body. She launches into a conversation, in heavily accented English; smiling broadly, she promises to be available every morning of the upcoming week.

"I'm sorry, but I have rehearsals in the afternoon; my new show begins soon." She's a professional tango dancer and moonlights as a guide only when someone pays her as generously as *The Travel Magazine* is doing. Tango is a difficult way of making a living and it will take some time before she can earn enough money by just dancing. If ever, she confesses.

"*Que querés ver?* What would you like to see, exactly?" She spreads a big map of Buenos Aires on the wooden table in front of us. In a yogalike pose, she folds her torso over her legs to better show the position of the hotel, a tiny dot, smack in the center of this huge city.

Food, shopping, dancing, entertainment. Typical components for any travel piece, but Clarissa, my editor, has also made a specific request: I am to investigate the rumored link between tango and plastic surgery. Clarissa has a hunch that there are several new and inexpensive packages being offered to foreign tourists. A traveler in the know can find a surgeon and perfect their tango steps in one trip! I want to find out about these packages; it could be a clever twist to my article and would surely appeal to a certain section of our audience.

"Tell me," I ask Analia. "Is it true that people—women and men—come here to get all kinds of plastic surgery? Apparently with the depreciation of the peso, more people can now afford a tango-surgery package. They come, get done, and a few tango classes are thrown in for good measure."

Analia shakes her head in disbelief. She has never heard of anything like this.

"Can you imagine someone enduring hours and hours of travel only to have surgery instead of a vacation?" Analia wonders innocently. "Why would tango be part of their plans?"

"Well, it's kind of cool to tell people that you are going to take tango classes for a week, ten days. When you come back all your friends will associate your good looks with the endorphins produced by dancing and no one will think about your former wrinkles."

"*Bueno*. You know what? Tonight I'm going to take you to Canning. It'll be your best introduction to the world of Buenos Aires—a certain part of it anyway—and I'll explain all about tango. Surgery will have to wait, at least for today." Analia seems used to foreign tourists who flock to Argentina to observe the locals and pick up some steps of their own. "You should start by taking a walk around here," she said, pointing to the neighborhood nearest the little dot of the hotel on the map. *"El Microcentro."*

As our *café con leche* is brought to the table, Analia explains the *milonga*.

"Not only is it the name of a particular kind of dance—a sort of fast, happy tango—but it also designates the places where tango is danced. There are hundreds of *milongas,* all over Buenos Aires, some famous and crowded and some more modest, yet maybe closer to the heart of the people's tango."

There's a special *milonga* for each day of the week. Dancers will tell you that if it's Tuesday, it's Canning; if it's Friday, then Club Gricel is a must. There is no reason to show up at a *milonga* before midnight unless you are a real tourist.

"What time does it close, then?"

"Oh, four or five in the morning . . ." Analia shrugs, matter-of-fact. "Why not go back to the hotel now, and you can rest until ten. I'll pick you up later for a bite somewhere interesting. We should be at Canning by one a.m. Not before!"

I walk out of Confitería Ideal—once again alone in a foreign city, I take stock of my solitude—and begin to retrace my steps back to my hotel, the Castelar. I seem to be surrounded only by happy couples; they stroll arm in arm, laughing, kissing; knowing smiles light up their features. Could it be possible that everyone here leads a satisfied married life? Maybe it's just me and my paranoia. Once, years ago when my period was late, I was so terrified that it felt like I saw nothing but pregnant women on the streets. Today I'm experiencing the same feeling: these countless happy couples mock me and the shambles of my marriage.

I shake my head, trying to think straight. I need to clarify my thoughts, fix my life. But how?

As I push through the rush-hour crowd, I'm plagued by the same unanswerable question: Do other couples continue to have sex after twenty-five years of marriage? Do they still *do* it? I've never asked my friends, too afraid of exposing my flank to speculation. Everyone looks so happy, so *together* when I see them at the various cocktail parties and galas George and I are always attending. Can I possibly be the only unsatisfied wife? Maybe it's just me: eager, hopeful, needy, desperate Francesca. I've become a body starved of physical sensations. But the longing, the desire is still there, together with memories and regrets. The more I try to understand, the worse it is. Maybe I should just resign myself and thank God for what I have, but deep inside there is something that says: "I want more from life." Should I listen to that persistent voice?

I try to concentrate on the last few days in New York, a weekend that had started and evolved just like any other, an uneventful stretch of hours, a travesty of amity. My husband: a double-barreled belly and enough chins to match the Roman numeral after his aristocratic surname: George Farrington-Rhoads, the Third. Thank God for my editor's phone call. It injected some novelty in my life.

George, George, George, my obsession. Do I still love him? Too much ambivalence in my heart, too much confusion. I don't even remember exactly when it happened, but sex, the desire for real sex, got lost somewhere in George's brain. Now it's history, a youthful indulgence, something from the past. Somehow his sensuality shifted toward the worldly realm of gourmet specialties, of refined wines to be drunk in the religious silence of someone's cellar. His approach to the other sex, the pleasure he finds in admiring a beautiful woman's body or perfect lineaments, is that of an art connoisseur.

Our sex life ended imperceptibly slowly. I can't remember a specific date, a time, it just did, together with the companionship that came with it. George left me behind, and I am alone in my frustrations, my longings. For him, I am about as attractive as an amoeba: no shape, no fleshliness, no sex appeal. A few years after we stopped having sex, our spaghetti lovemaking began, which gave me hope and led me to believe that there might still be a spark of passion between us. But after only a couple more years of that, George finally admitted one day that he wanted nothing from me other than my culinary skills.

"Francesca, I'm not really interested in continuing an active sexual life," he told me. Just like that, addressing me with as much tenderness and concern as he would use with one of the associates at his bank, our physical relationship came to an end. "If—or when—you find someone to fill that void, please don't let me know about it. Only, dear, don't fall in love. That I could not accept. It would destroy me forever." That was it. All the passion, the pleasure we had once taken in each other, the three children we share, all gone; dismissed by a matter-of-fact conversation over dinner. Silent and ashamed, I tried to hide the tears streaming down my cheeks.

Was it me? What had I done wrong? Had I forgotten how to arouse a man? Was I old? Or was he too busy, worried about his work, plagued by too many business problems? *U' cazzo non vuole pensieri,* say the Neapolitans—anxiety is not an aphrodisiac.

And so I was left to my own devices, a freedom I never asked for. When our intimacy became an embarrassment, I moved to the guest room at the other end of the apartment. I could feel George's eyes scrutinizing me coldly as if he were judging me. It has been difficult to accept this change, to witness his once full-blooded sexuality metamorphose into complete indifference. Eight long years of drought are too much for any woman to endure.

Cooking is my best way out. As much as it hurts for George to have replaced me with his culinary ardor, food has become a sort of salvation for me as well. Cooking relaxes me, it allows for long moments of silence, when my fingers take on their own life and do all the work, and my brain disappears into a different world. It's conducive to better writing, and decision making. And, for just a while, I can forget about my solitude, George, and our failed relationship.

As a food and travel writer, I'm one of those people who can expound on the marvels of "the best pasta recipe, the best restaurants, the most luxurious and little-known hotels around the world." Aside from my children, professional successes are the only pleasure left in my life and they provide a much-needed diversion to my monotonous daily routine. It's no wonder I jumped at the opportunity to come to Buenos Aires, last-minute though it may have been. I needed to escape. I needed to throw myself into my work. I needed to think about my failed marriage and try to find a way to either recapture the flame or move on; leaving behind the life George and I had built together.

Boleo

(A Whip)

Así se baila el tango,
sintiendo en la cara,
la sangre que sube a cada compás,
mientras el brazo,
como una serpiente,
se enrosca en el talle,
que se va a quebrar.

"Así se baila el tango"

t exactly 10:00 p.m. Analia barges into my room, carrying with her a whiff of the freezing winter air. And to think that it's June!

"Analia! What should I wear? God! Jet lag doesn't really help." I complain loudly at my own reflection and reach for my makeup.

She laughs and emphatically suggests, "Black!" The tango color par excellence and the easiest way out, even in Buenos Aires. In a skimpy coat, a purple crocheted cloche pulled over her eyebrows, she's a figure from an Erté drawing.

"You must try some typical Argentinean dishes. I'm going to take you to one of the best meat places in town, La Cabaña."

Her eyes sparkle with anticipation as she briefs me. By now I'm ravenous.

The taxi cuts through the traffic, leaving behind the busy section of *el Microcentro* and climbing up to Recoleta, the exclusive area and the city's richest sector.

"This is where the millionaires live," says Analia. "Everyone here is blond, their children go to English schools and they play rugby instead of soccer."

A clear line of demarcation separates Recoleta from the area around the Hotel Castelar. It's like the difference between whispering and yelling. Quiet streets, lined with sophisticated boutiques—at this time of night already closed—are the same the world over. I squash my nose against the windows: even here money, lots of money is needed to afford the items behind them. We walk slowly along Posadas to Rodriguez Peña, checking out the stores full of extravagant fur coats, diamond-encrusted belts, high-heeled boots, and expensive jewelry.

We turn a lonely corner opposite Patio Bullrich and enter La Cabaña, which seems like a combination of Boeucc—one of my favorite restaurants in Milan—and the Post in New York, with a wink to a perfect gaucho fantasy. White tablecloths, dark wood paneling, middle-aged waiters, and a bread basket that is an open invitation to binge. The large-lettered menu doesn't disappoint either: it's exactly what I expected from my first Argentinean meal. "An Atkins diet paradise!" I jot on a piece of paper as I assess the knife I've been given. It's as big and sharp as a machete, a perfect weapon to attack the oversized steak in front of me.

Analia and I bond over the impossible task of clearing our plates as we begin to strategize about the next days: so much to see and report, so little time.

"And now your tango education. Are you ready?" Analia

moves her chair back. We are about to jump into a night of *música* and *milongas*.

"Two pesos for your future . . . only two pesos." Outside the restaurant a dark-skinned girl grabs my hand and pulls me toward her. I shake my head, loosening her grasp as she calls out, "You'll leave your past behind. Watch out. You'll dance and your soul will be carried away . . ."

Analia ignores the woman and hails a cab.

"Canning, 1331 Scalabrini Ortiz, *por favor*." Analia—shimmying over the seat to make room for me—urges the driver: "Quickly, please."

My black skirt brushes against my suntanned legs. How strange to wear boots in June! I tighten my down jacket to shut out the penetrating cold that has started to get to me. Maybe it's jet lag, maybe it's exhaustion, but I'm determined to explore the local nights. Fatigue can wait.

It's already past midnight, but here I am, running around wintry Buenos Aires in a beat-up taxi instead of going to bed. Suddenly George creeps into my evening, looming larger than life, reclaiming his presence inside my brain. What is he doing right now? Drinking his usual nightcaps? A well-aged whisky? Maybe he's listening to his beloved Bach. Why am I thinking longingly about him? He doesn't deserve it. While I know that resolving to dismiss him would simplify my life, I can't help but still have feelings for him. Distance can play tricks, and I wish we could rekindle our old passion. Why can't I just leave him behind? How disconcerting to find out that I still care. In New York I'm used to our life—so together and so disconnected at the same time. I've accepted the pattern. But here? Here it all feels different.

We stop in a large street crowded with double-parked cars and well-dressed people getting out of taxis. At one in the morning this city looks as alive as New York at rush hour. Analia and

I walk through a modest entrance onto a long corridor; a sort of senior citizens' club, an after-work meeting place. Ugly tiles, narrow hall—thousands of flyers advertising all kinds of get-togethers—tables piled with leaflets, pamphlets, photographs. I'm fascinated. Glasses balanced on my nose, I peer at pictures of famous tango dancers and scan ads offering sexy-looking outfits and dramatic accessories. I need one of each for my wardrobe!

At a narrow table near the glass doors, a lady sells entrance tickets: four pesos each, little more than one dollar. Her hair, featuring prominent dark roots, is in dire need of a good stylist, I think wickedly. All over the world, salt-and-pepper roots, the sprouting of straw-colored hair, signals a woman having reached a certain age.

Everyone embraces Analia and spontaneously stamps a generous kiss on my cheek. Argentina is the place for immediate friendship.

A ramshackle glass door leads to the *milonga*. The place is jam-packed with loud people and cigarette smoke, and the soul-stirring, blazing tango music assails my senses. Black—interrupted only by red and gold accents—unifies the crowd. A heavy potpourri of different perfumes and staccato, brisk notes mixes with the whispering that accompanies the beginning of every tango. Unable to take in the entire scene at once, I stand still, letting it wash over me. I'm used to assessing a situation within seconds but at Canning I feel unexpectedly helpless.

"*Disculpe!* Sorry!" A blinding smile, a hand lightly touching my shoulder, and an extraordinarily good-looking young man passes on my right. For a second I meet his shining eyes. Then he is gone, lost in the crowd.

The people sitting at the tables around the edges of the large, perfectly square ballroom are drinking, chatting, watching. Analia pulls my arm and I follow her through an ocean of bobbing heads to a table directly at the center of the first row. She introduces me to Yoli, a short, pudgy woman in her late sixties, who gives me a cold once-over.

"*Hola*. Welcome to the *milonga*." Her eyes project no warmth and her red lips part in a caricature of a welcome, before her attention is diverted by the others at her table. As the evening's well-known organizer, she wears a tight, low-cut red dress with black satin inserts. A few generous slits—which almost reach her crotch—show a pair of remarkably good-looking legs. Yoli is a Buenos Aires icon, a famous dancer with her own school and the attitude of a Hollywood star.

Analia is her protégée, and her beauty and talent attract much attention and many compliments. No one cares about me, not even after Analia's introduction. The jaded dancers and their groupies don't give a damn about my being a journalist or the fact that I'm covering the city for an important magazine. That's a refreshing change! Everyone goes on chatting in Spanish about families and friends, mentioning other dancers' engagements and occasionally discussing a couple parading in front of our table.

Tonight, though, being a nonentity is a plus, since it means I can focus freely on the room. Each of the dancing couples looks entranced, as if some weird spell has been cast. They drift effortlessly in complete silence, eyes closed, profiles joined in solemn intensity. The women seem to melt into their partners' bodies. The music infuses the room with its dream harmony, filling it with the voluptuousness of its notes, conveying a desperate longing for love and passion.

Love and passion. Will I ever feel them again? I look at the couples and envy their closeness, their embrace, their bodies enjoying an effortless intimacy.

The traffic on the dance floor moves in two well-patterned rings, the outside circle for the really good dancers, the inside for the less skilled. They slowly revolve around the room, seemingly lost in each other's pleasure. I'm riveted by their rapt expression. What must it be to let go like this, listening only to the feelings elicited by passionate tango notes?

A couple of young dancers—in their early twenties—pepper up their tango with a flourish of movements as they turn to the left of our table. They sail through the crowd—emphatically marking the beat by adding rapid, staccato leg accents, up and around like a whip lashing through the air. Are they trying to show off in front of us? But no, the outside world doesn't exist for them, the girl's slender body leans forward, her forehead buried into his cheek, her eyes closed. They are both lost in some kind of dream.

I arch my brows in a silent entreaty for enlightenment, desperately trying to engage Analia's interest.

"*Boleos.* Those are *boleos.* One of the most distinctive and difficult movements in tango. Too many people do it badly. The secret is in letting it go." Yoli, the grande dame of Buenos Aires tango nights, explains to me.

When I was younger I used to go dancing at the *balere,* the typical ballrooms in Italy, but this is different. I've never witnessed anything like it. A *milonga* feels more like a place of worship; its atmosphere more like a temple than a nightclub. Everyone is so serious. Do they ever laugh? And yet the electricity of the place, the magnetism between the couples is palpable, and exciting.

I skim the room, stopping at each table, checking every patron. The first row is occupied by men and women of every age and nationality. They sit watching the dancers, clearly relishing the scene. Blond hair and excessive weight give away the women's foreign origins, while the men are betrayed by their loose shirts and trousers: Americans! A large group of Japanese cluster together, cameras flashing as bright as their smiles, heads bowing imperceptibly. Hats, glasses, and bags pile up tidily on their tables. Their dancing is precise, each difficult step scientifically performed.

"Did you notice the pattern?" Analia asks. "The DJ plays a string of four or five tangos—*una tanda*—and you are bound to dance them all with your partner. If you stop and go back to your seat, you better realize that he'll never ask you again unless you have a good excuse for quitting before the end of the set."

"So many rules! So, if I were a man and wanted to test a new partner, I might then invite her at the beginning of the third song, right?"

"So you can get rid of her after a short time without losing face! You are a quick study, *querida* Francesca." The system is transparent, even to a newcomer.

Three or four fifty-something women sit drinking *sidra,* the local sparkling cider—*el champagne de los pobres.* And there he is! The young man with the shining eyes I briefly noticed at the entrance, standing among the group of Americans. Dark-haired and slender, he wears a bored expression, gazing into space as if he were not really in the room. It's hard to turn away from the curious setup, and I discover that I am ogling them without restraint. Very rude of me. But how fascinating they are: Why would such a gorgeous man surround himself by many middle-aged women?

From time to time the young man asks one of his companions to dance. Even I, the tango novice, can see that he isn't at all engrossed in his partner. After all, I am used to Manhattan clubs; I know when someone invites me out of duty and when real pleasure is involved. I lean over and shamelessly zero in on the group. Does he know how to tango? He seems skilled, but his movements are automatic and passionless, his eyes wide open. He holds his partner perfunctorily, his attention somewhere else, gazing over the crowd. He performs a few clever steps without any obvious joy; not once does he look engaged or moved. He glides around the floor ever so slowly, as if he has distanced himself from any deep emotion.

The contrast between his attitude and that of the others is conspicuous. The cheerful ladies at the table seem oblivious to his peculiar behavior and continue to laugh, drinking to one another's health. Tango after tango, the young man dutifully leads his companions through the steps.

"Analia, who's that guy?" I point at the table.

"Do you mean the guy in black? With the tight jeans? That's Luis, a tango dancer who now lives in New York and often brings groups of his students here. "

"Those women are his students?"

"You do realize that by now Argentina practically survives on the tango industry, right?" She launches into her subject excitedly. "At least sixty percent of the tourists coming to Buenos Aires from all over the world are here to improve their skills or just learn their basic steps. Once hooked, hooked forever. Tango is a disease. Watch out!"

"Is he good?"

"One of the best!"

"I wouldn't be able to tell. He looks so bored and detached."

"Well, trust me."

Now I turn back to Luis and his table. His cold mask has disappeared and he's laughing with the group as cameras flash. The white of his teeth lights up his features—his smile transforms his face completely and I get glimpses of a seductive inner life. But, wait. I suddenly recognize the petite woman proprietarily holding his arm. Putting on my glasses, I see that she's a friend from home.

"Ellie Goldberg!"

Maybe I'm so tired that I'm dreaming, but no! It is Ellie! What is she doing here? As I consider elbowing my way through the crowd between us to say hello, Luis gets up and adjusts the collar of his black shirt; even the simplest of his movements is smooth and fascinating. For a moment he stands still, like a dark bird of prey, then he comes straight to our table, his eyes on Analia. The happy notes of a quick tango *milonguero*, "Muñeca brava," bubble into a crescendo, a silk skein rippling through the room.

Standing just in front of our table, Luis and Analia look deeply into each other's eyes, already separated from the crowd, lost in another world, and Ellie is momentarily forgotten. I hold my breath and straighten up in my seat to watch them. A brief pause—then Luis takes Analia into his arms and starts dancing. His head brushes hers as he holds her close, his right hand pressing tight in the small of her back. She moves in unison with him, her torso performing a slow, rolling movement, emphasizing each note; her legs, completely abandoned to his will, stretch behind her, interpreting the music. Her feet occasionally tap the floor in quick, short movements, marking the beat and embroidering her tango with intricate accents. Both keep their eyes shut; their lips almost touch.

The detached look I had seen on Luis's face earlier has vanished. He dances gloriously.

I can't keep my eyes off them. I envy the way her body answers his requests—like a conversation in which he controls the dialogue but she has the privilege of responding.

I'm watching an incredible exchange. Is it sexual? Certainly it's almost disturbingly sensual. Slowly, a longing begins to creep in, grabbing me, knotting my stomach. I've never experienced such a reaction to a social dance. Salsa, swing, waltz: I tick off the various dances I know. But nothing has ever involved me at this powerful, intimate level.

It must be the *bandoneón*, the sound of someone crying his

soul out. My soul? Maybe I'm not as numbed as I thought I was. All kinds of feelings I believed were forever dormant resurface, overwhelming me. What have I missed in the past years?

I watch Luis and Analia stretch the final notes of the last tango, suspending them in rarefied sensuality, playing the silence with the stillness of their embrace.

George's arms holding me, his lips running up my neck, nibbling at my ears, his tongue suddenly filling my mouth. We, too, used to dance. That's how we met. Why am I still thinking about him? I'm painfully aware of how much I ache for all I've lost. And once again I ask myself: Where did I go wrong? How did I end up in such a desperate corner? I feel isolated, lost.

"The two of you dance as though you are in love," I tell her as soon as she sits down next to me. Having witnessed such an expression of intimacy and raw passion, I feel very close to Analia, as if I've known her and Luis all our lives.

Analia's laugh is lighthearted. "Luis?" She looks at me pensively. "No, not Luis."

After one of his nights of duty, Luis needs to restore his skills by sharing a few tangos with her. "Dancing is like a language, right? Easy to forget, and so easy to relax into the usual mistakes . . ." I laugh. "He must be like all my American friends, who claim that after some time with me they lose their English and start adopting my Italian phrases."

I scout the room, taking in the scene. I want to understand as much as possible about tango on my first night out. The dress code is intriguing in its variety: the gentlemen wear anything from business attire to jeans and T-shirts, while the ladies' clothes range from smart pastel-colored suits to evening gowns and transparent fripperies. The flimsy petticoats they favor expose all kinds of cellulite; their thick arms and shoulders quiver with extra flesh. Daring décolletés offer countless examples of the law of gravity, but nobody cares. Is the ability to dance the most important quality here? If so, I've finally found a place where good looks don't automatically equate with sex appeal.

I notice that men get up and invite ladies seated directly across the ballroom from them. No one ever refuses to dance. Is there a code? Or are tango dancers a particularly kind group of people? "How do they know that their invitation will be accepted?" I ask the table of connoisseurs.

"There is a system! And an infallible one at that. It goes like this . . ." Analia's years of dealing with foreigners helps her to answer quickly.

"The lady looks across the room and focuses on a gentleman she thinks would be a good dance partner. Once she has attracted his attention, he responds by arching an eyebrow and moving his head in suggestion. It's called *el cabeceo,* and that's his formal invitation to dance. The lady nods her acceptance and the gentleman knows that he won't be refused. A sure bet."

The music continues to play its melancholy, yearning tunes, interpreted by the dancers. Poignantly rapt in each other, they share tango and its suggestive lyrics, moving together to express something mysterious, something only they seem to understand. I shift uneasily on my chair; I envy them.

Tango, a sorrowful thought which is danced. Whose definition was that? I think of my father, who loved and collected popular music. I grew up listening to turn-of-the-century tunes, and now, in Buenos Aires, those notes finally come alive. This music isn't just something shelved in my memory, it's a reality, a pleasure shared.

My body begins to thaw at the sound of the music; my eyes glitter with tears. It's difficult to continue the conversation without crying. Damn it! I'm an adult. What's happening to me? Is

it nostalgia? I am miles away from my own country and yet this
place makes me think about home, my parents, my family.

> *Fue un ensueño de dulce amor,*
> *horas de dicha y de querer.*

"What's this song called? Papá sang it all the time!"

Analia, deep in conversation with her friends, is unaware of
the powerful emotions stirring within me. Yoli, on the other hand,
quietly checks my reactions and realizes that, once again, Buenos
Aires has done its damage, captured another soul.

"'Poema,' a good, old song . . ." She sighs.

I feel short of breath. Tango has just kidnapped my heart and
hit me like a thunderbolt thrown by some mischievous god. I wish
I could be in the arms of someone who loves me; I wish I could
translate my feelings into these intricate steps. I want desperately
to belong, to settle into someone else's rhythm, our two bodies
turning into one, fused by the power of this music. Instead, I feel
old, alone and discarded. Maybe it's my fault I haven't been able
to keep George's interest. Our life together has become nothing
more than a routine.

Yoli watches me silently. She's seen the longing; somehow
she's recognized my solitude and neediness.

"Would you like to try? You could come to my house tomorrow and see if you are interested or not."

Analia is excited at the prospect. "It would be great for your
article if you could get firsthand experience of something you are
going to write about. Yes! Take a class and you will understand so
much more." She elbows me to accept.

I shake myself out of my daydreams and reach in my bag for
my organizer, skimming through the week's appointments. Why

not? I can free one hour. But will Yoli be able to help me with my research into the connection between plastic surgery and tango?

Her stunned look betrays her ignorance of such an extraordinary idea. Why would anyone fly so many hours in order to be in a clinic, so far from friends and family?

"Think about it!" I point out how convenient it would be for a swollen-faced lady to escape the inquisitive eyes of doormen, coworkers, relatives, or acquaintances by going to a foreign country to have surgery.

Yoli's uninterested shrug shuts down any further prying.

Ellie has disappeared. Her table is empty and I didn't have time to ask Luis. My eyes are heavy with fatigue, and now it's me dragging my guardian angel, Analia, out of the *milonga*. Some of the couples are leaving too. Women tidy up their hair with their hands, men straighten their ties, holding the ever-present cigarette. It's such a peculiar mix of old and modern styles, with a surprisingly high number of young people wearing jeans. The older couples stick with a more formal look.

Before coming to Argentina, I had bought into the general idea of tango as an old-fashioned dance and I'd never imagined that young people would do it. Rudy Valentino's fault, of course. A rose in the teeth, black patent leather shoes, and lots of feathers—this is the familiar imagery associated with tango. Now I realize how little I really knew.

"Analia!" Luis emerges from nowhere and folds her against him, kissing her. He looks into her eyes, brushing her lips with his fingers. Up close he's even more handsome. I study him openly, with the brazenness allowed by my age. The unsuspecting object of my profound interest for the past couple of hours is in front of me, a character from my own private movie who has suddenly come to life. He even kisses *my* cheek!

His cohort of ladies approaches, smiling. "I can't believe it!"

Ellie and I hug in disbelief at the idea of meeting outside a *milonga* in Argentina.

"What are *you* doing here?" we both exclaim at the same time. I've met her only at social occasions in New York, but I've always liked her. Kindhearted and witty at the same time, with her what you see is what you get, but beware of Ellie when her eyes begin to twinkle. She's bound to burst forth with something outrageous.

"I didn't know you danced tango!" Ellie's impeccably cut hair swings around her slender neck; she's perfectly made up. Even standing straight on her high heels she barely reaches my shoulders, but she's so easygoing and bubbly that she lightens up a room with her presence.

Before I can answer, Analia interrupts. "If we keep standing here you'll collapse. Back to the Hotel Castelar, at once!"

"We are staying at the same place! Let's share a taxi," Ellie proposes.

A quick farewell and we are gone, into the Buenos Aires night, leaving Luis and Analia behind. I can't help but turn around. There they are, holding hands, leaning into each other. Analia's head is on his shoulder. Something is going on there.

"It's not what you think," says Ellie, watching me. "Are you going to take classes here?"

But I can't reply. My eyes are playing tricks by now and my lids simply refuse to lift. Argentina is heavy duty. I'll definitely have to suggest endurance training for prospective visitors to this country!

All kinds of strange thoughts flit through my semiconscious mind. I would love to seize them, if only to analyze them later. But I feel so drugged. I can't concentrate. For a moment, the afternoon's silvery wires reappear to trap me, lightly, but I'm too tired to worry. The taxi is warm and comfortable and I let myself go, resting my head on Ellie's shoulder.

Apertura

(Opening Step)

*T*he coffee is good in Buenos Aires, but have you tried their croissants?" Dressed simply in jeans and a sweater and brandishing *La Nación,* Ellie looks and sounds like an expert *porteña,* a real local. "Ask for *medialunas de grasa,* you'll see . . ."

I'm in the hotel dining room, typing up my first impressions on my faithful laptop. Already I feel overwhelmed. Maybe because the red button on my room phone keeps glaring at me, reminding me to check my mailbox? George must have tried to contact me several times but I'm still too upset and confused to do anything about it. The bright morning light has dispelled the romantic feelings I felt last night and now I'm just sad for all that George has done to me, yet a strange longing still fills my heart. Maybe this distance will do us good . . . Maybe he'll miss me.

"How *do* they manage?" I wonder aloud. It's emotionally and physically exhausting living this *tanguera* life.

"Manage to do what? Coffee? Croissants? Late nights?" Ellie laughs and sits down next to me at the breakfast table. "Have you ever danced tango?"

"No, but I love dancing. Many years of ballet classes in Rome and now lots of swing in New York, but that has nothing to do with tango. Unfortunately!"

"Ballet?" Ellie perks up. "That qualifies you immediately to try some classes. Ballet is usually the highway to tango proficiency. I wish I had the same advantage. Instead, I've been dancing tango for quite a while and here I am, still fighting to find a good style of *walking*."

Ellie comes from New York to Buenos Aires twice a year to improve her dancing—in March, during the International Tango Festival, and again in the early summer. For her as for many others, tango has become an obsession; it devours her days and fills her life with a passion she hadn't imagined she could feel as a single woman. Unmarried, she runs a well-known jewelry business inherited from her family.

"My theory? Look around and you'll see how many men and women in their fifties and sixties are taking classes here. They come from all over the world and dedicate five to six hours *minimum* per day to study under the best local instructors. I think tango is the greatest palliative for the middle-age blues . . . It's so difficult and frustrating that it makes you forget all about wrinkles and hot flashes."

"Great selling point! I might really need to dance tango then. But now I've got to ask you something which has nothing to do with the article."

"Shoot!"

"I want to hear about Luis. He intrigues me. What's the story there? And what about Analia?" I'm too polite to ask why Luis didn't really want to dance with Ellie and her friends. Maybe the indirect approach will reveal the answer. I know I'm being nosy, but Ellie and I have already found such an easy rapport that I'm sure she won't mind my question.

"First of all, last night Luis was tired and cranky after an entire day of rehearsals. Besides, he's gay."

"Gay? That's a surprise! I would never have thought so. He's so sexy!"

"What's the difference? Gay men are sexy; and it doesn't stop them from touching a woman's heart."

Luis teaches at Dance Studio, one of the best schools in New York. He performs and travels around the world and organizes events twice a year that take him and his faithful groups of students to Argentina and other countries. The world's fascination with tango has enabled him to turn an art form into a lucrative career. Now that he's about to star in a new show here in Buenos Aires, his students have come from all over the world.

Ellie has taken classes with him for more than three years and follows him wherever he goes. Their relationship transcends the dance, and she's now selling her gold and silver "Tango Line" on the web, accompanied by Luis's languid pictures and provocative video.

Ellie's fun and smart, and a precious source of information. Her tango theory fits in with my own interest in cosmetic-surgery-cum-tango-classes, but when I ask her directly she shrugs her shoulders; she's never heard anything so peculiar. Somehow, though, it makes sense. Why not? She stops midsentence and frowns, her dark eyes narrowing.

"Well . . . have you ever met Isabel Alexanders in New York? The Queen of Benefits? I'm sure I saw her sitting at the back at the *milonga* last night. She didn't see me, or at least pretended not to. And—she was wearing sunglasses. Inside the room! At night!"

"Who is she?"

Ellie explains that Isabel is married to one of the Masters of the Universe—as Tom Wolfe would dub him—and is one of the most prominent American socialites, a gossip-column fixture without the need for a publicist. She has finally reached the Olympus of social prominence, as she's about to give her name to a new wing of Sloan-Kettering Hospital. Her appearance in Buenos Aires, if it was really her at the *milonga* last night, is interesting. Is there a party requiring her august presence? Is she here for business? She's both a shrewd entrepreneur and a magnet for fluffy articles.

But right now this doesn't interest me in the least. Why would I want to hear about a New York socialite? I reach for one of the *medialunas* in the basket in front of me. Ellie is right: their flaky dough is to die for.

So much to do. The first day of an assignment feels terribly overwhelming.

"Will Analia be on time?" Ellie considers the affinity between youth and sleep.

"She'd better be. I'm not here to spend time in the *milongas*. I'm here to work. And by the way: How does Analia fit into the picture? I thought they looked more than friendly last night." Like a Jack Russell terrier, I persist until satisfied. But Ellie won't bite, at least not for the moment.

"Well, you won't be able to separate tango from your research. Tango is an intrinsic part of this city. Take some lessons and don't feel guilty about it. You should also do some shopping! Stick with me and I'll introduce you to the best boutiques in town. Manolo Blahnik would be jealous. The shoes here cost a fraction of the price. See for yourself!"

Balancing a croissant in one hand and jotting down notes with the other, I consider Ellie's suggestion: dancing and shopping are precisely what I need.

"Why don't you come with me while I visit this city? I have a car and a driver, it'll be easy," I offer, settling comfortably in my plush chair.

Unfortunately, Ellie's own addiction to tango dictates her priorities: each day she takes several hours of lessons and then, of course, she goes to the *milonga* at night. Her schedule here is more strenuous than a banker's on Wall Street. The answer is no.

"Talk to Analia about shoes and tell her to take you to Comme il Faut. You will thank me!" She stretches her well-proportioned legs to show a stunning pair of black stiletto shoes. Jeans and high heels? It's so seventies . . .

At this point Analia strides to our table with impressive energy. Whatever she'd done the night before, it doesn't show now.

"Lucky you!" I'm so envious. "My face was falling yesterday and it's still falling today. When do the Argentineans work and how can they manage this lifestyle?"

"This morning it'll be Palermo Viejo, then a class with Yoli, followed by lunch somewhere nice." Analia changes the subject, paying no attention to my query. Not even a day into the job and I can already see that she's an incredibly difficult person to pin down. Tiresome questions slide off her like oil from a Teflon pan.

"Lunch?" Ellie interrupts. "We're having lunch with my group at El Desnivel in San Telmo. Why don't you come? It'll be interesting for you to meet a group of crazy *tangueras* and Luis, their guru, if he can make it."

"We'll try . . ." Analia checks our schedule, nodding approvingly to Ellie.

I don't need much convincing. After all, San Telmo, with its open-air market and great antiques stores, is one of the areas I need to check out.

"See you at two. Which by local standards is still an early lunch!" Ellie collects her bag, bulky with dancing shoes. "A real *tanguera* can't possibly travel light . . ." She winks at me.

The cold winter light of a brilliant day carves a sharp edge along the city's skyline. The trees are greener, the sky a perfect blue. The sun is trying its best to heat up streets and squares. An ideal day for walking and exploring Palermo Viejo, the revivified *barrio* of old Buenos Aires. At every corner, hot restaurants and bars promise a busy nightlife.

"Come! I've got just a couple of hours before rehearsal." Analia takes me through the narrow streets, pointing out her favorite stores. Fallen leaves on the sidewalk hide broken tiles and holes and turn our walk into a veritable hurdle. If I'm not careful I'll fall and my tango days will be over before they've begun.

An impressive bunch of young designers has transformed this modest *barrio* into a vibrant area. This is fashion with a sense of humor, quirky and different. We walk slowly, taking notes, while my well-trained shopping eyes strain with the effort of memorizing as much information as possible.

"Careful!" Analia yells. Too many dogs roam the area, leaving behind their souvenirs. A young waiter stops—hand on hip, broom in midair. "Been cleaning the whole morning. Damn them . . ." He laughs good-naturedly.

Later in the morning, I sit sipping coffee alone with Yoli before we begin my first private class. Her townhouse opens onto a quiet street flanked by trees and with no traffic at all. Visiting a real *porteña,* in her own place, makes me feel as if I'm finally connecting to this city.

"I love Palermo! Even its name conjures up all kinds of early childhood memories. It sounds and looks familiar, as Sicilian as my own grandmother."

"That area is the only positive legacy of Juan Manuel de Rosas, one of the many dictators of Argentina. Now the *porteños* use the parks he originally designed for himself and other rich families."

Yoli gets up to lead me to a large space where a few mirrors, a wooden floor, and a ballet bar form the perfect in-house classroom.

"The most difficult feature of tango dancing is walking." The class begins with the quintessential introductory phrase used by every good teacher.

Walking is indeed the basic of tangoing with elegance, without hurrying, using the foot as an expressive tool, controlling the stride. Walking is the dancer's opportunity to respond to her partner with the simplicity of a perfectly executed step.

"Francesca, in my days I had to walk for two years before being allowed to dance." Yoli sighs.

Silently I bless Ellie. She was right: all those years of ballet training are a boon. Keeping the posture, aware of the subtle differences in how to shift my body weight, remembering to always keep my axis aligned, holding the torso still while the legs move independently. I follow the unfamiliar instructions by recalling the old teachings, my old routine. I brush the floor with the tip of my foot, my toes work their way in—toward the ankles—and slide back in a perfect *tendu*.

"Drag your leg; don't ever lift it. Imagine that you are walking in mud and your feet are heavy. One leg passes and drags the other. Keep yourself up! You have a spring on your head; it's sprouting toward the ceiling. It's pulling you up to the sky . . ."

Yoli is a demanding teacher and an hour goes by quickly, leaving me tired and empty inside—a peculiar feeling, exhausting and exhilarating at the same time. She played a slow tango, "Bahía Blanca," and took me in her arms. A delicate, ethereal dancer, she is nonetheless able to convey strong signals, allowing for no mistakes, showing the way a good partner would lead and how the follower should listen and execute.

"You are more than ready to start dancing seriously, if you

wish to do so. You should continue to take classes, but especially go out and watch. Look at the others, learn, copy. You're trained as a dancer and your eye is good at picking up clues. Loosen up your stiff ballet posture and just dance. The more you dance, the better you'll become."

I step out of the darkness of Yoli's house into the sunny day, still in a dream. Words and notes whirl inside me. I feel dizzy.

I'm late for lunch. "Quickly, to San Telmo!" I rush the driver, anxious to meet Ellie and her tango group. Automatically I reach up to adjust my hair, always in disarray, always escaping from underneath my velvet beret. My calves hurt and the tension in my neck is killing me. I must have put all my concentration into the class, trying to learn some basics. Tango is as difficult as everyone said it would be, but the pleasure of interpreting the music, repeating the new steps, has left me under a spell. I've been bewitched and—once again—I'm exhausted. But—at least for the moment—I've forgotten all about George. Strange: until coming to Argentina I hadn't realized how hurtful his indifference was or how I'd numbed my heart to avoid suffering.

At the entrance to the restaurant—a small place crowded with tables and people—a picture-perfect *parrilla* is fired up, with all kinds of meat already cooking on it. From the night before I recognize *bife de chorizo,* the succulent local steak, and a tray of tender-looking ribs.

"What will this beauty try today?" The chef flirts with me, holding out a thin strip of meat. It smells delicious. "Will you try *chinchulines?*" Sure, my looks have always attracted male attention, but to be lured with a delicious plate of intestines is definitely a first. What a great opening line! I thank him with a smile: a positive answer could prove dangerous. I may be adventurous in my food choices, but I've never had the stomach for innards. It's a limitation and my journalistic reputation may be at stake, but I'm adamant: no tripe for me, no kidneys and no sweetbreads.

The restaurant's few tables are already filled with customers, but no trace of Luis and Analia. They must be rehearsing for tonight's show. Still enraptured, I start describing my lesson to Ellie, only stopping midsentence when I realize that the entire group is listening to me. Shyness has never been one of my characteristics, but the twenty pairs of eyes trained on me are intimidating.

"Did I say something wrong?"

"Oh, no! It's just that for all of us there was a beginning—and then a definitive moment when tango got inside our systems. It's great to listen to someone who's discovering our passion. It's a feeling somewhere between joy and pain. Joy because you're a new addict, and pain because we remember so well what we've been through and know what we still have to endure." An imposing Californian woman smiles, sipping a glass of *tinto*.

I look at Ellie, astounded. It sounds like the speech of an early Christian martyr under a pagan Roman emperor. Is tango dancing a sort of cult and the *milongas* the equivalent of the catacombs in ancient Rome? It's all ridiculous and yet—deep inside—I know I understand these people. After all, I've just been deeply affected by a one-hour class. Yoli made me *hear* those desperate old lyrics and, through a few simple steps, showed me how to *dance* those heart-tearing notes.

The waiter passes a basket of bread and a tray with typical spreads.

"Here! *Parrilla* and all kinds of empanadas, with meat and cheese. This is *real people's food*. You must taste it." Ellie is already devouring one and it smells delicious. She's right, the delicate dough crumbles inside my mouth and the tasty combination of cheese and onions is enough to instantly seduce me.

Luis and Analia rush in, looking exhausted, and I find myself sandwiched between the two of them. Not bad. I eye Luis: he wears a perfectly ironed yellow shirt and a pair of jeans. He is so handsome.

"Do you dance?" asks Luis. He leans toward me. Boy, is he sexy. I feel like a schoolgirl with a crush.

"Not really—or at least not tango. But today I took my very first class with Yoli."

"She is great, *qué bueno*. Good for you. Is this your first time in Argentina?"

Usual questions, usual answers.

I zero in on him, engaging him in conversation, excited by the sparkle in his big eyes; he's happy to be the center of attention. He looks like an impertinent schoolboy. Long dark hair curls up on the back of his neck. Steel-framed glasses make him look younger than he is.

"I love New York, and would never exchange it for any other city in the world. But I enjoy traveling too, and if someone invites me, my suitcase is always ready. I don't know what's wrong with me, but I could spend my life going from place to place. I'm a real Gypsy."

He definitely looks the part, a romantic character from a Hungarian operetta. It isn't hard to picture him springing up from the table, dancing to a crazed string quartet.

His smile is contagious. I find myself warming up to him and wanting to talk longer. But his groupies are already gathering their things, ready to go back to the studio where classes are held.

"Do you want to come with us?" Ellie asks. "You could see the whole shebang, get a better idea about tango instruction in B.A. Come!"

"San Telmo! You wouldn't believe the way it looked just a few years ago: a very poor area full of crime. Now it's the Soho of Buenos Aires." Luis takes my arm affectionately and we wander past the old buildings, their patios, and rundown grocery stores with Coca-Cola cases piled up outside. There is Plaza Dorrego, where the famous weekend market is held. "You must come back when the antiques dealers are out. You'll go crazy!"

Only *dos cuadras,* two blocks, and we come to a spacious loft in a Spanish-looking street. Most of the buildings—no doubt in better shape in another era—are quietly crumbling. The Domus de la Danza is a large white space with a magnificent wooden floor. Pediments, rosettes, and crests hover just above the mirrors or wherever fantasy has inspired the clever owner to splatter them. Old wooden fans hang from a high ceiling and the light filters soothingly from a wrought-iron veranda that opens out onto a narrow balcony crowded with a magical green jungle. The bench on the longest side of the room is a perfect inspection point, and from here Analia explains all that goes on in a group class.

Sacadas and *barridas* are the order of the day. Luis divides the group into two—men and women will dance on opposite sides of the room. Only when he's sure that his students have learned how to lead and follow will he join the two groups.

Still a novice, I'm fascinated by each student's movements, and I already notice—and mentally separate—the good dancers from the bad. Ellie, for instance, is very precise and harmonious in the execution of her steps.

"Stretch! Stretch those legs!" Luis grabs one of the men and shows how, suddenly moving like a follower, executing *ochos* and *giros*. The change in his attitude is mesmerizing: his eyes become liquid, his lashes at half-mast, and he looks provocatively at his student. He acquires sharp, feminine cheekbones; his lips widen in a mysterious, sensual smile, and he stretches with the elegance of a cat.

I can't take my eyes off him. The transformation is incredible. His feet never leave the floor: they glide on it sketching intricate patterns, until he puts in a meteoric double *boleo,* the rapid whip-like movement I admired the night before.

"Bravo!" I clap enthusiastically.

Analia smiles and turns to see Luis's self-congratulatory reaction. "Just what he needs! After this, he will be insufferable."

Laughing, Luis comes toward us holding his arms open for Analia. Why not take advantage of such a dancer? It isn't every day that he can introduce his dancing partner to his American students. And it's a treat for us—a little preview of what's to come tonight when they'll dance in the new tango show at the Astral.

"Tonight it's opening night," Luis explains. "Here's our first number, 'A Evaristo Carriego.' "

They come together in the center of the room, Analia fitting into his arms as if she were meant to be there forever. Her eyes close before the music starts; her arched torso forms a playful counterbalance to his powerful embrace. With a movement of her head she lets her hair fall on her shoulders, a shiny, jet-black mass that slowly echoes the movements of her body. They dance as if they were alone in the room, lost in their own world. Their performance is simultaneously electrifying and intimidating. Is this the level one should hope to attain? How disheartening to think that probably none of the students in the class will ever dream of reaching it. I yearn to be able to experience, at least once in my life, that same union of body and soul.

Analia and Luis continue to dance, lost in their passion, forgetting that they are there to show just a few steps, to demonstrate a couple of technicalities. The group admires them silently, enjoying their exhibition, envying their passion; each of us is lost in our own private dreams.

Luis holds Analia with unequaled tenderness; together they draw their emotions into marvelous movements of precision and elegance. Their pauses mean more than a thousand words and the miraculous sensuality of their dancing captivates their devoted audience. He puts his hand around Analia's neck, tenderly cupping her long hair, watching her as if she were the only woman in the world. His lips mesmerizingly close to hers, together they write the emotional phrases of their tango conversation. A murmured *Oh!* rises like a chorus from everyone's lips, releasing the tension, stirring old sensations and spawning new yearnings. I look around, checking expressions. There is not a dry eye in the room and no one is embarrassed by the nakedness of their feelings.

Enrosque

(A Twist)

Fue lo que empezó una vez
lo que después dejó de ser.
Lo que al final, por culpa de un error
Fue noche amarga del corazon.

"Desde el alma"

*P*uchero for my friend!" Luis directs the culinary choices of his students with the precision of a ballet master. Having been officially adopted by the group of tango aficionados, I sit with them at Lugar, the restaurant behind Teatro Astral where yesterday we admired Luis and Analia in their successful show. I'm still stunned by the brilliant dancing, the perfection of the choreography and the music.

It's cold outside and I need comfort food. *Puchero* is a local specialty that hits the spot. A strong winter dish made with selected meat cuts—chicken, beef, and sausages—and cooked slowly for hours with vegetables and legumes, it is akin to *lesso,* the exquisite pot-au-feu so famous in north and central Italy. I plunge in with my fork and the meat, as tender as butter, melts under my touch.

At the shriek of a cell phone everyone dives under the table, searching their handbags for the shrill, insistent gadget we can't live without: our crucial link to the lives we lead away from B.A.

"Francesca, it's yours!" Luis nudges me gently. I search around in my backpack until I find the annoying phone in the special internal pocket.

"Hey, finally! How many days were you going to go without answering my calls?" It's George's teasing voice, coming through sharply from faraway New York. "Remember? You have a husband."

"Yeah, sure. A husband!" is my immediate reaction, but then it turns into instant guilt. When did I last think of calling him? George's been bolting in and out of my consciousness like one of those internet pop-up ads. I stand up and walk away from the table to get some privacy.

George misses me, or at least that's what he says, and the apartment is empty. What to do with the enormous Spanish ham DHL has just delivered? What to say to the many social invitations? How should he cope with the dry cleaning? He sounds like the spoiled husband he is.

"You mean the refrigerator is empty, right?" I joke, sensing his longing for our dinners together and my food. "Don't worry—this cook will be back before you know it . . ."

"I was only calling to say that I'm leaving in a couple of days for Europe. You won't find me when you come back."

"Ooh? Ah, well. Fine . . ."

My immediate reaction is one of relief. I was right to accept Clarissa's assignment, and I shouldn't feel guilty. See? He's off again. A welcome and unexpected sense of freedom unfurls inside me. Sometimes I feel shackled by the legacy of my traditional Italian education. I came from a Neapolitan family that moved to Rome in the 1920s. Rules, etiquette, customs directed almost every minute of our days. *This is unheard of, a girl like you can't behave like this* was all I constantly heard growing up. My father, a judge, exacted complete devotion and obedience from everyone, including my poor saint of a mother! Even these days my family regards feminism as an ill-bred, working-class disease and considers my behavior quite extravagant. How can I leave George and travel the world by myself? In the first years of our marriage, an old aunt scolded me for not packing my husband's suitcases every time he traveled.

I would never accept a marriage like that, I used to vow to myself. And look at me now? *La legge del contrapasso,* punishment fits the crime, as Dante said.

"Oh, then there is no need for me to rush back, right? You don't really miss me."

I return to the table and resume my attack on the *puchero.* The plate in front of me could feed a regiment of hungry marines. Argentinean portions remind me of some Italian restaurants in the USA: these huge quantities would horrify the chefs back home in Europe. I toy with my food, hoping not to insult the sensibility of my local friends. I'll never be able to eat it all.

Analia leans against Luis like a cat lounging in the sun. In her tight jeans and a red T-shirt, she looks barely old enough to drink. Luis plays with her long hair, gently twisting a curly lock around his finger. His hands move slowly over her shoulders, feeling her skin, delicately stroking her neck. He kisses her collarbone, reaching down along her thin, well-toned arms, tenderly brushing her delicate hands with his fingers. Analia smiles languorously, enjoying his touch.

"Ellie, you've got to explain this," I plead sotto voce.

After only three days in Argentina, I'm experiencing an entirely new sense of awareness. I feel alive, something I haven't felt in a long time. My body, my mind, my soul have finally reclaimed their space, and I've started to relax. First I already feel as if I belong to the place. Being Italian, or *tana* as they say locally, makes things easier. With very few language barriers, it's easy to slip into the city's daily life; the *porteños,* the inhabitants of this port city, greet me warmly day after day, generously helping me with my discoveries and research. I've visited every relevant *barrio* in Buenos Aires, eaten at the best restaurants, and quickly drafted page after page about the city and the world of tango for my article. I've even braved the dance floor at the various *milongas* I've visited with my crazy group of *gringos tangueros.*

I scan my hotel room, coldly considering the huge difference between this tiny space and my large New York apartment. The vast distance from Fifth Avenue has also given me some much-needed perspective on my relationship with my husband. I can't help but wonder if I renounced physical love too soon and too easily. I don't know what to do with our situation. Here I'm much more aware of how hurt and discarded I feel. Is tango to blame for this unexpected awakening of the senses? Now, more than ever, I miss the George of the past and the love we once shared.

My other great frustration—infinitely more pressing right now—is the difficulty of tracking down information about cosmetic surgery. The real *tangueros* and the teachers know nothing about it and laugh every time I bring it up. The only solution is to call one of my friends, Sarah de Villaperosa. A New Yorker by birth, Sarah married an Argentinean and moved to Buenos Aires. She took the helm of the family's agriculture empire after her husband's death and is now the owner of a huge *estancia* in the north of the country. I deliberately waited before calling on her, wanting to see a different Buenos Aires, not just its sophisticated, wealthy sections and rarefied social life.

Spontaneous invitations—to luncheons, cocktails, and dinners—tumble out of Sarah. Her delight at hearing from me is heartwarming.

"Of course, since I'm working, I can't possibly accept, but what about lunch today?" Patience is not one of my calling cards and I am growing increasingly frustrated, stymied by my fruitless research. At least at lunch I may be able to concentrate solely on Sarah and find out something about plastic surgery.

Walking is my way of immediately getting the pulse of a city, the fastest route into the heart of a place, its well-kept secrets and its moods. So I get my car to leave me on the corner of Avenida Huergo and Dique No. 2, at the entrance to Puerto Madero. Once a merchant port, it's now the hippest destination for restaurantgoers.

The first warm day since my arrival in Argentina allows me to finally take off my hat and zip down my jacket. I hurry along, skirting the docks, enjoying the sun on the newly restored buildings housing fashionable bars and restaurants. The soothing notes of the Buena Vista Social Club come trickling out of an Italian pizzería; a black cat stretches luxuriously in the middle of a pedestrianized street. A thicket of tall cranes on the horizon betrays the new real estate delirium: freshly minted buildings sprout up like young trees, filling every empty lot in the area. A new skyline for an old city.

Sarah asked me to meet her at the new Philippe Starck hotel, the Faena, which was constructed in a converted grain depository. She assures me that this is the best introduction to this side of the city, proof that the country is coming out of its deep troubles. A bevy of smartly dressed young men, complete with dark sunglasses and tight T-shirts showcasing impeccable six-packs, greets me at the door. If not for their solicitous courtesy I would have taken them for nightclub bouncers rather than doormen. The rest of the pretentious entrance—heavy with curtains and gold furniture—puts me off at once and I go straight to the restaurant, hoping for good food and better interior design.

"See? Look around! Don't you think this is positive? Imagine, they are opening up a new hotel, just in front of this one. What it means is that the Argentineans are finally getting back on their feet." Sarah kisses me warmly, offering drinks, food, and friendship, as ever.

The room resembles what I imagine the inside of an igloo must look like, lit from within with an eerie incandescent hue. The exquisite menu, veal carpaccio rolls and roasted *magret* with quince strudel, is a triumph of minimalism. The simple elegance of the food clashes with the opulence of the white and gold unicorns protruding from the walls.

"Who's that woman?" I nod as inconspicuously as possible toward a faraway table where a blond lady sits in complete solitude, reading the list of dishes with apparent difficulty. She keeps shifting the big menu, alternatively distancing it and pulling it closer to her. Encumbered by a dark red fur turban and a pair of bulky sunglasses, she bends, rummaging through her huge Hermès Birkin, sprawled out next to her on the floor and spilling over with newspapers and magazines. I feel her pain; restaurant owners should always write their menus in large print. After all, who pays for these expensive places if not the over-fifty crowd?

"You mean Isabel Alexanders?" Sarah lip-synchs a congenial *Hola!* at Isabel, who looks back unblinkingly. I remember what Ellie told me after seeing her at the *milonga,* and a wave of dislike washes over me. Seconds later, Isabel, dragging her paraphernalia under the imperturbable stare of those weird unicorns, steps like a queen onto the bright vermilion rug and slowly sails out of sight.

We look at each other, mystified. "Why the sudden departure?"

During lunch I expound on my favorite subject, checking Sarah's expression, hoping to find some reaction.

"I definitely know something about it," she answers matter-of-factly. "I don't have the exact details and figures, but lots of foreigners fly here to get *done*. It's so cheap, compared to the prices in their countries. I heard that for twenty-five hundred dollars you can buy a tango/hotel/brand-new-breasts package! Of course, if you need to have a complete face-lift, it costs a little more, but it won't exceed four thousand. All included, naturally." Sarah laughs, touching her perfect cheekbones in a propitiatory gesture to the God of Wrinkles.

"Do you think that's why she's here?" She returns to the question of Isabel's looks and her hasty disappearance. "Why would someone with so much money fly to Argentina to have surgery? She doesn't need to come here. She could hide in Manhattan or Los Angeles, or wherever she wanted."

"Well, well! Look who's here instead of writing in her room." Ellie, in a sumptuous fur coat, has entered the dining room with Luis. "So much for not taking classes today . . ." She pulls a fluffy shawl around her shoulders with a dramatic flourish.

I hastily introduce my new friends. "This is Luis, a great tango dancer, and Ellie, his alter ego." Will I ever escape these social encounters? Complete privacy doesn't exist, not even on a first-time visit to Buenos Aires.

Sarah turns to Luis with the attention of an entomologist. Before her is a real specimen from a world she has seldom—if ever—encountered. Upper-class Argentineans have always considered tango an ethnic extravaganza, and Sarah is no exception; even though she was born in the States, she has wholly adopted true local prejudices. But Luis's smile is captivating, and she laughs and flirts outrageously. Already a willing victim of Luis's charm, I note the change in my friend's behavior. She clearly relishes this unexpected encounter. Luis's sex appeal is at work.

"Isabel was here!" I grab Ellie's elbow and fill her in on the disappearing act.

"Are you sure you want to find another table?" Sarah invites Ellie and Luis to sit with us. The waiters and the maître d' flutter about solicitously, wishing to impress *la Señora* de Villaperosa with their attentions. But Ellie needs to discuss the new publicity campaign for her jewelry line with Luis.

"Will I see you later? After tonight's show Analia, Ellie, and I are going to a friend's apartment for drinks and a casual dinner. Join us! It's a breathtaking space on the sixth floor of an old building, built inside and around a cupola, one of the many you see on the Buenos Aires skyline. You'll never have another chance to be inside one. Please say yes!" Luis kisses me goodbye before Ellie drags him away.

Sarah's eyes follow Luis, admiring his easy gait. He keeps his back as straight as a rod, his feet sashaying smoothly, as if he were gliding on ice. I'm delighted to be invited, surprised to find that I'm even on the radar of this intriguing man.

Sarah turns back to me. "Let me introduce you to an acquaintance of mine, a surgeon who owns and directs Pluribus, the most exclusive clinic in town. If there's anyone who knows about these surgery-tango packages, he's the one!"

The pleasant, warm morning has given way to a miserable afternoon. Rain falls insistently on a gray city, while a somnolent fog rises sluggishly from the canals surrounding the Faena Hotel. The Río de la Plata, its murky brown waters swelling under the ocean's powerful tides, seems suddenly dark and menacing.

Sarah's Mercedes purrs quietly in front of the hotel's entrance. Two of the staff, flashing movie-star smiles, make a beeline to hold the doors open for us. "Fernando, *vamos enseguida a la* Recoleta, corner of Montevideo and Vicente López."

"We'll be there in a few minutes." As her driver follows her instructions, Sarah phones Roberto Hellzinker, the owner of Pluribus. With the question now a matter of personal pride, Sarah has decided to crack the secret surrounding Isabel's appearance in Buenos Aires.

"I'm not particularly interested in the work she has done. What I want to know is, why Argentina? It doesn't make sense.

"The obvious reasons—and the one that would appeal most to my readers—is that it's cheaper here. Even for a millionaire, a buck is a buck, right? But how good are they here? Are these doctors and their clinics safe?"

"*Son divinos!*" Sarah replies. "They are wonderful! In B.A. we have some of the best plastic surgeons in the world. Once we get to Recoleta, take a look at the women shopping and having tea. They are all exquisitely made up, with very few wrinkles. Having cosmetic surgery is as normal as drinking *mate* . . . Everyone admits to getting some kind of work done. It's as gratifying as letting your best friend know that you have found the latest Armani jacket on sale at Saks!"

At this time in the afternoon, Recoleta isn't busy at all. Only a few customers pass through the glass doors of the famous Patio Bullrich, the top-of-the-line mall in B.A. Taxis cruise along hushed streets, stopping at corners in search of fares. And the rain continues to fall, shrouding cars and pedestrians.

The entire façade of Clínica Pluribus is covered with reflective blue glass, enormous panels that capture the sky, recording B.A.'s dramatic weather patterns. Luscious palm trees line the entrance hall, where a young nurse in a white polyester uniform politely assists a couple of affluent-looking clients. A large-boned, middle-aged woman fidgets nervously, scanning the latest issue of *Hola* and concealing herself behind her stack of Louis Vuitton suitcases.

"*El doctor* Hellzinker is waiting for you. Please follow me." A blonde in a tight dark suit and high heels leads us through a succession of halls, corridors, and elevators. The doctor's office, soothingly decorated in pale wood and filled with pictures of horses, leather saddles, and stable finery, looks like an interior designer's hacienda fantasy. Handwoven saddle blankets in magnificent colors are strewn with studied abandon over a large, dark-chocolate leather sofa and two Ralph Lauren wicker chairs. From behind an imposing English desk at the end of the immense room, a good-looking man in his early forties jumps up and strides to the door, both hands held out in welcome.

One of the most famous surgeons in Argentina, Roberto Hellzinker shuttles us into his office, quickly explaining that he opened Clínica Pluribus only five years earlier and that it caters to a particularly needy group of prominent socialites. Lifts, Botox injections, breast enhancement or reduction, and all kinds of tucks are the bread and butter that have helped him to become one of the fifty richest entrepreneurs in Argentina. His discreet and profitable clinics are popping up all over the country, making it the center of cosmetic surgery in South America, having practically overthrown the more expensive Brazil. His expert staff cares for people who fly in from all over the world, urged on by the devaluation of the peso. Who wouldn't be happy to shed a few years during the course of a morning? Patients begin taking tango classes a week later. A new look, a new neck, a few tango tricks, a new life . . .

"Our patients come from all over the world, but mainly Europe and the States. English patients are excited to get breast implants for a mere two thousand pounds, and the Americans think we are still very cheap. Plus, we are well known for our skills." His ease and confidence are impressive; I can see why he's so successful.

Tickled by Roberto's complete transparency and candor, I laugh. His intelligent, inquiring eyes focus on me, now holding my gaze. I feel an old stirring, a familiar warmth spreading in my groin, sensual and comforting at the same time.

"What did your doctors do with Isabel Alexanders?" I ask point-blank, hoping to catch him off guard. In an instant his demeanor changes from puzzlement to complete, impenetrable darkness.

"I've never heard of such a person. Would you like to take a look around the clinic?"

Terribly ashamed of myself, I quickly retreat behind professional behavior. I don't even know Isabel! Why am I probing?

Sarah jumps into the conversation. "Francesca was just bitten by the tango bug, I'm afraid." She turns toward me. "Roberto loves it too! You must take her out to the *milongas*," she adds for good measure.

"I've been going out every night," I admit proudly. "And Sarah's right; I have fallen in love with Buenos Aires and tango."

"Tonight it's Confitería Ideal, wonderful live music—will you be there?" Roberto looks straight at me, his professional interest mixed with obvious pleasure. A few minutes ago I caught him staring at my legs. Perversely I continue to cross and uncross them, playfully rotating my ankles. Men love a good pair of legs. Why not use them? Besides, I'm so out of practice.

"Wouldn't miss it!" I smile back, flirting openly. I could always go after the party. I'm a social butterfly who's just reclaimed her wings. How convenient, I think, that the *milongas* start after midnight.

I banish George to the back of my mind. But once again those silvery wires get hold of my stomach, squeezing it painfully. For just a moment my husband's scrutinizing eyes materialize in my consciousness, and then, just as quickly, they retreat, like a fade-out in a movie.

Why not, indeed? I coolly assess Roberto's muscular body and the long, prematurely silver hair. The contrast with his tan is gorgeous! He's exactly what I like in a man. I toy with the idea of making love to him. Again that warm wave washes over me.

Deliberately, Roberto takes off his glasses and puts them on the desk before ushering us to the door. He smiles.

Why am I noticing these details? Why do I suddenly feel so hot inside? I steal a look at his hands, with their long, strong fingers, no sign of a wedding ring. Bad news: a successful lover is in love with his own wife. An affair should be without feelings, without attachment, and especially no falling in love. I hope no one has noticed me.

I giggle inwardly as I kiss him goodbye and, arm in arm, Sarah and I exit the clinic.

The sky has by now cleared up and taken on the mixed pinks and blues of a Chagall painting. A rainbow links the city east and west under a magical, ephemeral arch. I feel like a movie star on my own Hollywood set.

Back in the car, my arms tightly crossed over my chest, I lift the collar of my jacket—as if to hide my expression—and I close my eyes. I need some silence. I need to dream.

Sarah drops me in front of the Hotel Castelar, her kiss and funny look more telling than words.

"Careful, dear. He's married . . ." And she's gone.

I close the door behind me, ignoring a floor littered with trousers, scarves, and T-shirts. My room is a mess, a *quilombo* as they say here. Even my children never behaved like this! But Luis's invitation was serious cause for anxiety, and a last-minute fashion crisis is perfectly excusable. I must have tried on my entire wardrobe. Thank God I brought just one suitcase.

I walk five or six blocks on Avenida de Mayo, until I reach a graceful building on Montevideo. Slowly the old elevator, an exquisite iron cage embellished with heavy gold leaves, flowers, and cherubs, takes me to the sixth floor. The apartment, on several levels, is schizophrenically linked by winding steps and stairs and capped by a spectacular cupola which stands above the east side of a terrace boasting a 360-degree view over the city.

The party is in full swing. Everyone dances under the moon to the sounds of the Héctor Del Curto Quartet playing Aníbal Troilo and Pugliese, the two great tango masters. I have to pinch my thigh. I'm living in a dream: in the middle of winter we are dancing tango on a terrace!

Luis and other teachers are embroiled in a fiery conversation about the philosophy of tango. It could be a scene from a café in an Italian village—the only missing elements are a bar table and an ongoing game of cards. A crowd gathers around them, men and women, young and old. Some stand, quietly embracing each other, touching. Others hold hands—transfixed—and lean toward the speakers. They want to master the truth, to understand the dance's essence.

César Coelho passionately expounds his credo: "Tango is a secret between us, *una emoción contenida* . . ."

"The man's lead is the essential skill, without it there is no tango," El Negro Copello counters back with authority, snapping his fingers in his famous signature gesture. Maxi nods approvingly.

"But what is really important is to treat the lady with the due respect," Osvaldo insists, looking at Lorena.

"Beginners should avoid fancy movements. Precision and cleanliness are essential." María Blanco's hands draw precise tango lines in the air. There is no doubt that Italian blood still runs strong in this country.

"I think it's a question of love. When you dance you must accept the embrace. You must want to give back, to listen to the man's wishes and be able to answer. If this isn't love . . ." Mariela Franganillo whispers, shaking her jet-black hair.

"The most difficult task is listening to the music, because it passes through the ears, but it has to heat your heart before you can process it into steps. When you dance tango you propose, never impose . . . Feel it, love it!" Luis shouts fervently, to exploding applause. "It's the embrace of love. Mariela is right." The wind tosses his curls. "Tango is a true expression of love and intimacy."

By now the excitement under the tent is tangible.

"See? I told you so. If you don't lead, I can't follow . . ." Daniel and Melina, two of the most advanced students, are already quarreling.

The music flows, enveloping me, holding my soul and drowning out the teachers' debate. It's as if the *bandoneón*—poignant, yearning—plays for me alone. The violin's pizzicato—rhythmic and precise—pulls my heart to shreds. I melt inside, and tears well up in my eyes. I dry my cheeks furtively, hoping that no one has noticed.

"Finalmente!" Analia and Luis stop in front of me and we hug. Then Luis holds out his hand, an invitation to dance.

Taken by surprise, I'm horrified at the idea of dancing with him. My heart pounds in my chest.

"You had a Ferrari in your arms, and now you want me, a jalopy? How can you stand it?"

My legs drag me down and get in my way. My brain is empty of all that I've learned in the past few days and nothing remotely useful resurfaces to help me navigate the four de rigueur tangos. Neck and shoulders tensed, I clasp Luis's hand and arm, holding on tight.

"You might be Italian, but you dance like a robot." Luis stops me. "*No tienes corazón,* you have no heart," he adds, dramatically hitting his own. He wiggles to free himself from my iron lock.

"But I just started!" Now I'm offended, angry. I must show him what I'm capable of.

I want—I need—to interpret these tango notes. With George, I've tried to control everything inside me. I've set up a system to protect myself. Will I be able to let go now?

"Let's try again. Relax. Feel the music."

He maneuvers my body, gently directing me with a little pressure of his hand, shifting his frame as he leads, to get me to follow his wishes. I slowly let go, fear abandoned.

I close my eyes and let the music transport me.

Firulete

(An Adornment)

No habrá ninguna igual. No habrá ninguna.
Ninguna con tu piel ni con tu voz.
Tu piel, magnolia que mojó la luna.
Tu voz, murmullo que entibió el amor.

"Ninguna"

What a difference after just a few hours: the rain gave way to an almost balmy night, and now a crystalline darkness surrounds us. I free my neck from the constraint of a scarf. Having danced all night, I completely forgot Roberto's invitation to Confitería Ideal. Analia went home and now Luis and I, without a need for words, walk back to the Castelar, arm in arm. The streets are quiet and all the stores closed, except for a few kiosks selling cigarettes and phone cards, the daily essentials in this city.

It's past three a.m. and Buenos Aires belongs to us. Is there a better hour to see the city? Luis detours around Plaza de Mayo, just around the corner from La Cupola, as the apartment is called. I'm still floating in the dreamy moment of my first real tango. We stroll past the Presidential Palace, the Casa Rosada, its pink hue quite astonishing under the glare of the floodlights. It reminds me of some kind of sweet confection, an Easter Day treat. We turn back, crossing in front of the imposing cathedral, with its neoclassic columns, and El Cabildo, the old Government House, an exquisite leftover from the colonial era. Buenos Aires is a miracle of timeless elegance, a dream of architectural eclecticism. At the famous Café Tortoni, on Avenida de Mayo, I stop and plaster my nose against the windows to try and see the inside of this celebrated tango outpost.

"The best have come and gone through these doors," Luis assures me. I look deferentially at the colorful posters advertising future concerts and exhibitions.

He stops me in front of the Castelar's glass doors. "Do you believe in love?"

He had said nothing, hinted at nothing. We have spoken of history and art, tango and music, but I was not prepared for this spontaneous burst of confidence.

"I need to talk," he says. His eyes are darker than usual as they concentrate on me.

He leads me into the cavernous lobby of my hotel, and we sit on the ugly, but oddly comfortable, leather chairs. The night doorman brings us tea and a few *biscochitos,* left over from breakfast, a reminder that we are not on conventional time.

"Remember the Astral? The Tango Show?"

"Of course." I nod. Does he really want to talk about tango? It's almost dawn.

"It's about Analia. I think I'm in love." He scrutinizes me, checks my reactions.

"Ha! Of course, I imagined that much. What do you want to tell me?" Why is he talking to me instead of his best friend, Ellie? I'm tired and confused and I don't know where this is going.

"I'm gay. You know that, don't you?" A defiant opening line. I smile. Yes, I did know.

"Something has happened. It's Analia. She's the one. I'll marry her," he bursts out, needing to convince me. "Yes, I'll marry her. She doesn't care if I'm gay. With her I feel free, I can be myself."

"Tell me."

"That tango with Analia at Desnivel. I felt as if we were one person: one heart, four limbs, and a thousand spellbinding notes. For the first time I belonged to someone. Am I imagining it?"

His hands held her tight, he said, his heart beating with hers. He'd never experienced anything like it.

"I've found my dancing mate." Luis looks at me, almost imploringly. He wants me to hear him out. His eyes are wet with emotion. I bend over, my hand on his knee.

"Strange, how different it is working with her, compared to the other girls." Luis tries to find the right words to explain. During rehearsals he always helped her through the most difficult steps, he says. They've spent hours, days, and weeks together, rehearsing and relaxing in the wings waiting for their turn onstage. Analia would rest her feet—wrecked from too much dancing—by stretching her legs up against the wall to drain the tiredness away, as Luis chain-smoked, lying down on his back on the bare floor next to her. He would listen to her stories and chat with her about their lives: an easy, comfortable friendship. Analia would seek Luis out, desperate for a tender word of encouragement or reassurance that she was a fine dancer, that their director was just an artistic despot.

Preparing for their latest production, under the tough direction of the famous Valerio Perez, twenty dancers sweated and labored to achieve the perfection demanded of them. Valerio was determined to put together the ultimate tango show, something never before seen in a major international theater. In his search for unique steps, absolute synchronicity, youth and beauty, he drove the company insane with endless hours of practice and drills, perfecting each figure, embellishing each step.

While he had been relentless in his criticism of Analia—harshly correcting her placement, fluidity of movement, and musicality—he obviously favored Luis. What Analia could not have known was that Valerio also approached Luis after rehearsal. The famous director was notorious for his attraction to the lithe young men who starred in his productions. Luis knew he was treading in dangerous waters but as a performer, he couldn't do better than to curry favor with one of Buenos Aires's most respected artists. He just hoped that Valerio would continue to cast him.

By opening night, Luis felt—maybe without even really knowing it—that something was going to happen. Either the easy, supportive friendship he had with Analia or the master/protégé relationship he had with his director was going to become something more.

At 9:00 p.m., the company assembled behind the curtains, principal dancers and corps de ballet together, embracing in a mass hug.

"Mierda, mierda, mierda!" they whispered, heavily made up, eyes blackened with shadow and mascara, lips a tinge too bright for the lights that would shine on them.

Luis stood in the wings waiting for his entrance. Seemingly void of emotion, he focused somewhere in the distance in front of him. Underneath a gray felt hat, his eyes were as dark as ink pools, hidden by dramatically long eyelashes. A white silk scarf was tied around his neck. He was ready to take his place onstage, to dazzle the audience with his bravura, when he felt Valerio standing behind him, his hands touching his hips.

"Scary. You look exactly like Gardel when he was your age!"

Valerio whispered in his ear, his breath sweet and hot on Luis's neck. "Just as sexy. Just as irresistible."

Only seconds after the director walked away, Analia approached. *"Mierda, mi amor,"* she said lightly, adjusting his scarf.

The violins' plaintive sound gave the *A* to the orchestra and tango notes filled the space above and around the dancers. Analia followed him to the spotlight. They were on.

Lights, shadows, dancers running in to change, the frantic slipping in and out of costumes. No time for hesitations, for thinking.

The last notes of the finale: Luis held Analia in his arms, her left leg vertically projected above his head, the right one stretched behind, her arms around his neck. With her entire body leaning against his—her profile an Egyptian drawing—she flashed an exaggerated performer's smile at the audience, catching her breath after an exhausting performance.

He looked down, and saw her for the first time. He noticed her silken skin, the full, sensual lips enhanced by dark red lipstick, her black eyes, the perfect breasts so voluptuous on her slender body.

The moment the curtains were down, Luis covered her mouth with his. Washed away by a strong tide, swept into uncharted territory, he beamed at her in wonderment.

The curtains parted again and he was obliged to recover his composure. Analia stood trembling next to him, staring at him with wide eyes. Luis, totally depleted by the difficult routine and this unexpected passion, and unable to understand what had happened, stared back, his heart exploding inside his chest, his breath coming in short gasps. Analia? Could it be?

The crowd, unaware of these brief life-changing minutes, erupted with applause that seemed to go on forever.

Luis dragged Analia out of the theater and to Corrientes, where they jumped on the bus and rode all the way to his Boedo apartment, never allowing their hands to unlock. They traveled in a dream, without realizing how long it took to cross the city. Forty-five minutes, holding their breath, staring, unable to say a word, sensing each other's soul, yearning for each other's body. They trembled at the idea of what was about to happen, overwhelmed by something they'd never imagined they wanted so much.

He undressed her tenderly and she abandoned herself to his hunger, arching her body to meet his. Her breasts, once freed from the T-shirt, wanted to be teased, caressed. Her nipples hardened, begging for his touch, longing for his lips. Luis slowly unbuttoned his shirt, pinning her down with his weight but in full control of his movements, enjoying the thought of what was to come, watching her. Spellbound, he harnessed his desire, waiting to take her with gentleness, preparing to unleash his own sensuality to give her pleasure, to fill her with love.

As his fingers traveled the velvet of her skin, an old song—a silly bolero—came fleetingly to his mind: *piel canela,* cinnamon skin, it sings. Impatiently Analia dragged him down, moving her hips to meet his hardness. He slipped into her, surprised at how much he wanted her. Lost inside her liquidity, Luis possessed her, filling her as if they'd been made to be together forever, their bodies matching in the ardor of their desire.

They rode high, still intoxicated by the dancing, the applause. They still felt the public's admiration on their skin, frenzied with lust, longing for hours of unrestrained pleasure. Together they surged and flowed like dark waves rolling on the ocean.

When it was over, they held each other silently, spent. Empty of all, except for the extreme pleasure of the aftermath. They slept hugging each other, adjusting to the curves of their bodies.

The Buenos Aires night, its sirens and horns muffled by distance, wrapped them in suspended silence. They'd both come home.

Sacada

(A Displacement)

Subject: New plans
Date: 6/12/2008 08:01:02 A.M. Eastern Standard Time
From: Francesca.Rivabuona@aol.com
To: George.Farrington@aol.com

George!
How is life in New York? Have you packed? Are you ready for Milan? Your trip to Europe has inspired me. Since I'm completely absorbed by my tango classes and you're going to be traveling, I've decided to extend my stay here for another week. Ellie Goldberg (I told you I ran into her here, right?) and I will rent an apartment in Abasto, a great area developing around the old covered market, which has been transformed into a mall. For the moment, though, I'm moving all my belongings to the Alvear, the oldest and most exclusive hotel in town. I will be staying in Recoleta, an area comparable, say, to Fifth Avenue in New York. Lots of chic people and expensive real estate. I'll let you know what I think of the change. In the meantime I have to admit that I've fallen in love with the Castelar. When I come back (after my self-indulgent tango nights . . .) it feels like home.

I'm constantly improving my dancing. At my tender age I've found a new passion. It's never too late . . .
Write as soon as you land in Milan.
Love you
Francesca

"It's such a pain to change hotels. But I guess I have to. I'm here to work, after all, even though it feels like a vacation."

"Don't worry, soon enough we'll be in our own apartment."

"Do you think we'll be able to find something for just a week?"

"Let me call my friends. I'm sure we can find a place to rent." Ellie sits on my bed, watching me as I fold my T-shirts and place them tidily inside my suitcase, flattening out wrinkles and straightening the hems of trousers and skirts, buttoning up shirts and jackets, doubling up my cashmere sweaters.

"Baires is full of visitors right now, but the Tango Fest is just about to end and everyone's leaving. There'll be plenty of inexpensive choices."

An extra week in Argentina with a friend. How much better could it get? I'm looking forward to living more like a resident than a tourist; it will feel different. Food shopping, *milongas* until dawn, a kitchen to cook in, and our own sofa to crash on.

"I love that dress. It's perfect for tango. Look at the skirt. It dances by itself—still on a hanger! Francesca, you've got to wear it tonight, since you never managed to hook up with Roberto at the Confitería Ideal last night. . . . Maybe you'll see him at Club Gricel tonight. Make him pant for you."

"Do you think I should have called him when we decided to skip the *milonga* and keep dancing on the terrace?"

"No, and the proof is that he already left you two messages."

This newfound freedom—even if only for a week—has unleashed unexpected feelings in me. Energy, excitement, a new appetite for life. I love the change of pace. I'm buoyed up by a new challenge. And also, an unexpected problem. Since yesterday I've been thinking about Roberto constantly. We've only just met, but he hasn't left my mind for an instant.

"This Roberto must be something. Look at the sparkle in your eyes. It's as though thinking about him has made you even more beautiful," Ellie teases. "But what about George? And didn't Sarah say Roberto is married?" Ellie's eyebrows arch to question me lightheartedly.

"Roberto is a professional contact." I stuff my no-nonsense cotton underwear into the outside pocket of the suitcase. "I'm definitely writing a blurb about plastic-surgery-and-tango packages." *What a good excuse to see him again.* I smile to myself inwardly.

"I have to finish my piece by the end of the week, but I hope to be able to wrap it up sooner," I remind Ellie. I'm halfway through the article. Soon the magazine will contact me with questions and requests, and I need to be ready. Paulo, the Brazilian photographer I work with, has done a dazzling job of capturing the city's mysterious soul, the darkness underneath its brilliant appearance. The pictures he took at the Confitería Ideal are sensational. By using a slow exposure, he caught only the dancers' legs and feet. Each picture, purposely grainy and out of focus, reveals the couples' intensity and documents the dancers' vibrant passion.

Smiling, Ellie helps me zip up my bag and gives me a hug. She'll work on finding us an apartment while I sequester myself in my new hotel to finish my assignment. Life could be worse.

"Where else in the world would one choose to lunch near a cemetery besides B.A.?" I'm sitting at Café de la Paix, overlooking the cemetery of Recoleta. "No wonder you Argentineans have been writing desperate tango lyrics for so many years! No wonder you have the highest number of psychiatrists and psychologists in the world!"

Under the canopy, the bougainvillea is still in full blossom, its purple flowers a striking contrast with the yellowing leaves of the nearby trees.

"This city constantly reminds me of Rome. Even in winter we can eat outside." The sun warms its way through the awning. Analia and I have ordered the usual *parrilla* and a bottle of Malbec from Luigi Bosca, one of my new favorites.

"I must take you to another cemetery, La Chacarita. A week from now, on June twenty-sixth—the anniversary of Carlos Gardel's death—it will be flooded with crowds of people from all over the world paying their respects. It's a veritable pilgrimage; Gardel is Argentina's icon, its most famous tango singer and an everlasting legend." If I ever wondered about tango-as-a-cult, here's the proof.

"Look how beautiful." Analia points toward the brick wall of the cemetery. With its monuments, angels, statues, and ornate chapels, it resembles a baroque village. "Did I tell you that Gardel's life-size statue can make miracles happen?"

"So, if I pray and maybe even leave some kind of offering at the base of his monument, does that mean that I'll be able to dance like you?"

"Yes, definitely! Hey, the Romans may have had numerous miracle-making popes, but here in Argentina we have Gardel, the tango pontiff."

The telephone takes me by surprise. I've learned to appreciate my handbag's emphatic silence; it's been so nice spending a week with a quiet mobile.

"La Señora Rivabuona? Francesca?" Roberto isn't sure he's dialed the right number.

My eyes open up in surprise and I gesture *shhhht* to Analia. I am annoyed by my own teenage behavior, but at the sound of his voice I can't help it. Now I'm even blushing.

"At Gricel, tonight. Hmmm, *sí*, yes. At eleven thirty, midnight. Ha—no, not before. Can't possibly have dinner, because . . . well, I just can't . . ."

"*Cazzo!* Why am I so stupid?" I ask Analia after hanging up. "I am bloody fifty! Why am I behaving like a virgin?"

What am I going to do now? I think of George, but only momentarily. The freedom he's given me is a bit complicated, after all. I want to let go, I want to experience passion again, to open myself to lust—and yet I'm afraid. George has given me permission, but I've never taken advantage of it. This time, I swear, I will stop being chicken and see where this adventure takes me. Matriciana lovemaking—fine for the first few times— has become tedious. I know I deserve more than the sensual sensations evoked by spaghetti.

Tango notes swirl around in my head, a frisson runs the length of my spine, and I shake myself from reverie. I inhale deeply. I've decided.

Analia watches me, smiling. She's read all that's going through my mind as easily as if it were showing on a high-definition TV.

"A cigarette, please!" I'm sweating like a horse. I strip off my sweater and throw it on the chair next to Analia, pleading.

"The least I can do is smoke a cigarette." I just accepted a date with a man I met yesterday. And I'm married.

"See? You're all set to go to the *milonga* tonight. Carlos Gardel has already performed a miracle: you even have your own *caballero*," Analia teases. "Do you need me to come with you?"

I puff furiously on my Marlboro, shaking the ashes in the wind.

Tango. What will it do to my life? Sometimes I feel as if something significant is already happening. Everyone says that Italy is the country of drama; but I am wondering if the reputation belongs instead to Argentina.

At a table nearby, a group of men in slick business suits argue with one another loudly enough to practically silence our conversation. I eye them wearily, noting how they keep sneaking admiring glances at us, probably curious about what could possibly bring such a flush to our cheeks.

"I want to know; I *demand* to know why you can't have dinner with me tonight."

Startled, Analia and I look up to see Roberto staring directly at me.

"What are *you* doing here!"

"This is my area, remember? My clinic is just around the corner. What brings *you* here in the middle of the day? This is far from the Castelar, from *el Microcentro*. Your *barrio* . . ." Amused at my attempts to compose myself, he takes hold of my arm. I reach up to fix an imaginary curl; I straighten the collar of my shirt.

"I think you need to see Buenos Aires with different eyes. And there is no better way than by having dinner with me." His hand sends great warm vibes into my skin and I feel as if I were burning, every nerve raw under his touch. Even my hair feels electric.

He's taller than I remembered. And those eyes!

"You know she's at the Alvear? You won't have far to go." Analia starts out joking, but she shuts up as soon as she sees my annoyance.

"Then it's settled. I'll pick you up at nine and we'll go to Club Gricel later on." Roberto kisses my hand, nods to Analia—and he's gone.

"I will kill you. Kill you! What do I do now?"

"You've been saying that drama belongs to the Italians? Well, live it up then! I have enough of my own problems. I wouldn't mind witnessing someone else's hot tryst."

"Tell me, does this happen to a lot of women when they come here? Is this a place for love affairs?"

"Well, a lot of single women often come to Argentina to enjoy a fling, a flirt with fantasy. There are people who never experience such freedom. They live their tidy lives in their own countries with their neighbors, families, social ties. When they land here they are freed of all that baggage and they suddenly open themselves to new experiences. I see it happening all the time."

"Do tango teachers get lots of easy lays? It reminds me of the fifties in Capri. Women of all ages and social levels would come to Italy and look out for lifeguards, waiters, porters. Anything, in order to be held in the strong arms of a macho Italian man. It might be the same here with tango dancers, they have a similar kind of earthy quality, the physicality of a great body . . ."

"Tango dancers have incredible sex appeal. First, they dance so well; then at the *milongas* they are absolute heroes and gods. Women like it. In their arms they bask in everyone's admiration. And at five a.m., there aren't many barriers left. Things happen. Maybe there's a fat husband. Maybe they have no sex lives."

I cringe. That's a low blow, and it hits home. But Analia, of course, can't possibly know.

"I, too, am going through something strange. Francesca, you can't imagine what happened. Luis and I . . ." She averts her eyes, silencing herself. "Anyway, will you come again to the show one of these days? You should bring Roberto."

"Luis?" I interrupt her, feigning ignorance. "I had a feeling there was something special between the two of you. I am new to this world, but it was quite clear to me that there is more than dancing there."

"I don't know what's happening to me, to us . . ." She throws her hands up helplessly. "Luis . . . he wants to have children with me. Do you think it's possible? I want them too. I don't care if he's gay, he'd love them." She's almost pleading.

Oh God, she's so young and naive. "That was fast! Analia, you have to be careful. Live in this magic moment and enjoy it. A family at your age? Children? You are a kid yourself. Please, don't ruin your career chances. You never know."

Analia looks anguished for a brief moment. "But, nothing wrong could ever happen. Luis loves me . . ." She smiles knowingly.

What does she know about life? I don't want to be the one to kill her hopes.

"A bisexual man? Attracted to both sexes? My trainer in New York always says: You are either gay, straight, or you are lying . . . Who knows where the boundaries are? Careful with your hopes with Luis: you need to try to keep some perspective."

"Maybe Gardel will make a miracle for me. Maybe I'll give a baby to Luis. He wants a family." Should I point out that she's a woman and not just a womb? Analia is too young to allow her life to be trapped into motherhood just to please Luis and he doesn't strike me, at least for the moment, as a solid father figure. This affair has just begun, it's too soon to make these types of irreversible plans.

Having finished our lunch, we slowly walk up Alvear, window-shopping and enjoying the beautiful balmy day. Everyone is out. *Los porteros*—the caretakers—watch the world go by in front of their buildings, leaning against the expensive cars parked in the Recoleta streets. Elderly ladies, with their zinc-white hair, walk their dogs around the block, solemnly greeting one another. Recoleta shines with the renewed hope of a stronger economy.

We stop for a cappuccino at Caffè Cantinetta, Analia's favorite Italian bar, just a few steps away from my hotel. Here the shelves are filled with Italian products: the best pasta—De Cecco, Barilla—bottles of rare Umbrian and Tuscan olive oil, refined vinegars from Emilia e Romagna, cans of tiny tomatoes straight from the hilltops in the Neapolitan countryside, and Amedei's world-renowned chocolate.

On the other side of the globe, in Milan, George is probably doing the exact same thing. Is he drinking his afternoon coffee at Cova, in Via Montenapoleone? He likes it straight, not even a drop of milk or sugar to disturb the exquisite bitterness of his favorite blend. How come I can't stop thinking about him? Baires has unearthed thoughts I've tried to control and deny for so long: my own weakness baffles me more than he does.

I stand among all these Italian goodies, frustrated: I have no kitchen to play in. Going without cooking for more than a week has been extremely difficult. In Buenos Aires, eating at the local restaurants has been part of my assignment. Too much meat, too few vegetables and mushy pasta—instead of the al dente stuff Italians favor. Lashings of cream and butter are definitely not my choice. I miss those long hours spent cutting, assembling, stirring the ingredients while I let my brain ride free in order to find my bearings and restore my sanity.

It is time to reclaim my place in front of a stove, at least for one night. As soon as we find an apartment, I'm going to organize a full Italian feast. "Do you have a vegetable market here? I must get my hands on the best possible ingredients. I will show you how real Italian food should taste, *querida* Analia. The heavy sauces your compatriots love so much spoil the perfection of a simple pasta dish."

Whom will we invite? I want Mariela, Lorena, Carolina, María, the group who had been so passionately discussing tango the night before. And of course my new group of friends, Ellie, Luis, Analia, and Roberto—if I dare.

Cunita

(Cradling)

*f*rancesca, do you think it's real love? It happens every time we dance. It's as if she is inside my body: Analia becomes mine and I'm hers; her soul is in touch with mine. That must be what real love feels like, right?" It's strange, but Luis seems to have selected me as his new confessor. It always happens while we walk around town. He's a true nomad; he could cross this city on foot a thousand times and never get tired of it.

He loves to take me to new places and today he's proclaimed that my local education would be nothing without a visit to Boca. I've already been here with Analia, my official guide, but he wants me to see it through his eyes. Tango lyrics resonate around me as we sit at a hidden bar, just off the beaten path of the tourists. Even in this famous area there is a safe haven, removed from crowds and noise. We've skirted busloads of eager visitors, shopping for postcards and mementos, we've left behind the busy market and the many little stores. Now I feel like a true Argentinean: leaning against my chair, I sip my *mate,* the local tea made of *yerba mate,* enjoying my new friendship with Luis and the insight it's giving me into this city.

Thousands of poverty-stricken Italians and Spanish disembarked at this very dock, a no-man's-land at the beginning of the twentieth century, and it's here that they composed the music that would make Argentina famous around the world. Tango was born in these tiny streets, among garishly painted houses, with their roofs and doors made of corrugated metal. Red, orange, electric blue, yellow, green, an entire rainbow of colors sets this *barrio* aside from all others in the city.

Luis launches into his virtual confessional. "After the show, last night, Analia and I ended up at my apartment in Boedo. It has become our refuge from Valerio and the rest of the company, our secret safe place." He tells me that they've been going there every night, as soon as they can, after the curtain call. It's the only place where they're free to drink, watch TV, listen to the music they love, and where they share the occasional joint. He's completely open and honest about it.

"A bit of *porro* goes a long way," Luis assures me seriously, his eyes absent, still rapt in his thoughts. But he can't keep silent.

They spent the entire night lying in bed, caressing, savoring each moment of their passion. Analia draped her legs around his belly, her left hand stroking his arm. She brushed his face, tenderly tracing his lineaments.

Luis passed her the remainder of the joint, a minuscule sliver of white paper.

"No . . ." She shook her head.

His arm rested on Analia's breast as he looked up, lost in endless scrutiny of the ceiling. Under the effect of the *porro,* the wooden beams faded in and out, dilating and extending to the windows and beyond, and then, quickly vanishing, swallowed whole by the walls of the small apartment. Luis felt Analia watching him as he drew in, filling his lungs with the sweet, tangy smoke. Unhurriedly he turned around and bent over her, putting his lips over hers and gently exhaling into her open mouth. Analia closed her eyes and took it in, surprising Luis with her new willingness.

"It was a sort of communion, a connection, a way to get deeper inside her."

Drowsy, Analia reclined against the pillows and draped the duvet over her body. Sitting in silence next to her, Luis let his mind float far above the ground and register each of the musical phrases wafting in the background. Astor Piazzolla's brilliant light notes separated over their heads, a few cascaded down for them to breathe—in their marijuana-induced lethargy—others floated above, glittering. For them to dance.

Luis slowly moved around the bed and took Analia into his arms. *"Bailamos?"* He needed no answer as Analia blended into his embrace, rounding her shoulders to submit to his desire.

Luis led her in the simplest of the movements, feeling her breath, sensing her lips close to his, looking at her. He held her tight, as light as a leaf, suspended in midair, weightless. Stage tricks forgotten, they danced the fundamentals of tango, simple steps of pure perfection. Their bodies became one, their feet never once left the floor; catlike they emphasized the lyrics and each silence, enhancing every pause of the music.

"Magia," Luis murmurs, "pure magic."

At a brisk variation of the music, Analia whipped her leg up, emblazoning the air with a slow arabesque, tenderly sliding down to stroke Luis's left side. Tantalized, Luis was filled with a lust he'd never experienced before for a woman, and endless desire. While the *bandoneón* lamented old losses and suffering, Luis's lead became firmer, even more precise, marking the sadness of "Ojos negros."

"You are an emotion that lingers," Luis whispered, tightening his pressure on her back. "When I see you dance, I see the aura of your movement trailing you. I wish it were true of all my partners."

His senses recorded every moment, every word of this evening with Analia. What would happen? He couldn't separate the present from the future. He's gay, and she knows it. He looked down at her exulting face, her lowered eyelashes, her contented smile.

"What will happen with us?" she asked hesitantly, breaking the magic of the dance.

Luis gently took her back to the bed and lay on top of her, playing with her hair, reaching her neck and shoulders, kneading her muscles with his fingers. Analia closed her eyes, inhaling the raw force of his touch, his presence.

"Don't ask. I have no answers. Let us simply *be* for the moment. We'll have to confront Valerio, and the others. Don't forget . . ." As if to banish these thoughts, to silence his own doubts, he kissed her hard on her mouth, demanding. He cupped her breasts in his hands and sucked on her nipples, hurting, pulling, biting. He stopped to look at her, and then continued, intent on giving pleasure. She wiggled underneath him. She wanted more, she was ready for him, again.

Barrida

(A Sweep)

Soñar y nada más
con mundos de ilusión,
soñar y nada más
con un querer arrobador,
soñar que tuyo es él
y vive para ti,
soñar siempre soñar
que dicen que el amor
es triste despertar . . .

"Soñar y nada más"

id you sleep at all?"

Ellie bores right into my thoughts—I don't even want to say "my soul" because I have no idea what I did with it. I might have lost it last night at the *milonga*. And afterward.

I feel vulnerable and slightly unhinged. What happened to fierce Francesca and her stoic attitude?

"Should I repeat the question?" The corners of Ellie's mouth twitch; she can barely control her laughter. Okay, okay, yes, she knows. After all, I didn't even say good night, for what is a farewell worth at three in the morning?

I wrap the belt of the robe tight around my waist; I return her enquiring look coyly and purr, purr.

"I demand details!" Ellie laughs at me. It's only ten a.m. and she's already here for breakfast with me at my hotel. *La curiosità è donna;* curiosity, thy name is woman, as my grandfather used to say.

I'm dying to tell her everything. But doing so would be risky—we have so many mutual connections in New York. Ignoring the thought, I sigh and we sink into the sofa. I've always trusted my instincts, and if I don't tell someone about last night, I'll burst.

A trolley, covered with a starched white tablecloth, is piled high with all that two spoiled women could dream of for breakfast. Freshly squeezed orange juice, all kinds of *biscochitos,* and the usual perfect *medialunas de grasa,* to which I'm now addicted. And I'm definitely going to need that huge silver pot full of strong Argentinean coffee.

I shrug sheepishly. "What can I say? Does it show?" Voracious, I reach for more croissants. "Delicious! No guilt in this country about using lard . . . Good for them!"

I haven't even checked the mirror today. Do I carry the external signs of my depravation? Deep wrinkles, under-eye bags, and dark circles?

Am I the only person in the world to have an affair? Why do I feel so strange? One minute I'm frozen inside, the next, a delicious wave of sensuality interrupts my thoughts.

"You are impossible. I have never met anyone like you. Please, tell me! How was your night? You look positively radiant. It shows, definitely . . ." Ellie demands full disclosure.

How difficult to explain what has happened. It was so sudden. I like the idea of putting the blame on something specific like tango; it kind of makes me feel better about the whole situation. It's true that as soon as I arrived in Buenos Aires something changed inside me. Maybe being in the southern hemisphere felt like a way out—a good release for my frustrations—and I grabbed it. If that's the case, I should behave like the adult I am and take full responsibility for my actions.

"Okay, Ellie. Here I am: The Sinner! And, to tell you the truth, I am not the least bit remorseful. I'm just tired and confused, in exactly that order."

"Have you ever heard of the torments of Tantalus? That's what you are doing to me. I'm hanging on every single word you're saying, and so far I'm getting nothing!"

And so I spill the beans.

Roberto met me in the lobby of the Alvear. Towering over me, he immediately planted a kiss on my cheek, but that doesn't really count, as the Argentineans do it anyway, even if they've never met you before. For someone who is supposed to have a wife at home, he seemed remarkably calm and self-possessed.

He's intriguing, well traveled, and full of interests, passionate about far more than his clinics and polo horses. I stole a few looks at his body while we stood at the bar. His tight jeans revealed quite a lot of useful information . . .

"I saw you together at the *milonga*," Ellie insists. "He seems to know what he's doing."

"Well, I'm not an expert, but I loved dancing with him. He's the perfect height."

Music and cigarettes, a few glasses of champagne, an intoxicating cocktail, and then, dancing. At first I made an effort to use all that I've been learning—steps, posture, embellishments—but then I remembered what Luis had said: listen to your partner, feel him, follow his lead, don't anticipate; the single most useful secrets of tango.

It's interesting how an independent woman can be conquered

by the quite medieval idea of being silent and obedient to a man's will. I'm surprised to realize that I enjoy it. It makes me feel frail, vulnerable, feminine. *El abrazo,* the close embrace. That's what it's called, and it feels just right. I took refuge in Roberto's arms, as if he belonged to me and I belonged to him. I nestled against his chest, closed my eyes, and listened to his heartbeat, his body. My cheek against his, the slight rasping of his growing beard, his lips brushing my hair.

"Your hands . . ." Roberto traced my fingers, briefly holding them in his. In the early hours we had to leave.

He wanted me. That was clear from the moment we stepped into the *milonga.* No words were exchanged. At the end of each tango we simply stood, looking at each other, waiting for new notes to resume our courtship ritual.

"Details to come?"

"Of course. Be patient." I'm enjoying the power I have over Ellie. She's a butterball, all soft and blond. Perched on the sofa— her arms circling her knees—her dark eyes shine with curiosity.

"In Rome we used to call it *lo scannatoio.*" I'm not sure an American will understand the concept; we Italians can be so graphic and cynical. *Scannatoio,* or the slaughterhouse, typically described those apartments used by gentlemen of means to conduct their affairs.

"That name is *so* un-PC!" Ellie laughs.

Roberto drove fast. We were both quiet, savoring the hours ahead of us. I had anesthetized my soul, silenced my mind, and concentrated only on the idea of pleasure. I didn't even have to look at him; I felt hot sparks coming from his body, scorching me with the strength of his sex appeal. I studied his profile, taking in his white hair and boyish, suntanned golden skin. Yes, something was definitely moving inside me, down there. The tingling, the anticipation nearly made me faint with desire.

A perfectly luxurious *scannatoio* awaited us—in a loft overlooking Puerto Madero, converted from a huge factory.

"Will you stop sounding like a bloody interior designer? I demand facts. What did he do?"

"He licked me."

"Excuse me?"

"Yes, you heard that right. We didn't make love in the real sense of the word. He licks."

"No penetration?" Ellie's eyes nearly pop out of their sockets.

It was one of the most extravagantly erotic nights of my life. Telling Ellie makes me red and sweaty, but it also helps me to relive those delicious hours, and once again feverish shivers ripple over me from deep down.

As soon as we closed the door, Roberto took me into his arms and started undressing me. I allowed my body to go almost limp, enjoying his hands pulling my sweater off, unzipping my skirt. He looked at me and slowly unfastened my bra. I stood there, happy to be watched, to be completely naked.

"Ellie, keep in mind that he was still perfectly dressed. I was naked, he wasn't." Like me, she flushes.

"Amores de Estudiante," a tango from the forties, was playing softly, delivering the romantic notes of Hugo Diaz's harmonica. This was rapidly turning into the most lascivious Argentinean fantasy, and I certainly wasn't going to stop it.

He took me in his arms and laid me on an enormous round, red sofa. Everything in the loft was over the top, and yet refined. Fellini would have approved.

He started licking me, while stroking my shoulders and my breast with his fingertips, gently. I mean, in my life I have certainly had many experiences, but nothing had prepared me for this.

He licked my eyes, covered my mouth, slid down to my neck and finally my nipples. When I thought that the pleasure had already reached its peak, Roberto knelt in front of me and took both my feet in his hands. Slowly, he touched them, licking my toes and that particularly vulnerable part between them.

He took off his trousers, removed his shirt, all the while concentrating on the pleasure he was giving me. My entire body was like a violin string—taut and ready to be played. He opened my legs and was there. And he stayed . . .

I came in bursts and eruptions, screaming, convulsing with pleasure.

When it was all over I was still an electric circuit, with my hair standing on end, skin as raw as if burned. At that point Roberto came over my belly, my thighs.

Ellie looks at me, her mouth open. She barely remembers to breathe. I can't blame her. Last night seems like a dream, and telling a friend has fixed it as reality. It's like a black-and-white picture, before and after being dipped in the developer fluid. Only at this point do I realize that it really happened.

"And now?" Ellie asks.

"Now? Now we have breakfast and then we go out and shop. I feel so alive and yet so exposed. I need to immerse myself in mindless activities."

"No! I mean: What's the next move with Roberto? Will you see him again?"

"*Non lo so.* I don't know. We kissed good night and were too exhausted to plan anything. I'm not sure I want to get embroiled in a relationship. I'm leaving in a week and I have a husband, back home. It's better if this stays what it is: an adventure. But I must admit that there are a few constants in my life: my love affairs always begin with a dance."

Suddenly the Gypsy's words resound clearly in my memory.

And a nagging thought unsettles me. "He is only forty, you do realize that? And I am fifty."

"Francesca! That's the most idiotic remark. Look at yourself! He is lucky." Ellie joins me in front of the mirror, rapidly dabbing her flushed cheeks with a Kleenex. "See? I'm still gasping."

With a sense of guilt, I switch off the computer, left running since last night. It can wait. But when will I complete the article? Clarissa's e-mails are becoming increasingly frenetic. If I can possibly come to my senses, I'll be able to send it this afternoon.

And George? Where is he? It's my very first time as an "adulteress" and I'm not even conscience-stricken. Is there a God somewhere, ready to skewer me with his sword?

"I've had a couple little encounters in Buenos Aires myself." Ellie's Cheshire-cat smile appears suddenly from behind the coffee cup. "I assume this is the reason why I never married: I love my freedom. I was too terrified to belong to someone else or to have children. Being tied up by duties, responsibilities."

"I keep thinking I've become like the English ladies in fifties Capri. I feel dated."

"Has the world changed over the past few decades? No, it's the same, and flesh continues to be weak. Think of it like this: it's good for your complexion and conducive to better sleep." Ellie grabs her fur coat and a large cashmere scarf. She feels the cold more than any other person I know.

"Do men talk about these things? Apart from boasting about their conquests, do they indulge in the gratifying routine of the morning-after analysis with a good friend? I doubt it." I stretch languorously. I've decided to relax now and worry later. I'm going to concentrate on these floating impressions. For now I am a Venetian gondola, soundlessly navigating the canals of my senses.

"Shoes, we have to buy shoes. Perfect timing! What's more relaxing than that?"

We spot Luis from across Esmeralda, turning the corner of Viamonte. His shining smile betrays his happiness: the Tango Show is already a success and everyone's talking about it. The prospect of spending a few hours together is even more appealing.

I've been intrigued by Luis since my first night at the *milonga*. Add to that the way he seeks my advice about his situation with Analia, and it's as if I've known him forever; as if we've always been friends. Even though I'm continually surprised by the dark, liquid eyes which he will focus only on you, before gazing over your head, in order to concentrate on some invisible place.

I glance at him. Today he looks like a kid who just woke up, and I want to run my fingers through his curls and straighten them.

Luis joins us at Neo Tango, where we are shopping for shoes. All one needs for dancing is here—including those sexy dresses with the asymmetrical hem that many *tangueras* seem to favor. I need one too!

While the young shop assistant expounds on the virtues of a new version of dancing sneakers, Ellie whispers: "Mariela Franganillo says that *those who can't dance buy shoes*."

I'm sure Mariela—a great dancer—is right, but who can resist the lure of such splendid footwear?

I look defiantly at Ellie. "As far as I'm concerned, I could shop all the time!" And now, as part of the tango pleasure, I want the appropriate clothing: shimmying trousers—in delicate chiffon, silk, and gauze, to better enhance a *boleo* or a *rond de jambe*—and pencil-straight skirts, adorned with ruffles and pleats to reveal the shape of the legs.

Ellie's eyes widen in alarm as she checks her watch. "Oh God, I'm late. Now you and Luis can spend quality time together. Without me." She's always in a hurry, as if she never learned to plan in advance. Appointments and meetings materialize at the final hour, leaving her frazzled. Those around her get dropped on the spur of the moment. "You two have fun! See you at dinner."

Luis laughs and draws me close, with his usual easy confidence and warmth. "She'll never change. Let's continue to explore the city! I can show you places you'd never see on your own."

Why not? I'm thrilled at the idea of having him to myself. For a moment I feel a bit unfaithful to my friend, but I chase the idea away and step out into the busy street of La Capital Federal—as the locals refer to their city—ready to get to know Luis better.

My article? I swear: I'll finish it tomorrow morning. No Robertos, no tangos, no *milongas* will keep me away from my desk. Besides, tomorrow will be my last day at the Alvear. The assignment is officially over and I'm moving to my new *civilian* apartment.

"You're a writer?" Luis turns on me, a mixture of admiration and curiosity.

"I write about travel, food, interior design. It's an interesting job."

"Writers usually have a different dimension. They understand people's minds, don't they?"

"Oh, *mamma mia,* I don't know. I suppose some do. I'm not so sure about myself. Why?"

"Because I feel as if I can talk openly with you. As if I can tell you all about my life. I sense that you might understand me."

"My favorite Italian author, Dacia Maraini, says that writing is like extending your hand; the readers will take it only if it is warm and friendly. I hope I can help you. I'm certainly happy to listen."

Luis drags me through Buenos Aires's *Microcentro,* walking fast. We walk at the same speed. I've never found a companion who likes to march through a city as quickly as I do. I synchronize my steps with his and find a ridiculous, childish pleasure in watching our feet move at the same tempo through traffic, without missing a beat.

He takes my hand and pulls me, almost rushing, through Retiro and Plaza San Martín. It's a meeting point, the chosen place for sweet rendezvous; it's Buenos Aires at its architectural best and Luis proudly urges me to admire the statues and fountains dotting the square. In the south corner stands a big *palo borracho,* the South American tree that decorates Buenos Aires with trillions of pink flowers each December.

"How strange! It still has a couple of flowers and we are in midwinter." Luis passes his hand across the big trunk. "A panacea for all evils: these flowers can cure anything, from back pain to alcoholism."

Under the tree a woman has set up shop. "Tarot, hands, Reiki," shouts the big poster she's propped against a table. A purple chiffon cloth, covered with faded gold stars, envelops the legs of her transportable practice.

"I'll read your future." Her hands trail over the tattered gauze. "I see changes . . ."

"No, no. Thank you." I quietly turn away, irrationally frightened. And if she is good? What if I discover something about George? Or Roberto? A Gypsy girl the first night, silvery wires appearing and disappearing; and now this woman. I feel like someone's trying to tell me something.

"Should we sit somewhere for coffee?" I'm beat; I can't really walk anymore. Coming back at eight a.m. after a dissolute night is not a good idea at my age.

A *pastelería* at the corner of San Martín welcomes us with its modern stainless-steel tables and soothing light from sleek, contemporary lamps. I deposit my tired behind on a cushioned armchair and briefly close my eyes.

"I don't know what to do. I need to talk to someone. I think you can help . . ." Luis begins, looking straight at me. I hear the pain in his voice, his desire to share, but I'm so tired that I hesitate to take the bait. Why do I always get ensnared in other people's problems?

He's just a kid full of hope. It's the dichotomy between this boyishness and his maturity that makes him so endearing. Maybe he's a Gemini, with two people inside him. Sexy and tough one moment, tender and vulnerable the next. Like all Geminis he can change quickly.

Before I can respond, he's begun telling me his problems. He's confused. He thinks he's fallen in love with Analia but it's been too quick, only a few days. How can he know if it's the right thing to do? He's gay, and always will be. He's not sure he can commit to life with her—or any woman for that—not the way she'd want it to be. And his work, his career, will suffer. Valerio is already making him pay dearly.

He reaches forward to take my hands, professing his doubts, and I see that he wants to bare his soul to me. "Life at the Astral has become impossible," he admits. He tells me that Valerio has begun torturing Analia even more than usual. He's verbally abused her and unleashed his fury by constantly insulting her and her dancing. Yesterday it got so bad that Analia ran to Luis, sobbing.

"Have you ever heard of *musicality*? What about following simple choreography?" Valerio spat words designed to hit her innermost feelings. Luis couldn't believe Valerio would resort to such maliciousness.

"It's okay, *mi amor*. We'll go through this together," Luis assured her, stroking her hair, kissing her. She sobbed quietly, curled up against him.

Is it real love, what he feels for this girl? It all started in a moment of passion, and it's been beautiful. At last he's attracted to a woman, a relationship accepted by society. Then why does he feel such a sense of dread? And he's nervous about Valerio. The life of an artist depends on too many variables: the right director, the right place, and the right moment. It's touch and go. Today you're a star, tomorrow you're nothing. Luis's anger toward him is mixed with fear.

Once again, trying to escape from reality, Luis and Analia left their tormentor immediately after the show, and went back to Luis's apartment and the safety of Boedo.

Once inside, he held her in his arms, slowly passing his fingers over her body, rocking her to calm her down, making her feel loved. He undressed her and ran a hot bath, filling it with tube-rose essence. He took her feet in his hands and massaged them with essential oils, his fingers stretching her toes, pulling them, stroking the tender flesh between them. Slowly, Analia seemed to warm up, abandoning her sadness and fear. Her slender body reached out to him, as his hands hastily caressed her buttocks, fondling her with slow, deep strokes, teasing her until she submitted to his desire. They made love until exhausted and then, once calmed and appeased, she fell asleep contentedly in his arms, her humiliation and shame temporarily forgotten.

I blink, flustered by his openness, but I can only offer a sympathetic attention. What else? He's confused and doesn't know what he wants. He's worried he'll end up hurting himself and Analia.

He tells me how life has been full of real drama. His mother died when he was twelve, his father when he was fifteen. Tango saved him. His immediate, unexpected success gave him the means to support his younger siblings.

Now I'm all ears; his words have stirred my maternal senses and I want to shield this handsome creature from life's harm.

"I was lucky. Early on I was offered prestigious roles and round-the-world engagements. Thank God for my godfather—*mi padrino*; I owe everything to him, the only person who believed in me. He pushed me and motivated me through my childhood and teenage years; the most difficult period of my life." Luis smiles shyly.

Gone is the internationally known dancer, the sophisticated New Yorker. In his place I see only a *piola*—a street urchin in his black pinafore and billowy blue ribbon—walking to school with his *padrino,* skipping around the plane trees in the ramshackle streets of Caballito, his *barrio.* Bitterness and desperation were his birthright; the burden of poverty and obligation was all he inherited from his parents.

"I'm at sea. I long for love, for normality. But how do you define *normality*? Sometimes I'm so proud of what I have become—through my own efforts—and yet I feel like Cinderella, still not really sure that the glass slipper belongs to me. And I continue to look for my prince . . ."

I nod and touch his hand.

I feel sorry for him. I know what it means to be young, unable to control your destiny; it's a debilitating sense of impotence. I may be fifty now, but I'm questioning the same things. The situation with George doesn't help either. I've loved him dearly and I can't imagine living without him, but I'm restless and want more. The children are gone, work has completely filled my life—and yet it's still not enough. I can no longer rely on my usual self-control. I'm a bundle of nerves, shaken to the core. And now Roberto . . .

"*Un conito para la señora, por favor.*" Luis points at a tiny chocolate cone in the display cabinet. The perfectly shaped mound of *dulce de leche* and chocolate is pure heaven, but I can almost see the cholesterol cluster around my heart. How do the Argentineans stay so thin? Are these gourmet delicacies made only for greedy tourists? Between the meat and the sweets, I'll probably fly back to New York with some serious extra baggage—and I'm not talking suitcases.

Luis moves his chair closer to the table and leans toward me.

"Every time I come home I ask myself: Who am I? Why am I here?"

His life is a string of contradictions, of longings and desires. I understand his ambivalence. Who is the real Luis? The man who wakes up in his apartment on 176th Street, starts his day at Starbucks, and rides the subway to an art exhibit, a concert, a new off-Broadway play? Or the *porteño* whose dancing shoes hang near the door, always ready to perform a tango he was trained to dance?

New York is the place to be, where things happen, where he can be himself without hiding, without trying to change, to conform. Six years ago—when he moved there—he felt accepted, understood. He made friends, had lovers, was offered career choices.

The strange thing is, I'm experiencing the same here, in B.A., enjoying a freedom I can't possibly have in New York.

For Luis, though, Buenos Aires is as tight as an ill-fitting tuxedo. Night after night, sitting at a crowded table, he looks around and sees the usual people. *Milongas* are frozen time capsules: same dancers, same *tangueros,* same couples, same music. He knows what everyone will do, what all of them are thinking. Nothing has changed. Yoli is still in charge and she still wears that defiant half smile. They go back several years, those two. And there is a history there, I can sense it. And yet Luis loves tango and all the emotions involved with it. He studies it; listens to its *letras*—those favorite old lyrics that still make him cry.

"Yoli?" My interest is piqued. "What's the problem with her?" He singled her out with bitterness in his voice, and his choice of words intrigues me. Luis sits still, looking off into the distance, ignoring my question.

I think about the conversations we've had in the few short days I've known him. Despite his charismatic, self-assured façade, he has slowly peeled off his layers, allowing me to see more facets of his personality, to glimpse his insecurities. Once again I'm surprised at how much I enjoy his company.

"Would you consider giving me a few classes, back in New York?" I take the plunge, deciding there and then that I will continue studying tango when I go home. Why not? I've given it a try in the past few days, and Yoli thinks I'm gifted. According to the *gringos tangueros*—my new best friends—*milongas* have sprouted up all over the world. I've even met many groups of Italians here and discovered that tango has conquered my own country as well. It doesn't surprise me.

"What about an hour right now? My friend José's studio is just around the corner. He might have space for us. Wanna try?"

Luis doesn't waste time and we take off like a booster rocket through Cordoba and Reconquista. I barely notice where we're going until we stop in front of an ornate iron gate.

"*Cazzarola* . . . and now?" I'm exhausted. Why did I accept his offer? Will I ever learn to hold back?

"I am *dead,*" I whisper, gasping for breath, hoping to be heard.

"In Argentina we say *calavera no chilla,* a skeleton can't speak . . . Come on! You're strong. Let's start . . ."

We have the room to ourselves, and Luis is a great teacher. He makes me *see* each note and the way my movements should interpret a tango, emphasizing every musical phrase.

"Remember, when you dance it has to be *your* tango. You have to imbue it with your own personality. Otherwise it's as if you were on a bus, always being driven by someone else. Listen, imagine, add . . ."

He asks me to pay attention to the music, shows me how to

interpret a pause, underscoring it with a quick tapping of a foot or the smooth swerving of my leg.

Ellie warned me—and she wasn't the only one—that tango could become an obsession and should be treated as such. Already those dangerous tango cells are multiplying like crazy inside my brain, invading my heart and my body with their relentless power.

And Luis compounds the problem. He makes me feel capable of anything, of dancing well. He gives me hope. Part of me is tempted to run as fast as I possibly can—from Buenos Aires, from tango, from risks. I'm already different and— even if still in a sort of haze—fully aware that I have lifted the lid on Pandora's box. As I dance with Luis, I shiver. I'm a little afraid, but alive again, finally.

Back at the Alvear I lie down on my bed, depleted. I wrap the soft hotel robe around my body, lost in pleasant reveries. Francisco, a short, vigorous man in his fifties—and the favorite of the tango dancers—has just left my room after pounding on me for an hour and a half. I closed my eyes and dozed off while his magic hands kneaded my tired muscles and restored my sanity. My feet have sustained my body weight for too long and now are clamoring for attention. I recognize physical exhaustion, but today the numbing memories of my evening with Roberto have added to the general fatigue.

I'm completely drained. But maybe not so dormant . . .

What's happening to me in this city? Is my body being rewired? How come I suddenly react to everything sensually? Have I been so deprived of physical touch that five hours with Roberto have unleashed all my demons? Have I turned into the Queen of Eros? My body was suddenly aroused when Francisco adroitly pressed the *shao yin,* a major meridian shooting up my thigh. What was

I supposed to do? *Moan?* Instead, I giggled to myself—and that momentarily reestablished my inner balance. I quietly enjoyed the ebb and flow of some intense and wholly unexpected pulsations. At least for now, my reputation is safe!

Only moments after Francisco slipped out of my room, the doorbell rings. "What now?" I need some time off. I'm going to impose a strict do-not-disturb regime before I join Ellie at the restaurant for the usual *parrilla*.

Warily, I crack the door to find a huge basket just outside. There, at my feet, is an incredible orgy of flowers, festooned with ribbons and multicolored paper. Red roses, dark-pink calla lilies, crimson amaryllis, fuchsias, and auburn orchids erupt in riotous chromatic intensity. Here and there—among the magnificent blossoms—white satin pouches emerge in bulky shapes. Awestruck, I motion to the porter to drag this marvelous extravagance inside my room.

A heady perfume surrounds me and I investigate the mysterious bags. *Comme il Faut* is written in gold letters all over the white satin. I lift one pouch and pull its strings; inside is the most exquisite pair of tango shoes, in lavender velvet and silver snakeskin. Never have I seen anything quite so striking, and they are even my size.

But, wait a moment: all of them are! There must be at least ten pairs of perfect shoes of all kinds, in every possible color and material. I stand in front of the mirror and try on two different sandals: a polka-dotted black-and-red number and a striped black-and-white one. I wiggle my toes; I parade, admiring the way the shoes show off my legs. This is crazy.

Who could have sent the basket? Was it . . . *could* it be?!

The accompanying note says simply: "I think I know your size . . ."

Parada

(A Stop)

Subject: Moved!
Date: 6/15/2008 09:01:02 A.M. Eastern Standard Time
From: Francesca.Rivabuona@aol.com
To: George.Farrington@aol.com

Ciao!
Haven't heard from you for two days. A really long time!
You must have been on the move from Milan to Hamburg.
How is Germany and what about those herrings? How
many hundreds of that blue fish did you ingurgitate? I am
sure that by now you've turned into the greatest *haringsfi-lets* expert in the world.

I've moved to the Abasto and I'm finally sharing an
apartment with Ellie. We have two bedrooms and a full
living room. It's a long old building, with large balconies
full of flowers and plants. The Argentineans have a funny
name for it: *casa chorizo*! A sausage house! We even have
una portera, controlling the tenants like a Gestapo.

The article is finished and Clarissa e-mailed me back
immediately. She's happy with it. I did what I came here to
do, and you should see Paulo's pictures: fantastic.

In the meantime, the tango bug has bitten me and here
I am; more worried about the position of my feet than any-thing else I've ever cared about before. It's scary.

Ellie is proving to be a great friend. By the way, have
you ever heard of Isabel Alexanders? She is another New
Yorker and last night we met in passing at one of the *milon-gas*. But I'll tell you all *a voce* when I see you.

Let me know when you'll be back home, and I'll coordinate my return flight.
Baci
Francesca

Breakfast with Ellie. Our daily conversations could be a book, or even a television series. There is something so comforting and cozy about having a friend to share secrets with, to laugh and plot with—first thing in the morning. In the couple of days we've spent in our tiny apartment in the Abasto, we've become each other's confessors. It feels so good to be able to tell the truth, to spill details and bare one's soul. I hope I won't live to regret it. One never knows. But for the moment I trust my friend, and besides, she's telling me about her own life too; I'm not the only one to have committed sins!

Every morning we wake up and make coffee in silence. I'm grateful for that, since I hate to have conversations—any conversation—before I drink my *caffè e latte.* Ellie is the same. She doesn't even open her eyes, just walks blindly to the kitchen. We've agreed on a routine: we both open the shutters; then one makes the coffee while the other sets the table. I go straight to the refrigerator to open a jar of *dulce de leche,* the horribly sweet and extraordinarily decadent milk fudge I can't live without.

I eat it in the middle of the night, when I come back from the *milongas,* and during the day when I need to indulge in a sumptuous treat. I love the entire wicked process. First there is Desire, then Anticipation—and finally Pleasure, as I grab my big spoon and plunge it into the pliant, satiny confection. That dense, golden mound of sweetness is a godsend at any hour, day or night!

Dancing and walking around this city are, for the moment, keeping away those dreaded extra pounds, but will I be disciplined enough to stop indulging once I fly back to New York?

Buenos Aires's sun streams through the windows, piercing through the cold air. This is the kind of winter I grew up with in Italy: blue skies and warm enough by midday to walk around without a jacket. All my new friends make fun of me, because I feel so at home here and I constantly compare it to life in Rome. If I hear a modern tango, I'm immediately sure I recognize the familiar sound of one of our contemporary Italian singers. I've even discovered similarities between our food and theirs.

The dinner party I've been wanting to host is scheduled for tomorrow, and I'll be cooking. Yoli—my impossible teacher who's perennially correcting my feet, my ankles, my balance and back movements—will see that I'm not just an *imbranata*, a klutz! After all, good food is an art and I will finally get to shine.

"I'm a bit worried about Isabel," I tell Ellie as we sip our coffee. "Not sure why, but my sixth sense is telling me that I should be wary of her." Last night, at the *milonga,* I kept catching her looking in my direction with a coldness, a kind of subtle fury. I can't easily put my finger on anything she's said or done; it's just that my antennas vibrate crazily, sensing her contempt, swiveling toward the red danger zone.

I don't quite understand why I'm talking about Isabel first thing in the morning when I have so many other interesting things to tell Ellie. But whenever my stomach gets knotted like this there's a reason. It's not always immediately clear, but sooner or later I'll know. Throughout my life I've learned to trust my instincts. George and my children respect my shit radar and use it all the time to assess situations, friends, risks, and possibilities.

What is it, exactly, that's bothering me? I don't know Isabel at all—I actually just met her—and yet I'm sure that something tricky is going on.

"Francesca, Isabel means nothing here. She doesn't even dance! She goes to the *milongas* because they are dark. They provide a good hiding place for whatever she's done to her face. Remember? That turban, those dark glasses . . . If I ever decide to go in for an overhaul, I won't venture out until my face looks like a baby's behind. Sorry, but it's true."

I burst into a fit of laughter. Ellie can be so funny in her straightforward way.

"Don't worry about her. I think it's just one of those things. She's famous for being cold and we're both too spontaneous to be comfortable with it." Ellie yawns, pouring herself another cup of coffee. "We need sunglasses in this kitchen!" She turns her chair around to escape the daylight that wraps the apartment in algid radiance. We've become like a pair of old owls, accustomed to flying around at night. Once again, this morning we came back at four a.m. How will I ever get used to my social life once I am back in New York? Fancy, sterile evenings that end at ten thirty because everyone is too busy and too bored to stay longer?

My last night at the Alvear—surrounded by ten pairs of delicious shoes—was as sweet as the previous one was wild. Roberto called me seconds after I received his extravagant gift, while I was still in shock and contemplating help from Ellie. His laugh immediately put me in a good mood.

"Hungry?" was his first question. And by then I was definitely feeling a distinct rumble in my stomach. A few *alfajores* and a *conito* couldn't be considered an ideal diet.

"Somewhere I read that one consumes about ninety calories making love. Is it calculated per minute? Per hour? So, yes, I am in need of good food, to replenish what I lost last night . . ."

"I accept my responsibilities then. I have a mandate to take you to a wonderful place." He was already on his way.

We ended up at La Cabrera, a new hotspot in the ever-changing panorama of B.A. nightlife. But where was his wife? And why doesn't he care about being seen with another woman?

It was a gentle evening and we relaxed together, talking, laughing. From time to time I blushed without warning: the mere idea of being seated in front of him brought back some embarrassing memories and I felt all hot inside.

"You are incredible!" Roberto brushed my cheek with his fingers. "Look at you, not even made up and yet so sexy. I love your eyes, green as emeralds; they shine all the time." He traced my lips, my chin.

Blood rushed to my chest and my décolleté turned as red as a tomato. He kept looking at me, smiling while I scrutinized him, too. I wanted him to kiss me, right there, in front of everyone. The old brothel rule—kissing not allowed—came to my mind. Maybe they had a point there. A kiss is a foray into someone's heart, a moment to wait for and indulge. With a kiss you let your defenses go. It's a preview of sensuality, a glimpse of desire, a first taste of eroticism.

Considering all of this while sitting in my apartment with my friend, I fall silent. It feels like a dream. Is Roberto for real? "Ellie, while we were at La Cabrera, Isabel Alexanders walked in and seemed surprised to see me with Roberto. Do you think this might be the problem?"

"Oh dear! I don't know. But it might be a good idea to start asking around about his wife. Maybe she's Isabel's friend? You never know in this town."

"I'm going to call Sarah. She must know something about Roberto's private life. I'll invite her to come to dinner tomorrow night and I'll ask her then. Do you think she'll be upset to see Roberto here?"

"No, she's far too sophisticated for that, plus she's your friend."

The more I think about it, the more certain I am that Sarah has the answer. She'll have the secret behind Roberto's quite open adventure with me. Is he famous for having affairs? He wants to see me again and he's been making all kinds of plans, which makes me both excited and nervous.

"What should I do about Roberto?" In order to persist with my reprehensible behavior, I need some encouragement.

"Relax! Go out; see him. If this makes you happy, do it. You've never told me much about your relationship with George and you rarely mention his name. Long-term marriages usually metamorphose into something else: routine breeds tedium, longing, and frustration. Enjoy what's being offered to you while you're here."

Easy for her to say. My body and my heart are not in synch right now. Intellectually, I know that I have nothing with which to reproach myself. After all, I'm not a robot. I'm a woman, made of real flesh, with all that it implies: I have needs, I have desires. My body is reacting to Roberto's sensuality, but my heart seems several steps behind. I keep thinking about George.

It's unsettling to be so preoccupied by thoughts of George in the midst of my affair with Roberto. I've never been one for reflection or nostalgia! I usually just plunge into the water holding my nose. But now that I've plunged, why do I feel so uncomfortable? Why do I remember that special night George and I spent in a train, crossing Europe, holding hands? Italy, Austria, and then Czechoslovakia; lying on our bed, close to each other, without sleeping, watching the stars going by. Maybe I don't want to give up hope, I still believe in a future with George. People seem to think that I'm the strongest woman in the world, with a will of iron and no weaknesses. If only they could see me now.

I concentrate on my toes, stretching them. I rotate my ankles. Although it's still early, I am, once again, exhausted. I must relax, stretch. So I lift my right shoulder, then my left, bringing them down slowly. One, two, three and four. I repeat the same movements; DanMichael, my trainer in New York, would be amused to see me using his exercise routine to help alleviate my hangover.

It would be nice to spend an evening without going to a *milonga*. Should we stay in tonight? I miss reading. I'd love to sit down with a great novel or an absorbing biography and spend silent quality time. All by myself. I know that Ellie would understand, even if she is the most tango-obsessed woman I've ever met.

"You can make fun of my obsession all you want, but you are still a novice. Wait and let's see if one year from now, you aren't as crazy as I am. You have a leg up—no puns intended—since your formal ballet training helps you understand positions and movements of the body. You know how to think in terms of balance." Ellie shakes her head, bewildered by the memory of all her effort and the long journey she has undertaken in order to become an accomplished dancer.

"This is such a huge difference from, say, the salsa or swing world in New York. The atmosphere there is completely relaxed, different. Even when you're learning everyone is much kinder to you. *Milongas,* on the other hand, are intimidating." I wave my finger to underline my fears.

There, I've said it! *Milongas* terrify me and I can't understand why, but I feel intimidated as soon as I find myself surrounded by all those expert *milongueros*. Just days ago I wasn't so self-conscious and I accepted every invitation, allowing my body to simply move. I didn't concentrate on the position of my feet; I wasn't trying to be perfect. Last night, though, when Roberto— who had to be in surgery early in the morning—left me in front of Canning's door to join Ellie, my legs were wooden, stiff and heavy as a pair of old logs. I didn't feel like dancing and a sense of inadequacy almost swallowed me whole.

"Francesca! The more you know, the more you understand how much you have to learn. It happens to everyone." Ellie identifies with my apprehensions and my sudden moments of shyness. "Take me, for instance. Do you know how much I hate to go to a *milonga* when nobody asks me to dance? It makes me feel so naked; as if everyone around can see that I am a wallflower. It kind of reminds me of when I was a teenager and none of my schoolmates ever asked me to dance. And those bat mitzvahs were torturous. It lasted until I turned sixteen and then, suddenly, I was intensely popular. I think my boobs grew, and my confidence with them." Ellie voices our shared feelings of insecurity.

"If I have to sit alone for too long, I start crossing and uncrossing my ankles. I feel conspicuous; I fidget and busy myself by listening to the music, and looking around. I love studying the odd life-forms that populate these places. I drink too much, for lack of better things to do. Beer, Coke, water; you name it. But then I always have to rush to the bathroom, which is actually a good distraction since it gives me an excuse to get up from the table." Ellie's giggle is contagious and we both laugh. Getting everything out in the open makes the *milongas* feel much less worrying, and we start to dissect the dancing crowd.

"Tango works incredible miracles. I've seldom seen a more swinging group of geriatrics! Look at the Confitería Ideal."

"Okay, take the hair: for women of a certain age it has to be blond, preferably platinum."

"And it usually goes with extremely tanned skin and wrinkles as deep as the Grand Canyon." Sparkling fabrics and cleavage, as massive as the wrinkles, are displayed with skintight trousers and body-hugging skirts. Local men fancy their hair, always perfectly combed, gelled on top and cleverly trimmed. At least they have lots of it.

A strong perfume is also de rigueur, Ellie points out. Is it because of the so-called close embrace, the tango style that envelops a couple in a tight *abrazo*? But a pleasantly fragrant clutch is preferable to the indignity of a smelly, sweaty partner. Bring on the scent.

Finally I can ask her about my first night in Buenos Aires at Canning, when Luis's behavior fascinated me and I wasn't able to take my eyes off her table. I'm so lucky to have made such a fast friend. An easy silence falls between us as we sip our coffee.

"Speaking of Luis, that first night I saw you, he looked so bored." I continue, "How could you enjoy his company? He invited everyone to dance but you."

"Well, when Luis doesn't feel like dancing it's really obvious. There's nothing anyone can do to change his mind. It's as if he isn't even holding you in his arms; he's simply not *there* with you. His eyes wander, roaming around the room. In those situations it's actually better not to ask him to dance."

Analia had once told me the same thing about Luis: there are times when he must be treated with *kid gloves*.

"But," I insist, "don't we all occasionally indulge in reproachable behaviors? I mean, look at me! I'm behaving like a teenager in love."

"Hey, I thought turning fifty would free me from all desire. Instead I'm discovering that tango has awakened me to something I'm not sure I want." I'm as perplexed as Ellie, and I've just started dancing. What can I hope for? I shouldn't have been encouraged by Yoli and the others. I should have stuck with my writing, my recipes, and George.

Breakfast table cleared and confessions exchanged, it's now computer time: I need to check my e-mail, keep in touch with my children, George, and my family.

"Ellie, look at this!" I call her from the bedroom, where I'm staring at my computer.

"What is it?" Ellie ambles in wearing a pair of silk pajamas. How can her hair be perfect at this hour?

"Take a look at George's e-mail. Apparently he knows Isabel! He says she's a fellow trustee of Eaglette, his old boarding school in Switzerland."

Now, that's interesting. I wonder if she has realized that I'm George's wife. My name—di Rivabuona—is not that common; she might have.

"Hmmm. Does he say if they're friends? Did he give you any details?" Ellie's eyebrows have a life of their own: they arch or nosedive according to her inner thoughts.

"No, he just answered my question." With the fingers of both my hands I straighten my forehead, massaging the skin sideways. My dermatologist has warned me that if I continue to frown every time I am worried, I'll look like a tortoise when I'm sixty. Who wants to risk it?

"George and Isabel . . . See? I've never met her before because I hate those school functions; I go only when he really needs me to put in an appearance. Besides, no one there ever wants to talk to me; they're too busy with their own feel-good pet projects. God, I wish I knew why she's decided to come here to Argentina for her treatment, instead of the States, but Roberto will never reveal anything. Him and his Hippocratic oath."

Banishing these questions to the back of my mind, I grab the phone and follow through on calling Sarah. I'm sure she might be able to tell me something about Roberto's wife; after all, wasn't she the first person to help me link cosmetic surgery and tango?

"This is nothing short of amazing, Francesca. I was just about to call you. Guess who I had dinner with last night? Isabel! We ran into each other at a cocktail party."

It turns out that Isabel has been asking questions about me, and while delivering her passionate description of my culinary wizardry and my writing successes, Sarah was able to dig a bit. Why was Isabel so curious? Apparently she often travels with George to Switzerland. The two of them have spent many days working together on school projects. So now she's curious about his wife.

And I'm curious about Roberto's wife. Hmm, interesting . . .

"This is puzzling. How come I've never heard about this woman? George never mentioned her before." I don't know what to think or how to respond to the news. I feel as though the lust fest with Roberto has dulled my wits and numbed some of my reactions. On one hand I believe I have no right to reproach George. After all, what can I say after my own crazy, erotic night? On the other, if Sarah is talking about *trips,* as in plural, well, maybe I should be asking some questions about Isabel.

"They were in Lausanne, together, a month ago." Sarah delivers the news with some hesitation. "I'm sorry, but I thought I should tell you. Maybe there's nothing suspicious about it, but it's better if you know."

Ellie's looking at me, eyebrows raised. The term *poker face* certainly doesn't apply to me! My thoughts are whirling a mile a minute inside my head. Maybe they're projected on my forehead like those news strips in Times Square.

In retrospect I think of insignificant moments, suspicious incidents, odd phrases here and there. Trips I didn't know about, a relationship—professional or otherwise—with a woman I've never met. Is it possible that George has been lying to me all these years? Has he been unfaithful? His extraordinary passion for food and the subsequent absence of sexual activity, could it all have been a smokescreen? As usual my mind flies off in a million directions, before I can answer Ellie's silent question.

I hold my breath while I consider this news. Can it be?

If something has happened between George and Isabel, it's

also partially my fault. I've always refused to travel to Switzerland for the Eaglette meetings. Who wants to attend those maddening a cappella concerts? Chirping, trilling notes, polyphonic and polyrhythmic effects, pulsing tremolos performed for the trustees by a bunch of overzealous teenagers.

When it rains it pours. News cascades like strings of pearls, one after the other, or in this case more like a hailstorm. I'm astonished by my own sense of calm; I'm not even horrified by what I've just heard. Surprised, yes, and curious, but nothing more. Have George and I reached the point of no return? Why am I not reacting in a more dramatic way? He seems so far away. His image comes to my mind as if from an old film, grainy and unfocused. All this distance can't be good for us.

In the last few minutes my entire world has capsized and I am suddenly drowning in insecurity. All my points of reference, my psychological landmarks have suddenly been swept away by this news.

There is another woman in George's life. Was I not sexy enough to continue to attract George? Where did I go wrong? I'm like a broken record: I failed, I failed, I failed.

"Are you still there?" Sarah asks anxiously. "Should I have kept quiet about it?"

And of course the answer is no. She's a good friend who's just delivered baffling information. And I'm probably heartbroken, but I'm too numb right now to know it.

"By the way, remember that Buenos Aires is a small town. Last night people were already saying that you and Roberto had been spotted having dinner at La Cabrera . . ." Sarah continues. "Well, Isabel immediately spread the rumor. Don't tell me anything, if you don't want to. But of course I'm curious; especially considering that I'm responsible for introducing the two of you."

"Sarah, I don't have much to tell you. There is nothing scandalous in having dinner with a man." A city of almost twelve million inhabitants, and they saw me eating with my hours-old lover?

"My dear, think about it: Roberto is married. His wife is one of Argentina's most famous actresses and, while she's filming in Punta del Este, he's taking out an Italian woman. You're lucky you're not on the covers of *Hola* and *Gente*."

I make a mental list of everything I've learned in the last few minutes. I now know that my husband flies regularly to Switzerland with a New York socialite and billionaire, and that he's never told me about the trips or his company. I also discovered that my lover (what a delicious word!), who just happens to be married to a celebrity, is openly unfaithful to her. So, not only have I been shortsighted for years about George's secret activities but now—as soon as I'm offered the opportunity—I've eagerly turned into a full-on adulteress.

It's mind-boggling. And it's only ten a.m.!

I walk to the window in a daze, still holding the phone and listening to Sarah. I love the palm trees that grow in crazy bunches at the end of our street, erupting into the plaza with exotic enthusiasm. Buenos Aires's vegetation is part of its charm. What incredible urban art the *porteños* could create if only they had enough money to tidy up their avenues and streets.

I know I'll have to come back to Argentina when it's warm and sunny. One week from now, when I board the plane for New York and return to my life, my heart will stay behind, parked in Buenos Aires until the next trip. I'm experiencing an intangible sadness mixed with desire and loss. I am stunned by the latest news and homesick for a country I don't really know and haven't even left yet.

"And so, how many for dinner?"

I'm off to market with Analia. I can't believe I've decided to cook, and now I need to get the ingredients for tomorrow's party. With my world crashing around me, I've completely lost track of time. I'm not the slightest bit prepared for my debut as a hostess in B.A.

I've made a list: what to buy and when to buy it, and how to space the hours allocated to cooking. Like a general on a battlefield, I plan each move, every moment. My strategy is always, make it simple. Anyone can cook a good meal if they prepare in advance. I heed my own advice, but this time I have to juggle all kinds of unknowns since I've never gone shopping for ingredients in Argentina.

I've planned a traditional Italian menu. Exquisite *spaghetti alla Matriciana,* of course, as a kind of private jab at George. And then a risotto with porcini mushrooms—maybe I'll add a few sausages if I find the right kind—and a veal stew—a perfect companion to a big bowl of polenta.

My day is full. Later in the evening, after my private class, I have to go to the Escuela Carlos Copello, to begin my intensive tango workshop. Yoli has suggested that I enroll in a group course with Maxi and María in order to progress more quickly. Back in New York, I'll be able to join the advanced level.

"Are you ready? *Lista?*" Analia pulls my elbow, asserting her position as my official handler. It's fabulous to have her back in my life after a couple of days. I've missed her mischievousness and her loving, quizzical nature. If she were a punctuation mark, she'd be a question mark. When her smile shines on me, she reminds me of a dark-haired Julia Roberts. She's a breath of fresh air, full of youth and beauty.

Piles of flawless fruits and vegetables are stacked vertically as high as the doors in Baires, or at least in this *barrio,* Abasto.

Oranges, apples, pears, all kinds of lettuce and greenery are arranged in a chromatic order: different shades of green compete with the red of tomatoes and radishes, while the brilliant orange of pumpkins—stacked up by the dozens—sets off the pale shades of fennel and turnips.

"Damn it!" I turn around, twisting my head to look at what has hit my legs. This neighborhood is the headquarters of loose street tiles. Whenever it rains, if you step on one, stagnant water splatters up the legs of the unsuspecting passerby. An instant douche.

"Welcome to Buenos Aires and its civic pride!" Analia is amused at my annoyance.

My cell phone rings and, as usual, it's hidden in the darkness of my coat pocket. I grab it and tuck it under my chin while I finger the tomatoes for the sauce. I want the ripest and reddest of all.

"News about Roberto's wife, my dear." Ellie's wary voice reaches me while I shop under the stony scrutiny of an Argentinean greengrocer. Never has anyone spent so much time touching, probing, and stroking the vegetables in her store.

"So? Tell me! I'm all ears . . ." But in reality I'm much more interested in getting the precise quantity of parsley I need for my *Matriciana*. "Francesca, I hope you're ready." Ellie is sounding more and more ominous, and I stop with a big head of garlic in my right hand. I drop it and get a firm hold on the receiver.

"Shoot . . ."

"Well," Ellie continues haltingly, "get to the nearest newsstand and buy the *Clarín*. It's all there. Roberto's wife has not only gone to Uruguay to film her *telenovela*, but apparently she's left him and run away with Fernando Sendra, one of the most famous young actors in Argentina. A sort of local Brad Pitt."

"Oh . . ."

"And you're in a tiny photo, having dinner at La Cabrera with Roberto . . . looking good and—may I add?—very young."

"*Oddio!* No!"

"Yes. You don't look a year older than forty." Ellie giggles suddenly. I want to kill her. "They also say that he's launching a new venture: a big hotel-spa for those who've been *done* and need to be shielded from society. Guess who his financial backer is? Or should I say: his international godmother? None other than our Isabel."

Analia looks at me, not understanding what's going on. I'm about to throw up. I switch off the phone and bend over the tomato display, holding on for dear life. A storm of doubt threatens to overwhelm me. He used me. Yes, Roberto used me to get back at his wife. And Isabel? After what I learned today about George, how can I be sure of anything? Roberto. Isabel. George. What is the world coming to?

Almighty God, with sword in hand, *really* is intent on skewering me. Wow! I didn't think that being unfaithful would bring down such quick punishment. At my age, how could I have been so stupid? I thought I was immune to those ridiculous situations young people constantly run into for lack of experience.

I shouldn't have.

I wish I . . .

Why did I do it?

Why did I fall into Roberto's arms? Why did I let down my guard?

Should a fifty-year-old give up her sexual needs? Now I'm beginning to see how fulfilling those desires can cause more trouble than it's worth. Maybe I've got it all wrong. Maybe women of a certain age should just relinquish full sexuality. Only a few decades ago, the Catholic Church would assign women my age to care for priests: they posed no risk of temptation or attempts on the chastity of the clergy.

Slowly I sink onto a pile of discarded wooden crates, ignoring the greengrocer, whose eyes still follow my every movement. I tell Analia that we need to get the *Clarín* and then I want out, back to the apartment.

Actually, no: I want to leave, go back to the States, forget about tango, forget about Roberto. But then I'll have to confront the George situation. I can't believe it. Everything is collapsing around me like a house of cards.

"That's definitely drama." Analia holds my arm and helps me carry the bags.

I stop to breathe deeply, inhaling the cold winter morning air. I think of athletes, overcome after completing their final run: I, too, bend over, pressing my hands on my knees. I wheeze.

"I don't really understand what's happened. Tell me what I can do for you." Poor Analia hovers over me anxiously, not sure what's caused my reaction. "Let's go have lunch, a coffee, something. You look green."

But then I remember the dinner tomorrow. What am I supposed to do? Roberto is coming, and Sarah. Everyone will be there. At least the tango people probably aren't aware of this story. But what if Roberto is really famous and they recognize him?

I stand up. I lift my chin. I'm strong. I can do this. With a deep breath Analia and I finish shopping. Leaving the store, I check my phone: so far four texts and several calls. All from Roberto. Good, make him suffer. I find a certain evil satisfaction in watching his phone number appear several times in the call log but I don't want to talk to him right now. The bar at the corner of Agüero seems the right choice to sit down and try to regroup.

I need to concentrate on my own problems. For the umpteenth time I whip out my phone and see that Roberto has called me again. His messages are sweet and kind; he sounds genuinely horrified by what has happened, he's sorry for the *Clarín* article, sorry he didn't tell me about his wife. He didn't think the shit would hit the fan so quickly. He wants to see me; he needs to explain.

I do want to hear Roberto's explanation. After all, he's only part of my problems right now. He certainly has nothing to do with my husband's potential affair. The fact is that he doesn't even know about George and Isabel. And I don't either. Everything is nebulous and I can't be sure of what's going on between them. Yes, I'll call him back. I'm suddenly horny: I want to be with him. It doesn't take much to get me going! But is it a solution or just a palliative?

"Come on, I'll drive you to class. Thinking about what to do with your feet will help your soul and clear your mind. Trust me." Analia gently stretches her hand to help me gather up all my things.

She drives slowly, uncharacteristically patient, caught up behind the thousand vehicles suffocating Corrientes. The big obelisk down the avenue is our destination, an unmistakable target that encourages us to endure the traffic and its crazy caterwauling.

> *"De noche, cuando me acuesto,*
> *No puedo cerrar la puerta,*
> *Porque dejándola abierta*
> *Me hago ilusión que volvés . . ."*

Analia intones with her limpid voice; she must have taken voice classes. Tango notes rise high, carrying with them those desperate lyrics.

"I need to talk to you. I know you've got your own problems, but I need help."

"With what?" Here we are again, and drowned in a river of cars, I'm her captive audience.

Corte

(A Cut)

Vida mía, lejos más te quiero
Vida mía, piensa en mi regreso
Y es por eso que te quiero más
Vida mía, hasta apuro el aliento acercando
    el momento de acareciar felicidad.
Sos mi vida y quisiera llevarte a mi lado
    prendida y así ahogar mi soledad.

"Vida Mía," 1934

*F*rancesca, it's been only a few days and my world has turned around. I'm not sure of anything anymore. I love Luis, I thought he loved me, but now?" Analia shares her doubts with less ease than Luis, but I want to understand her, too. Where does she think this affair will take her? I'm worried about her; she's so young, so naive.

"I know that Luis loves me. It can't be otherwise, you should hear the things he says to me or even the way he sang for me when we danced together last night." She smiles as the memory floods her mind.

"Oh, my life, from afar I love you more." An old tango poured its passionate lyrics into the emptiness of the studio. Luis—his hand on Analia's back—stood still. With a sigh, she settled into his arms. "This is where I belong," she thought. "This is where the wizardry of tango allows me to be one with him." Her cheek against his, his long curls tickling her skin, she lost herself in his powerful energy—inebriated by his smell—deliberately inhaling the essence of love.

"Oh, my life, think about my return."

They glided together, ready to be one, to interpret the notes they both know so well. He slowed her down. At the anguished entrance of the violins, he spun her tenderly, while her leg drew hypnotic curves behind her, her foot writing invisible poetry on the floor.

Whispering, he sang those sweet words, old, famous *letras* she'd heard before but never in this way. Now, as his voice conveyed the depth of his love, they had a real meaning.

"I stopped breathing. *And that is why I love you even more.* Can you imagine? He actually said it." Analia looks at me expectantly. I see the hope and energy of a young girl with love written all over her face. I recognize it well, I looked like that when I met George. I want to tell her to be careful, to remember that Luis was only singing the lyrics of a tango.

"Luis loves me. For sure."

They continued dancing, her eyes closed, her back fitting precisely into the semicircle of his shoulders; her senses awake under the curtain of her lowered lashes. A long pause heightened the intensity of their dance: they were one single block of musicality and emotions. A steady electrical current—not a jolt or a burst—ran through her spine. She submitted, interpreted his orders, obeyed each of his demands.

Yes, she'll be his forever.

"*Oh, my life, I breathe faster, shortening the moment for caressing happiness.*

Oh, my life, think about my return.

You are my life and I wish to carry you fastened to my side and thus to drown my solitude."

Luis sang sotto voce. Lightly he pressed his hand on her back to restrain her, stretching the notes of the violin into an exquisite pause. He rotated her torso until she twisted away from him, her legs still tantalizingly connected to his, pressing against him.

"*That's why I love you more . . .*"

Analia trusts her abilities as a dancer, sure that she's the best partner Luis will ever have. "He finds his *voice* when I nestle in his arms," she tells me. "When we dance together fireworks explode from our tango." She is his violin, his *bandoneón,* together they can make splendid music. He slowly lowered her down, her head almost touching the floor, and gently rocked her, one, two, three times. The dance over, she flushed with joy.

Arrastre

(A Drag)

Hoy tenés el mate lleno de infelices ilusiones,
te ingrupieron los otarios, las amigas, el gavión;
la milonga entre magnates con sus locas tentaciones,
donde triunfan y claudican milongueras pretensiones,
se te ha entrado muy adentro tu pobre corazón.

"Mano a mano"

We met a few hours after the article hit the newsstands—
and me—with a punch in the stomach. All day long,
Roberto had begged for forgiveness and proposed another evening out to make it up to me. For my part, I had steeled myself
against any degrading fits of self-humiliation: no recriminations,
no accusations, and especially no petty complaints. After all, I was
a willing partner in our brief relationship.

Roberto looked repentant when he arrived to pick me up,
and he held me with an unexpected tenderness. I took refuge in
his arms as if I'd known him forever.

We didn't say much to each other as we drove through the
bumper-to-bumper evening traffic. I looked outside, overwhelmed by the strangeness of my situation and resigned to the

existential earthquake I'd have to cope with once back in New York.

I can't sit next to him without feeling the urge to touch him, to press my leg against his, to draw my fingers over his long hands. Our dinner went by in a blur, and I cut it short, exhausted in my efforts to avoid the knowing looks of the people crowding the restaurant. In my new role as a local Dame aux Camelias, I've started attracting some undesired attention. I'll admit to feeling a kind of perverse pride at being involved in the latest scandal, but I would rather have been at an anonymous McDonald's than at this temple of high cuisine.

I'm also worried about George and what will happen to our lives. Isabel has surely let him know about Roberto and me. E-mail spreads news around the world in a matter of seconds. I wonder if George's breezy suggestion—*Go on, have an affair!*—will stand up to the reality.

We drove back to Abasto and I invited Roberto up to the apartment; no excuses, no faux pretenses. I wanted him. He wanted me.

I love the way he moves. Like a dancer, his head high, his body seductive and supple, he commands my personal stage with his presence.

I whipped out a bottle of good Marc de Champagne and put on some background tango music. Transformed by the latest events into a shameless, sex-obsessed time bomb, I stretched out on the sofa and leaned into his frame, setting aside my worries. My hands immediately reached for him, rubbing his shoulders, visualizing his body under the crisp perfection of his blue shirt. I touched his chin, his cheekbones, and closed my eyes, inhaling his smell, tempting, virile. His hands started playing too, wiggling in between the buttons of my shirt. The abrupt awakening of my nipples revealed my readiness and Roberto continued to caress my breasts behind a thin layer of silk. An unmistakable conflagration shot straight down there, in that mysterious place between my legs, and every last one of my nerves tingled, turning me into a state of liquid bliss. My hips rose and circled in slow motion, searching for Roberto's body; I needed him, I wanted to be penetrated. I wasn't ashamed of showing him what I lusted for.

Roberto held me tight and looked at me for a second; then he gently covered my mouth with his. His tongue explored my lips, at first without entering me, and then thrusting inside avidly, following an irresistible urge to dominate me, possess me. Breathless, I closed my eyes, once again accepting his domination. I found myself answering his kiss, softly biting his lower lip, sucking it and keeping it in my mouth for a few sweet seconds.

"Come!" I cuddled into his arms and—before things became too torrid in the living room—I pulled him away from the sofa. I didn't relish the idea of being found in flagrante delicto by Ellie. "For a non-*milonga* night, this might be better than the book I had planned on."

We undressed quickly and stood next to each other, in the half-light of my bedroom.

My hand moved to Roberto's hips, touching his strong buttocks and slipping in front, searching for his penis. I felt his glorious erection and let out a faint murmur of joy, proud of being the cause of his arousal. I knew I was attractive, sexy; I desired and was desired.

I lay on the bed, and he hovered over me. I studied his sculpted belly and small waist. My fingers outlined each muscle on his chest, exploring them; I closed my eyes in order to capture his frame, to fix it in my memory. Suddenly Roberto scooped me up, his hands behind my waist, and he pulled me toward him into a standing position. He opened my legs, wrapped my thighs around his and penetrated me with a forcefulness I didn't expect.

I gasped, surprised at the extreme pleasure of being filled, of feeling his power. He started moving, at first slowly and then rhythmically, his penis gliding smoothly inside my wetness. His strong hands held me tight, and, abandoned against his body, I finally felt safe. I let go of my hesitations, answering his movements with mine, calling his name loudly, moaning. There was no one to hear me; I surrendered to Roberto and all my frustrations flew away with each struggle for breath, each of my cries.

When it was over, he let me down delicately on the bed and lay next to me, his hands on my belly, and me cradling his spent penis. Sweat trickled down his chest. I was content, sedated. No need for words, no promises to be exchanged. Only the gentleness and sweetness of the aftermath.

We must have slept for a few hours, lulled by the still notes of our peacefulness, reveling in the pleasure of skin on skin. I opened my eyes and saw him resting on his elbow, watching me. His hands trailed gently over my head, unhurriedly feeling my earlobes, massaging them and then migrating all over, checking the tip of my nose, my cheekbones. I pulled the sheets over my naked breasts, suddenly feeling exposed, strangely affected by his smile. Blushing.

"You look so vulnerable and young." Roberto laughed, ruffling my hair.

"Well, I'm not, but you make me feel that way." With Roberto I experience a feeling of weightlessness. I don't worry. I don't think. As long as it lasts . . .

"I've got to eat something. You?" Whenever I make love I get hungry; I turn into a famished teenager. Roberto, definitely responsible for an even greater caloric loss than two nights ago, rolled over reclaiming the sheets. "Let's see what we can do to replenish your energy. You'll need it later on."

I can't even imagine the last time George looked at me in such a way. Maybe it's time for me to buy some saucy nightwear. Did my husband stop desiring me because I didn't wear chiffon nightgowns? Or did I stop buying them because he didn't look at me anymore? Which came first: the chicken or the egg? I threw on an old pair of exercise pants and a T-shirt and moved to the kitchen.

"Time for a plate of spaghetti *sciuè-sciuè!*" I laughed at his stunned look. "Comfort food: a simple sauce of tomatoes, garlic, and olive oil. Lots of basil. It will settle your stomach and afterward you'll be happy and sleep like a baby."

"You're really going to cook for me?"

And that's when I asked him. I find that the kitchen is always conducive to deep discussions and the truth comes out much more easily surrounded by the comforts of pots, pans, and a delicious smell.

"Tell me about your wife and about Isabel," I ordered him.

I watched Roberto struggling to decide what to say, how to answer, *whether* to answer.

"My wife left me a few weeks ago, but it was something we'd seen coming for a long time. We haven't had a real marriage for at least a couple of years. No children, no common interests. Imagine: we've *never* shared the same passions. We never liked the same books, the same films, the same activities. Our relationship was based on sex. Fifteen years ago we fell madly in love and our families couldn't have asked for anything better than our marriage." He is matter-of-fact and to the point. Once their attraction was over, Ana María and Roberto had had their fair share of adventures. There was no denying the fact that their relationship, based on initial attraction, had become stale; soon they were just a civilized and sterile married couple. It sounded familiar.

Roberto and Isabel first met at the opening of an exhibition in New York. Feliciano, the well-known Argentinean photographer, had introduced them, and Isabel, not immune to Roberto's dark, sexy looks, immediately decided to conquer him. She did all she could to grab his interest, but without luck.

Isabel is apparently the result of several surgeries undergone throughout the years in different parts of the globe. Dissatisfied with some minor wrinkles, she'd let a Parisian doctor persuade her that she needed another *tiny* intervention. Disaster! While she was mourning the passing of her cheekbones and the inevitable collapse of her eye sockets, she'd met Roberto and heard about his fame. And she decided that Clínica Pluribus would be her final savior.

"I'm coming to Buenos Aires and you, *darling* Roberto, must fix me. Only a simple surgery, will you, *dear?*" Her ruse had been quite transparent.

This was one of the most outrageous announcements I had ever heard. "You are joking, right?" *Wait till I call Ellie and Sarah!* was my immediate thought. How mad can you be to throw yourself under a surgeon's knife in the hopes of a good fuck? "*Olvidate!* Forget it! Roberto, I'd never exchange your sexual attentions for any kind of operation. I'd rather keep all my wrinkles."

"Wait, you have to hear the rest." Roberto laughed and shushed me with a finger over my mouth.

If his doctors were responsible for her inflated lips and her rabbit-eyed look, I don't think she made a great deal with Pluribus. Did she at least land him? "Ha! Now we know why she had to come to Argentina. Two good reasons: one—to get you into her bed; and then—to find a surgeon courageous enough to try and patch up the horrors of her previous attempts at eternal youth." I smile.

There's no getting around it: after radical cosmetic surgery, formerly good-looking women always have an unnerving way of twitching their lips. They pout every few seconds, as if to keep track of their newly plumped-up mouths—and Isabel was no exception. She actually looked as if some bitter doctor had suspended a life buoy under her nose, instead of a pair of lips. She gave me the creeps.

"No wonder she dislikes you . . . *Cin cin!*" He toasted my viciousness.

"What do you think she did to poor George? Are her inflated lips a bedroom advantage?"

"Francesca!" I loved his shocked reaction.

I served the spaghetti al dente, coated with the delicious tomato sauce of my childhood summers in Positano. "A preview of tomorrow's dinner. You must tell me what you think about my *sciuè-sciuè*. This is the essence of Italian cooking." Roberto inhaled the plate of pasta, reveling in the perfect simplicity of its ingredients. It slipped and swirled off our forks and into our ravenous stomachs.

"It's the first time a woman has cooked for me after making love . . ."

Making love. I liked the sound of it, and I felt glad that Roberto thought it was the right label for what we had done. But I knew I'd need to harden my heart against our future separation. There's nothing for me in this relationship; I can't expect it to last and I don't want to set up expectations that will result in my suffering. My heart is full of question marks. I can't believe what's happening to me. Francesca, the tough, well-traveled, experienced Francesca is fully immersed in what a women's magazine would call a midlife crisis. If she were smart, she'd go back to her New York routine immediately and forget all about Buenos Aires.

"What will you do with Ana María and Isabel? I heard that Isabel is investing in your Well-Being Hotel." In his Oxford shirt Roberto was as delicious as my spaghetti. I sat on his knees, leaning against the body I was getting to know so well. I raised my hand to touch his silver hair, his strong jawline.

"Ana María's okay. We're friends. It's only the press making it into a big story, simply because they never have enough scandals and Fernando Sendra is a famous actor. Once they understand that we're cool—as you say in America—they'll leave you and me alone. At that point, they'll only want pictures of the two of them and they'll leave me in peace."

"Yes, and Isabel?" I persisted, convinced that my worst enemy is now this blond sixty-something woman who won't accept her own physical reality. "If she is—or was—my husband's lover and then your rejected lover, she must hate me all the more." A powerful woman dedicated to creating trouble in my life? I really didn't need that.

"Isabel is just a business partner. At least she was until today, now I'm not so sure."

Baldosa

(The Box)

The telephone's insistent ringing pulls me out of a deep sleep. Drunk with fatigue, my eyes semiclosed, I fumble on the bedside table trying to shut down the fracas. My bed is empty, sheets rumpled at my left, the blanket hoarded at the edge, drifting to the floor. Roberto left early to go to the clinic. I roll over to his side of the bed, hoping to find a bit of his warmth, his smell.

"*Hola?*" I can't even recognize my own voice; raucous, it sounds as if it emerges from a well. It's Analia. I look at my watch: eight a.m. What is she doing up at this time of the day?

"Francesca, I need to talk to you. *Podemos hablar?*" Her voice sounds urgent.

I get up and sit on the ugly futon that dominates the living room, hoping to shake my brain of its torpor. I kick my slippers off and arrange the cushions to better support my back. I can tell from the anxiety in her voice that this is going to be a long conversation. Barely a week in Argentina with these two young people and they can't make decisions without seeking my advice. Eight a.m.: I yawn. I should have told her to call back later, but now I'm resigned and I listen.

"Yesterday Luis didn't call for the entire day, so I went to his apartment," Analia starts, her voice heavy. "I flew up the four flights of stairs, running to tell him my news."

She knocked at the door, urgently. Unshaven, wearing a mismatched T-shirt and sweatpants, thin as a rail, his curly hair a crazed halo, Luis immediately pulled her into his arms, smiling.

"What happened to you? You won't answer the phone." Analia dragged him and pushed him playfully onto the bed, falling over his body and hugging him. "Guess what? Guess what!!!" She straddled him and laughed.

"What?" He held her by the wrists and shook her frail body. "Tell me. Skip games. I'm curious!"

"I've been chosen for a show in New York! On Broadway! Yoli did it, can you imagine? Yoli, my teacher. Fuck Valerio! I was cast yesterday and they just confirmed an hour ago. Just enough time to take a shower, jump on the *colectivo,* and rush here; I had to tell you immediately. If all goes well, I'll get to spend several months in Manhattan." Her enthusiasm was propelled by her desire to share her happiness with the man who had become the center of her life. "We'll be together. Forever."

"You never told me anything about this. When did all of this happen?" Luis smiled at her, flabbergasted. Analia focused on his mouth, on those lips designed to be kissed; once again she found herself unaccountably dazzled by his teeth, pearly and perfectly regular. She touched his cheek and ran her hand over his unruly hair, pulling his curls.

"Francesca, I love every inch of his body, I know it so well: the nose he'd wanted to change since he'd become a man, his strong arms, his stomach with its bit of softness around the waist."

While she delivered her triumphant news she nibbled playfully at his earlobes, massaging them delicately with her fingers, the way she'd learned from Siri, her Thai masseuse. Soon they fell silent, and in the quiet of the bedroom she could hear her own heart pounding inside her chest. The pleasure of responding to each other's rhythm took over and they acknowledged the inevitable, giving in to a lust neither of them could restrain. Analia's hand slipped under his T-shirt and playfully stroked his chest, her fingers tickling his back and each vulnerable point on his body. This time Luis was passive, waiting for her next move. She quickly undressed and pressed her firm breasts against him, her erect nipples already straining painfully. She slid down and pulled off his pants, just enough to expose his penis. There was no doubt that Luis wanted her. Gently she took him in her mouth and loved him.

"But then he wasn't there anymore. He, he . . . It went away." Analia sounds dumbfounded over the phone.

Luis moved away, turned his back to her, cradling his softness, hiding his failure. Ashamed.

"I can feel it. You don't love me anymore. What happened?" Analia whined.

"Analia, you know I'm gay. I love men, all men. I am attracted to them, I desire them. Sometimes I might feel like having sex with a woman, but the older I become, the less I want it. I'm sorry . . ." Luis had stopped her abruptly, a finger over her lips, sealing the words that gave away her desperation.

"He took me into his arms with such tenderness, he covered me with millions of kisses. Francesca, I don't know what to do. He says he doesn't want to hurt me, that he loves me but he's not *in love* with me." I consider my response, not sure what she would like to hear from me.

"How can he say he loves me! How can he go to bed with me and have sex with me? I've seen him come, I've given him orgasms. What does that mean? He found it in himself to want me . . ." Analia's desolate, silent tears break my heart, but I can also see Luis's side of the story. He probably vowed to end their affair, stop once and for all what has quickly turned into a difficult situation that could destroy their friendship and their work together. They had only a few nights and days together. But what do I know? These are just my conjectures and I feel for both of them. I, too, have no idea of where I'm standing and what I should do. The only difference is that I'm so much older and should know better. But do I?

Colgada

(Suspended)

Y cuando de los bandoneones
Se oyen las notas de un tango,
Pobre florcita de fango
Siente su alma vibrar
Las nostalgias de otros tiempos
De placeres y de amores,
¡Hoy sólo son sinsabores
Que la invitan a llorar!

"El motivo"

I adore being in a kitchen. Any kitchen. I get a sense of comfort from stirring a sauce, cutting vegetables, assembling pungent herbs to marinate a piece of meat. Each activity brings a great sense of peace; a welcome moment of self-absorption. George likes to say it's the only time I keep quiet. Instead, while he watches me cook, he's the one who instantly turns verbal. Sometimes *too* verbal.

"You are *so* sexy. I'm falling in love with you, all over again." His expression changes as soon as he sees me making a risotto or baking one of his favorite cakes. His eyes sparkle with renewed passion and he circles my waist with his arms. He squeezes me in a bear hug. I am his kitchen goddess.

"Stop it, George. I bet you're convinced that the Kama Sutra is an unusual curry sauce." I shake my head, bemused by the sudden explosion of lust, which, unfortunately, can't make the journey from the kitchen to the bedroom door.

Thinking about this as I begin preparing my Italian feast for my Argentinean friends, I wonder if Isabel has had a different experience. But I don't want to go there. It hurts too much.

I will myself to focus on the present, where, in my Abasto apartment, Luis helps me prepare the evening's meal. His jeans strain across his butt as he washes all the dirty pans and pots I leave behind as I cook. Yesterday he begged to be allowed into the mysteries of Italian gastronomy.

"Francesca, please, let me help you. Italian food fascinates me. I promise: I'll be your slave; I'll cut, wash, and tidy up all you want."

It didn't take much to convince me, since I love having him around and I'm flattered that he wants to keep me company. From time to time, I catch him glancing at me with curiosity. I, too, have stolen a few looks at him; Analia's call replays vividly in my mind.

I quickly slice two big yellow onions and a few strips of pancetta and throw everything in a pan; I add red pepper flakes and a couple of spoons of the best olive oil I could find at La Cantinetta.

"Para Los Rumberos," a lighthearted, well-known salsa, blasts from Luis's iPod, which he's hooked up to the apartment's obsolete stereo system. Leave it to him to fill a place with music. He sneaks up on me from behind and takes me into his arms, dragging me around the living room, following the fast beat of the popular Cuban song. Our bodies move in unison and we laugh when my long apron gets entangled with his legs.

"Small! Small steps, Francesca! Quiet down your hips." Once

a teacher, always a teacher. I shimmy around in the narrow space still holding on to my wooden spoon. This is definitely the best way to cook.

The sharp aroma of slowly sautéing onions fills the apartment. The pancetta—releasing its fat—turns a warm caramel shade, while juicy tomatoes wait in a bowl, already diced and ready to be tossed into the sauce; it'll simmer for another two hours over a low flame, until it's thickened. At that point a few tablespoons of Parmigiano Reggiano or pecorino will add a welcome bite to the *Matriciana*.

"To George!" I fill two glasses from a bottle of Nicolas Catena—a rich combination of Cabernet and Malbec with a bold, sophisticated nose. "This is to you and your flying around Switzerland with plastic millionaires! You claim that my *Matriciana* is the best in the world; let's see if Isabel can provide you with the same." I lift my glass to the ceiling. Am I jealous? Of course, but I'm also sad. And furious. And scared. I feel inadequate.

Thank God for Luis. In his presence, I'm forced to hide my feelings of weakness. I offer him another glass of wine while he—true to his promise—busily cleans up after me.

"Bravo. You are very neat. Who taught you? Was your mother an accomplished cook?"

"Actually, I learned from my godfather, certainly not my mother. She was too busy ruining her life with drugs." There's not a hint of bitterness to his words as he relates what must have been a major trauma in his life. I stop and look at him, my trusty wooden spoon dripping sauce all over the kitchen floor.

"Oh! What have I done!" This kind of distraction is enough to turn me into a sloppy cook. I mop up the crimson puddle, wishing I could clean up my life just as easily.

"On his way back from work, my godfather, *el padrino,* would pick me up at school and take me to his home, where he'd prepare a plate of *pasta al pomodoro* for me. His name was Rossano Bruni: you can't get more Italian than that."

"Gnocchi, pizza, lasagna, *milanesa*. They were the staples of my school days." Luis grew up with the dishes loved by the immigrant Italian families in Argentina, who came straight from the old country with nothing aside from their traditions.

While the sauce simmers, I spy on him. He searches for plates and glasses, opening and closing drawers and cabinets. His energy lightens up the kitchen and it's helpful not to have to direct him all the time. The tomatoes are almost dissolved. I love how scents can create instant atmospheres: today I am at home. "Tell me about your mother."

"What is there to say? I loved her. She was so beautiful and kind, but also young, unhappy, and foolish. She didn't want to live hand to mouth; she wanted glamour and riches. She wasn't born to have children or to take care of them. I think I took a little from her." Luis's shoulders slump, sadness filling his eyes. For a brief moment he hides behind a mask of quiet reserve.

Not an easy life. The more I talk to him, the more heartbreaking details I hear. He seems willing, even eager, to open his soul and let go.

At the age of sixteen, his mother, Nelida, married Gustavo, a former policeman in his late fifties. After a few years of happiness, Nelida—saddled at twenty-five with four children—started to look around for something different: a change, anything that would help her out of the boredom she had sunk into. Barely a kid herself, she had never had the chance to indulge her own youth and she resented the constraints of her daily life—she craved a freedom she had never tasted.

"My parents ran a small pension at the corner of Boedo and

Humberto Primo, almost exactly where I have my apartment today. Funny, I've never thought about it and all of a sudden talking with you brings back all these memories."

"You can unload as much as you want and I'll keep cooking. Otherwise tonight we won't be able to eat."

Nelida, dark-haired and passionate, with large coal-black eyes and the body of a teenager, soon discovered an irresistible diversion. Heedless of the inevitable consequences, she ran into the arms of Amilcar, a *carnicero*—a butcher—who worked the night shift at the biggest meatpacking company in Buenos Aires. Handsome young Amilcar knew how to tango and make her laugh.

"My fifth brother is the result of that encounter." Luis carries a pile of plates to the table. He has an eye for style. He's decorated the room with candles, putting them into glasses and empty pitchers, making use of anything that catches his fancy.

"Five kids? How did your father react?" Maybe I shouldn't have asked Luis to reminisce. Have I lifted the lid of someone else's Pandora's box?

"Papá left her. No, actually she ran off with her boyfriend and left us with her sister, Tía Mirtha. So Papá, too, deserted us, since he couldn't take care of four children and his pension at the same time."

I impulsively place a kiss on Luis's forehead. I'm afraid of probing for more but the floodgates are open; it's clear that he needs to talk.

"My childhood was not so different from that of other kids from the poor *barrios*. I was happy, actually, because I had *el padrino* and Tía Mirtha. They were like strict parents, and since they didn't have children of their own, they took care of us."

Luis went to a good school and enrolled in the local *parroquia,* where he studied the catechism and followed the customary path to become a perfect Catholic boy. Rossano, *el padrino,* devoted to

Jesus and *la Madonna,* took him and his siblings to Mass, instilling in his nephews uncompromising moral principles and a healthy fear of God. Each day of the year had its own *santo* to worship; a separate one dedicated to every possible need. Luis learned to invoke Santa Lucia, the patron saint of eyes, in order to make his so sharp that he could immediately find any lost object.

On one of her rare visits, Nelida offered to take Luis with her, for a special afternoon and night together.

"Francesca, I was so happy that Mamá wanted to spend some time with me alone. I felt so important."

After dinner, Nelida took hold of Luis's hand, dragging him through the streets, which became emptier and emptier the farther they moved into Villa Soldati, a *barrio* known for its poverty and roaming bands of menacing youths. "Are we there, Mamá?" ten-year-old Luis complained, dragging his feet and trying to keep up with his mother's pace. Darkness shrouded the buildings around him. Only a few windows gave out a feeble light in defiance of the full moon rising behind the church. He eyed Nelida's big purse, which seemed to bulge with a life of its own.

"Maybe that's how you learned to walk so fast." I do my best to lighten up the suddenly darkened atmosphere of the kitchen. I fear what I am about to learn.

"Mamá knocked at the door of a dilapidated house for what seemed an impossibly long time. I was used to a *barrio* where doors were left open all the time and friendly people invited you in as soon as they saw you coming. We may have lived in semipoverty, but our neighborhood was safe, full of God-fearing families."

The door cracked open and they were let in by a fat woman dressed from head to toe in white. Nelida murmured a few words of greeting and hastily opened her bulky red bag. Out popped a live young cockerel, as bewildered as Luis was at its sudden appearance. Ruffling its white feathers, the bird tried to get its balance and stand up on the wooden table, but its feet were bound with rope and its light body kept toppling over.

The woman, veils flowing behind her oversized body, led her visitors to yet another room, larger and darker than the previous one, and motioned for Luis to sit on a chair against the wall.

"The room was full of people, men and women, sitting around in a circle. Everyone smoked Havanas and drank rum from small glasses." Luis's voice is dreamy, lost in the memory.

It was barely past midnight, and Nelida knelt on a rug, in front of a makeshift altar decorated with ornate images of Jesus Christ and Our Lady. Plastic red hearts twirled from the ceiling, while the walls were covered with icons and colorful religious images.

"The statuettes of red devils—men and women—with long, pointed horns scared me." But Luis, stupefied, had also recognized many of the familiar saints he had learned to venerate. He reached in his pocket for *l'estampita,* the holy picture the priest had given him the day before, for his services as an altar boy at the Church of San Pancracio, and stroked the image of Saint Joseph for reassurance. In front of him, plastered on the altar, there was good old Saint George, together with Saint Cosmas and Saint Lazarus. White candles, bright flowers, and beaded necklaces surrounded the garishly painted portraits of the orishas. Although at first frightened by the somber atmosphere of the room, Luis felt better once he recognized all those saints. They wouldn't harm him. He had always behaved, and the *cura* had praised him last time he had assisted at Mass.

"I wanted some of the candies the faithful offered to the gods, but Mamá wouldn't let me have any." Luis smiles for the first time.

"Bay y May," murmured the *iyalocha,* invoking Saint Lazarus, the orisha patron of the sick. Slowly rocking back and forth, she passed her hands over Nelida's head, purifying her aura of past and present dangers, readying her for great luck and fortune, guaranteeing her future health.

Nelida echoed the *iyalocha*'s chant. "Give me protection, give me advice."

Men and women threw alcohol on the floor and walked over it, to purify their souls. Words flew sweetly in the air, a monotone chant accompanied by swaying hips, hypnotizing movements, and rhythmic sounds.

Luis was soon overcome by a kind of heavy drowsiness. Tired by the long walk, he drifted to sleep.

"But the cockerel's shrieks were enough to jolt me out of my peaceful nap and I woke up to a living nightmare, the bloodiest scene a child could possibly imagine. My mother held the poor animal's legs, firmly pressing its body down, while the woman struck at it repeatedly with a knife, each time plunging into its throat."

"Was she mad? How could your mother take you to such a terrible place?" I look at Luis in complete horror.

Its own feathers swirling through the darkened room, the rooster twitched in its final convulsions until its limbs gave over and its body lay still on the altar. A cup of precious blood was collected and immediately offered to Bay y May, who would bring good luck and absolve Nelida from all her sins.

"I had previously seen Tía Mirtha kill a hen—twisting its neck with a swift movement of her strong hands—but somehow this struck me as totally different. Francesca, you can't imagine how scared I was!" All color has drained from Luis's face and he looks at me, as white as a sheet.

"And then? Why did your mother take you with her?"

Nelida, by now seriously addicted to drugs and alcohol, was

severely ill. A few days before, the doctor had shaken his head, pronouncing the verdict that robbed her of all but a few months of life, if she were lucky. She had been struck by *la Terrible Infermidad,* the Terrible Disease, the euphemism used almost like an exorcism to avoid uttering the word *cancer.*

"You must see an *iyalocha,* a priestess," her friends had advised. "And you should take your firstborn." It was well known that the orishas, the gods, would have compassion for a woman accompanied by her son and might grant her a miracle.

"I had no idea that macumba was practiced in Argentina too. I thought it existed only in Brazil." Shocked by the story, I've completely forgotten my dinner. I eye Luis in disbelief. How much misery has he gone through in his young life? I think about my own safe childhood in Rome—protected and spoiled by the love of my normal family—and those of my own children, who spent many serene years in stable surroundings.

"Francesca, don't be upset. I don't even know why these memories came to my mind. Look, I'm a happy man now. Don't you see? I'm successful, with a great life in New York and here." For a moment Luis holds me tight, flashing his warm smile. "I shouldn't have upset you like this. Stupid me."

Could I ever have imagined that my days in Argentina would bring so many surprises? Will I be the same when I go back to my luxurious home and pampered routine? I repeat these questions incessantly. So far tango has ushered in an avalanche of changes: a different approach to life and new friendships that feel as if they've existed forever. I'm starting to look at my relationship with George with new eyes and it's finally clear to me that I don't deserve the way he's treated me. A welcome sense of strength brews new resolutions to find a way out: I'm going to fight for a better life. I want happiness, if indeed it exists.

"Never mind cooking. Now I want to know what happened to

Nelida. Did your aunt and uncle discover what she had done with you that afternoon?" My motherly instincts have rallied again.

"I felt as if my legs were about to give way like the rooster's. I held my mother's hand in a painful grip and refused to move."

"*Niño,* you must walk by yourself, I can't lift you. You weigh too much. Come on! You are not a baby anymore, you're a man. Move, *mi amor,* we must go back home. What you've seen were only prayers. Saint Lazarus and Our Lady of Las Mercedes will help me. You want your mamá to be happy, don't you?"

"Yes, Mamá. Yes." Luis brought his hand up to cover his mouth. A groan from deep within his thin frame cut off his words as he doubled over to throw up in the middle of the street.

"Promise you won't say anything. Will you? It's nobody's business. Promise?" Nelida held her son's scrawny body in her arms, rocking him up and down, trying to comfort him. She took a big handkerchief from her bag and lovingly wiped Luis's mouth.

"I remember staring at her and suddenly noticing how gray the skin under her eyes looked. I felt as if life had evaporated from her body." Luis shivers and covers his eyes with the back of his right hand.

"Luis, I had no idea. I am so sorry." I don't know what to say.

"Mamá died two years later. The orishas had granted her more than the few months the doctors had predicted." Luis swallows hard. "Probably worth the rooster."

Darkness has settled in the apartment. I break the spell by putting on every lamp in the living room and lighting more candles.

"Luis, come on. The guests will be here any moment and they can't find us looking like this." I dry my eyes and gently take him by the shoulders, trying to snap him out of his memories.

I close my bedroom door and look at myself in the mirror. I bend over the table, sustaining my upper body with my hands. I scrutinize my image, impartially, as if I were studying someone else. Now and again, danger brews in Buenos Aires, and an impalpable fear seeps through one's bones. Today a macumba story. And tomorrow? This city attracts me and terrifies me at the same time. I think back to my very first day—a little more than a week ago—when silvery wires suddenly encircled and captured me as I crossed Avenida 9 de Julio. I knew they signaled important changes, but I certainly couldn't have predicted everything that has happened.

And the main question is still the same: What am I supposed to do with my life with George? The anger, the resentment I feel inside me at times washes over my soul like the sea at high tide.

Perched on a high kitchen stool, I survey the room like a movie director, guiding my actors through a performance of friendship and good times. Will Roberto come? He said he would. I check the clock, listening for the bell.

I wish he'd get here soon.

I wish I wasn't yearning so intensely for his presence.

The notes of Piazzolla's "Cafetín de Buenos Aires" create a vibrant atmosphere and a young couple, Maxi and María (my new teachers), dance slowly, as if in a dream, highlighting each musical phrase with well-delineated, graceful movements. They come together as one, their feet sketch intricate lines on the floor as if it were a canvas on which to draw their passion, their bodies become the physical expressions of the romantic tango lyrics. Immersed in their reverie, they're washed away by the music, their feelings revealed, their profiles coalescing dreamily into each other. She drowns in his eyes. He envelops her in his arms; tall and powerful, he gazes down at her, enraptured. I envy them and the emotions they share.

Ellie elbows me, distracting me. "Luis is such a flirt. I recognize his Salome mode. Look! Just watch him and this new guy in his life. He's smitten and Luis only encourages it." The two men dance languorously, Luis, in a purple shirt and a dark blue velvet blazer, as a ravishing Lord Fauntleroy. He is smiling at Oliviero Carés, the well-known theater director, and fluttering eyelashes that grew an inch the moment he set eyes on him.

"Oliviero has to be about sixty—or maybe less? He's one of South America's most famous literary pundits. He also produces the most widely attended, deeply intellectual plays and has a hand in the film industry. Quite frankly, Luis could benefit from meeting him, but he should be careful. Oliviero has a dark side, and I remember hearing about a torrid affair he had with Valerio a while ago."

"Oh, leave it to Luis to get himself involved in a messy situation like that. And what about Analia? How can he do that to her?" Ellie and I are back in the kitchen, and I'm giving the finishing touches to the *polenta al ragù,* adding heavy cream to my *risotto ai funghi porcini.*

"What does he think he's doing? I wouldn't want to be Analia, poor thing." We exchange glances. No need for words when it comes to those two.

Carés has never met Luis before, but something happened when they were introduced and they didn't bother to hide it. Even I can see the transformation: Luis instantly became sensual, provocative, flirtatious. He ogles Oliviero and sashays back and forth from the kitchen, performing for only one man in the room. Tight black jeans hug his perfect behind, a fitted blazer and ornate cowboy boots lend him a kind of macho swagger. With his gelled hair combed back, Luis is a Hollywood dream. No wonder Oliviero can't take his eyes off him.

I take the big bowl of polenta into the dining room, where

my poor Analia is curled up in a fetal position on the sofa in one corner of the room. She follows every one of Luis's movements with the precision of a laser probe. Her head has sunk between her shoulders; her face is an island emerging from a sea of dark hair.

"It's heart-wrenching to see her suffering like that. I'm not sure she can handle it." If Luis is a Hollywood dream, tonight Analia is a New York bag lady, with desperation and embarrassment evident in her crazed eyes. There are miles between them and they've hardly spoken a word to each other all night. She has hardly said a word since she arrived.

"Francesca, you can't do much about it. They're both adult and Luis has always been straightforward—well, one way or another." Ellie—always fiercely protective of Luis—defends him. I'm not so sure I agree with her.

Analia is in a difficult situation, but it's a problem of her own making. She's barely a teenager and desperate to believe in love, to trust Luis. By refusing to accept reality, she's going to dig herself deeper and deeper into a painful situation.

As I consider the *telenovela* unfolding under my eyes, I miss Roberto's entrance. He catches my eyes as he greets Sarah, all the while staring at me. I can see how he wants to cross the room, abandon all social conventions and take me in his arms. I understand him so well, even after just a few days.

Before he can disentangle himself from the warm embrace of my guests, I steal a glance at the tall window, checking my reflection. I look great. My new moss-green dress suits me; it brings out my colors and I love the way it moves, dancing around my body.

"Francesca—" Roberto silences himself, folding me in a tight embrace. I see Ellie and Sarah watching us and feel embarrassed. Then I let go, I breathe slowly, and I close my eyes. I allow myself to slip into my own private world. Trillions of beautiful notes are in front of us, to be danced, interpreted. Tonight is a blank page on which we can write our own story. I feel as if I'm about to embark on a long journey; in front of us a swerving empty road we can travel together.

Traspiés

(A Slip)

*I*t's that time of the day: breakfast with Ellie. But today also Analia is here, having landed at our front door after a brief pleading call. Shuffling, I drag myself to the stove, putting our morning ritual in motion.

"Coffee for everyone! Aren't we lucky there are no men around?" I show off my horrendous pajamas for Ellie and Analia.

"Freshly baked *medialunas*." Analia holds the white paper bag in front of my greedy eyes.

She looks thinner than ever, worn out and with dismal blue circles under her eyes, her subdued *"Buenos días"* is a sure sign that something is wrong. Ellie and I glance at each other, understanding. She's a discarded Pulcinella, bereft of life and barely kept together by strings; a Neapolitan puppet at the end of the show. No colors today, no red shoes, no purple boots; she wears only a bleak dark-gray pantsuit under her customary black coat. We say nothing, instinctually feeling this usually vibrant young woman's sadness, and we each kiss her cheek in greeting.

She crumples up on our sofa, silently sobbing, rattling like a willow tree in a storm. I kneel in front of her and shake her, brushing the hair from her anguished face. For the moment the *medialunas* will have to wait.

"Tell me. Let me help you. What did you do? Did someone harm you? What happened?"

"I'm so ashamed of what I have become. I've been totally blindsided by this whole thing. I never thought I'd suffer so much. I was living a peaceful life and now I'm in constant agony. I didn't ask for this. If only I could turn back the clock, two weeks, even a few days." Analia looks ravaged, her eyes lost in the distance as if she were trying to see through an invisible barrier.

"I know. I know." What else can I say?

"I can't stand it anymore. It's as if he's haunting me. I see him everywhere: his walk, his frame. When we aren't together I physically miss him. It's as if I'm torn to pieces every time we're apart." She shakes her head, crushed by her own suffering.

"Luis, right?" I stroke Analia's hair, as I've done so many times with my children, soothing her, hoping to stop the flood of desperation, trying to quiet her frail shoulders and stop them from convulsing. But she's lost in sorrow.

She's finally realized that there's no place for her in his future. Dancing with him is torture and yet, for those brief minutes, it fills her with perfect contentment. Closing her eyes and settling into his arms, drawing in his smell, touching his skin, burying her nose in his curls; it's a reminder of what could have been but will never be.

"I am the walking example of a cheesy tango. I represent the most banal, trite lyrics ever written by a bad musician," Analia adds, convulsed by a fresh round of sobs.

Her life has become a nightmare. Even the simple act of walking through the streets of Buenos Aires brings memories of the past days and she turns to ice.

"On my way to your dinner, last night, there was a *bandoneón* playing a random song on a corner of Abasto. Immediately my legs gave way as if disconnected from my torso. I didn't think

I'd be able to make it upstairs." Her black eyes well up with pain.

"I feel at peace only when I'm with Luis. I forget everything else in the joy of our togetherness, the thrill of his hands on me— holding me. But now I always ask myself *for how long?* Since yesterday I've been living my personal hell."

Ha! Oliviero, of course. Or is it something else?

Analia is trying to shut her heart to the violins' cajolery, the *bandoneón*'s lament, spurning the music, determined to hide her feelings. Tango is no longer her ally.

"I wish I could be the first one to flee. But how can I exist without Luis?"

Will she ever dance with someone else the way she dances with him? Is there no one else with whom can she walk, hand in hand, arm in arm, happy just to have her body brush against his? His mere presence sends electric shocks through her entire being. *"Cuando bailamos mi sangre está junto con él,"* she adds, when they dance her blood runs with his. What a powerful description.

I look at her, overwhelmed by the sudden theatricals. Indeed, this is eerily similar to so many of the old tangos I've been listening to. I can't help but think about some of the meaningful lyrics I've read in the past few days. Drama, passion, despair, grief. Although they are formulaic, the powerful, tragic words suddenly come alive in my Abasto living room. Does tango ever equate with happiness? It seems it always expresses people's everyday feelings, misery, life's losses, the eternal ups and downs of suffering humankind.

"Talk about it and maybe together we can ease your pain, at least for right now. Letting it out can help, you can confide in us." Moved by her suffering but also puzzled, Ellie and I fret around her.

Analia sighs heavily, closing her eyes as if to seal off her memories, her pain. It must be heart-wrenching to give up her love, her young dreams. If she loses Luis she'll have lost the magic they create when dancing together, that rarest unity of body and soul. Tango doesn't only translate in steps, but also in the emotional response to those dancing it and those watching it. At times, after the violin has rendered its last supplicating note, Analia feels faint, as if all she has inside had been sapped away by the dance.

I suddenly understand why she's so devastated. To experience a partnership like that onstage and to be denied it in real life has broken her heart.

This is unsettling and I feel vaguely uncomfortable, without knowing why. The last few days in Buenos Aires have rekindled some old emotions. I consider my own situation, the uninspiring life I lead in New York, with its predictable schedules and obligations and its complete lack of sexual stimuli. These past days in Argentina, my exposure to tango and the passion it has unleashed, have changed everything. I am determined to keep this dance and its sensuality at bay, or at least I'll try. But I'm afraid something has already changed inside me: Analia's sense-stirring descriptions— and Roberto, of course—have awakened a load of emotions I had all but forgotten. Damn him! And damn tango. I thought I had accepted George's abrupt annulment of my sex life, I thought I had found an inner peace, but hearing about Analia's predicament has once again opened the floodgates of my emotions. Now I, too, feel like crying.

"Let's go out. I need a new dress and I'm starving." Ellie breaks the spell of my thoughts. A mixture of shopping and eating is a surefire recipe for beating misery, at least in the short term. We usher Analia down the stairs and onto Corrientes. The Abasto mall and its myriad stores might finally prove useful.

Llevada

(A Lift)

La vida es una herida absurda,
y es todo, todo, tan fugaz
que es una curda, y nada mas!
mi confesión

"La última curda"

*I*t's three o'clock and I'm exhausted. Today I was made to walk up and down the length of the studio for at least an hour. It was frustrating and even humiliating at times, but I'm definitely improving.

"Stretch those legs. You've got a pair of long ones, so what are you saving them for?" At the Escuela Copello, María and Maxi never relent. "*Armá este brazo.* Keep that arm strong." How can they be such skilled instructors at barely twenty years old? Just as I was starting to feel foolish, María uttered a "not bad," which to me sounded like "Margot Fonteyn is nothing compared to you."

At times I become so exasperated by my uncooperative body that I think I should just give up. The rules are clear: the foot should *always* rub the floor, one knee must *always* be bent while the other has to stretch, and the all-embracing arm has to be *soft* and *strong* at the same time. Go figure. Why am I learning tango at my age? Why do I insist on torturing myself this way? Or is it that for the first time in ages I'm actually *feeling* something? I've been taking hundreds of pictures at my new school. I need to go back to New York with visual instructions, literal memories of all I've learned since I came to B.A.

Today, just before the *milonga* class, a young man—I'd never seen him before—invited me to dance. As he took me in his arms and led me around the room, it was as if we'd known each other forever. Weightless, exhilarated, I closed my eyes and enjoyed the sensuality of the embrace, that special feeling of belonging, of listening to a stranger leading my body into the happiness of the music. At the end of "Milonga vieja milonga"—a light, joyful song—we stopped and looked into each other's eyes, wordless, aware of the miracle we'd just experienced. I knew that for the first time I had really danced. When the music ended it was as if someone had brutally shone a bright flashlight on a magically somnolent room. For a few minutes we had closed our eyes and appropriated the entire space; now that we had separated, we wanted more.

Then the teachers arrived and the lesson began.

Now, at the end of a grueling day of classes, and delighted by finally having let go and danced, I wait outside the school for Luis. We're going to Caballito, his childhood *barrio*. In a long black coat, his backpack slung over his shoulder, he walks as if there were a gale behind him, pushing him forward.

"And Ellie?" He kisses me on both cheeks, attuned to the Italian system. In New York it's so embarrassing to go for another kiss while your unsuspecting friends have already altered the angle of their head and the only thing that is left for you is to bump into their noses or chins.

"Ellie has decided to stay longer and take a salsa class." I'm bemused by her stamina. She never tires. What's her secret?

"Typical! Okay, you and I will take *el subte*. It's nothing like the subway in New York, but it's definitely the fastest and cheapest way around the city. Rest assured: you won't be seeing many tourists."

The *subte*—with its blue cars with yellow stripes and wooden interiors—reminds me of Italy. It's a strangely familiar sensation that doesn't leave me until we finally get out at Acoyte. Here Luis blends in with the crowd. The black baseball cap planted firmly on his head is no different from the hundreds bobbing around in the station. He is always at ease everywhere he goes, but now—standing on the platform—I see how he really belongs to this country.

We walk through Caballito's busy streets, exploring new food stores, boutiques, and small bazaars.

"Get this one: *Tangos famosos*. There! Now you have many of Carlos Gardel's famous *letras*." From one of the stands along the main avenue Luis picks up a thin volume with a brilliant yellow cover. Antique books and old prints are thrown here and there haphazardly. One of the vendors has filled a large basket with booklets; I stop, searching for something special to take back to America.

"*Si yo tuviera el corazón . . .*" Luis sings, spinning me into a tango pose. That's Argentina! Here I am, dancing in the street; I doubt I'll ever be the same again.

We wander into a park swarming with people. The benches are as crowded as a rush-hour 6 train in Manhattan. Young couples kiss passionately, vigilant parents eye their children while they play, and a group of elderly men puff on their cigarettes, engaged in their endless game of cards. Winter and the feet of too many children have nearly obliterated the vegetation. The last surviving strands of grass have given way to dirt and gravel and dust.

"This is my favorite bench. My mother would sometimes bring us here after school."

"Luis. I need to talk to you about Analia. I know I am a *chusma*—a total busybody—but I feel I have the right to interfere in your lives now that I know you and love you both. I mean, what can I do to help her understand what's so clear to the rest of us? This situation is killing her."

"I'm not sure about anything myself anymore. I always wanted a *normal* relationship. Do you know how difficult it is to be gay in the tango world? Always having to hide behind a lie, always performing even offstage. And with me it's never been a secret: I love men." Luis is so serious and worried that my heart leaps inside my chest.

"And you've told her that, right? I worry you're sending her mixed signals."

"I don't know what to say. Analia excites me. I love to have sex with her and I've always hoped for marriage, children, a life my own family could accept and be proud of. But I finally had to tell her. About me, about my desires.

"Anyway, it's not like she doesn't have a past of her own," adds Luis, getting catty.

"What will you do?" I insist.

"Can't say. Let's not talk about it today, I'm *so* tired. I woke up early to clean my apartment. It was such a *quilombo*!" Luis has changed the subject with his typical fickleness. He and Analia definitely have that in common.

"Why? Were you expecting someone?" Luis is full of surprises but I'm afraid I might know where this is going.

"Remember Oliviero?" Luis stretches his arms high above his head, arching his back seductively. His eyes are black pools and for a moment his eyelashes shut out his more impenetrable thoughts.

"Oliviero? Sarah's friend? The guy who came to dinner? Yesterday?" Ah! Once again my instincts were spot on.

"He showed up at my apartment at eleven this morning. We had fantastic sex. Francesca, I like him a lot. I might even be falling in love," Luis says as if to test me, flashing his impertinent, defiant smile—but I happen to know that behind it there's a lonely man who's been looking for a companion, a real love, for some time.

"Well, that was fast. No time wasted between dinner and lunch." I shake my head, thinking that Oliviero's fairy godmother has been on active duty. I have been out of the loop for too long: being married and working hard is a sure way to forget how these kinds of instant affairs work. Buenos Aires seems to be fertile soil for romance. And I should know, my fling with Roberto developed in less than twenty-four hours. Is it something in the air? I remember a woman from Bologna once telling me that the vast fields of hemp around her city were responsible for the sexual prowess of its inhabitants. Hmm . . . I wonder if there's any growing around here?

"Maybe I should go for older men." Luis nods his head appreciatively. "They know what they're doing and they've already had a lot of experience. And you should see his chest and his butt. Muscles a twenty-year-old would only dream of."

Luis had been frantically cleaning up his place. He plumped up his many exotic pillows, moved the old Afghani chair in front of the window and, as a last touch, lit an expensive tuberose candle. At Oliviero's first knock at the door, he rushed to welcome him. Oliviero stood holding a shopping bag in his right hand, waiting. He took off his beret and smiled. Luis immediately kissed him full on the lips, and hard.

"*Buenas!* And hallo to you, too! That was some welcome." Oliviero walked into the minuscule apartment and looked around. He took in the space and the boldness of the whitewashed walls, interrupted only by a brilliant ruby red partition. Luis invited him to sit down on the sofa, readjusting the rich Indian striped brocade he had *casually* thrown over the cushions.

"Quite a collection of pictures from tango shows you have. You're definitely very photogenic. Well, I was sure you'd need to add this." Oliviero took a black-and-white picture book from his bag. It was Feliciano's last work, tango candids seen through the lens of the famous photographer.

"I can't believe you bought me this." Luis was enchanted. "I was saving up to buy it as a gift to myself!"

Suddenly the air became lighter. They ended up in each other's arms; lust and tenderness playing equal parts in the desire to be together. Luis undressed Oliviero, whose extraordinary body had already been on display the night before; he didn't look a year older than forty.

They stood, holding each other, waiting, breathing slowly, taking in each other's scent. Despite his active sex life, Luis felt as if it were the first time, as if he still had a certain kind of innocence. His heart cavorted furiously inside his chest and he almost fainted with sheer desire. He looked at Oliviero and waited. The older man's strong arms seized Luis's waist and he bent to kiss him, at first pressing lightly on his lips, then gently parting them with his tongue, playing with the soft inside of his mouth.

"Oh!" Luis moaned, answering Oliviero's desire. Oliviero's tongue was already searching for his, teasing, holding it in the softest grip.

Luis had never kissed anyone for so long; he went entirely soft, pliable, yearning for love, craving what was to happen. Oliviero moved him into the bathroom, against the washbasin, and gently folded Luis's body, pushing into him at first delicately.

"Relax . . ." he whispered in his raspy voice. Luis breathed deeply, his body greedily accepting his partner's urge. Oliviero's cadence improved; he held Luis tight, pinning his belly against the cold marble, aware of the pain and pleasure he was inflicting. "There, take it! Good boy . . ."

With both hands Oliviero grabbed Luis's butt forcefully and they came at the same time. Luis convulsed, crying silently as he reached climax. They collapsed on the floor, holding each other, exhausted. Oliviero touched Luis, surreptitiously, whispering how lucky he was to have him in his arms, to have possessed him. Luis curled up, leaning his head on his shoulder, one arm flung across his chest.

"I didn't even have time to leave my fingerprints on the mirror." Luis winks at me. I burst into a fit of uncontrollable laughter, his words captivating my imagination.

"Oliviero is strong, and prodigiously big . . . It hurt, but then it turned into pleasure. I love to be dominated."

"Okay, okay, enough details!" He can be so graphic. "Luis, when did you discover you were gay?"

"Hmm. I might have been around eighteen. Before then I tried to be as macho as I could: I even snuck into seedy theaters to see porno movies with my schoolmates. I did enjoy them. But of course, if I really think about it, it might have started before."

Luis had experienced his fair share of women. After all, it was what was expected from him at home and in the tango community.

"You wouldn't believe the number of times I've been asked to do *charity fucking*. Well, I don't do it anymore." Luis frowns, biting his hands. "Those days are over." His eyes stare into the distance.

This comment gets my mind racing. Was he ever a *puto*? One of those boys who sell themselves? No, I can't believe that. Luis strikes me as a straightforward man. Either he wants sex—and he's not ashamed of being open about it—or he simply has the strength to refuse. I eye him quizzically.

"I am talking about Yoli."

"Yoli? What do you mean?" I knew there was something strange about that woman. Didn't Luis once say something about Yoli not forgiving or forgetting? She hardens whenever she looks at him. I wait. If he wants to explain, he will.

"Men and women in power find ways to impose their appetite on those under them; it happens all the time. When I enrolled in Yoli's school, she took an immediate fancy to me. I was the teacher's pet, the future star dancer. Well, of course I was a quick study, but she wanted much more than just perfect steps. And my future was not her first priority." We stand up, leaving the crowded circle of benches, the screaming children and gossiping adults.

We pass under naked jacarandas and ceibas, skirting the majestic *ombúes,* and slowly following the gravel path to the other exit. We meander down a residential street, two tidy rows of three-story houses, dotted with mature plane trees, knotty and twisted. An elderly man sits in front of a door, a woolen hat firmly pulled down over his forehead; he slumps in his chair, his head shaking to the beat of some mysterious inner music.

"It was clear from the beginning that Yoli wanted to sneak me into her bed. So, for lack of better judgment, I fell into her warm embrace and against her enormous chest."

"I can understand that. It happens." Luis's inexperience had made him an easy prey to Yoli's voracity. He had no idea what he was getting himself into. For several months Yoli transformed him into her private sex slave. Day after day, performance after performance, she would nod and take hold of Luis in her uniquely proprietorial way. Off they would go, into the night—the stocky madam and her willowy boy toy—and straight into her bed. She never relented, and her hunger was legendary.

I'm horrified at the idea of poor Luis in the clutches of that harpy. "She ruined you forever, no chance for any of us," I say lightly. "Maybe someone should sue her—"

Luis turns on me, ferociously—I've never seen him like this. In his eyes there's fury. No, a profound rage.

"Look, I'm sorry. I wasn't making fun of you, only trying to lighten up the conversation."

"You're talking about being at a crossroads. If it's difficult to be one person, imagine being two. Man and woman under the same skin! Two different sexes, just one soul." He has relaxed again. But it isn't easy being Luis: yin and yang, black and white, a boy, a man.

"So, why Analia?"

"Because she's special. Because she dances like a goddess. With her I've had some of the best sex of my life. She could have been my trophy, my passport to *normalcy*. I felt gratified having her with me, proud of fulfilling her sexual needs, of making her happy. But it didn't work out." He simply couldn't deny his other desires.

Remembering everything Analia had said to me, I begin to feel uncomfortable about my place in their drama, like an old voyeur. Luis is sexy. Suddenly I can understand the power he holds over her. Here in Buenos Aires it's as if everything has taken a wrong turn. Sensuality seeps out of every corner of this city and I feel like I'm on an emotional roller coaster.

Our wanderings have brought us to a big white church. Santa María de los Dolores, says the sign above the door. Luis, alive with excitement, wants to show me the place where he had his First Communion and served as an altar boy; where Rossano took him to pray, taught him about the saints, and where *el cura*—the priest—rewarded him with *estampitas*. In front of the main altar is a sorrowful Madonna in a black-and-gold gown, flanked by two angels; a baroque crown hovers over her head, a large gold heart hangs over her chest. The Virgin's open hands express both her impotence and sadness at all she has to witness: pain, tragedy, loss, or just simple everyday suffering. She looks down at Luis with solemn love and he gazes back up at her like the innocent child he must once have been. Life placed a heavy weight on his young shoulders much too soon.

On a bench, second row from the altar, we whisper. If ever there was a proper place, the church is the fitting location in which to discuss the death of a loved one.

"I was twelve when she died. She spent her last months at home with us. Tía Mirtha and Rossano had taken her in. When she wasn't in agony, I was able to have daily conversations with her. After so many years, we bonded."

Nelida's beauty had vanished, and her body was swollen by the disease. Only her eyes, lost in the ravaged features of a much older woman, remained fierce and sensual.

"I wanted to make her smile, to help her forget those gnawing pains." So Luis started scavenging, selling all kinds of discarded objects at the market behind his home. "With the few pesos I earned I was able to get her chocolate and magazines."

At her bedside, he gently passed the brush a hundred times through her dark curls, spreading them on the pillow. "I wanted those strokes to hypnotize her, to assuage her pain and make her sleep."

The day she died, Nelida suddenly looked as pretty as she was before the disease. From a nearby vase Luis took a huge pink rose. In full bloom, it looked like a peony, its petals quivering around a yellow core. He tucked it behind his mother's ear, caressing her hair, holding her hand.

"She thanked me, beaming like a young girl." His silence breaks my heart.

"I called Rossano, Tía Mirtha, and my siblings. We all gathered around her. And she left us." I squeeze his hand. Hard. I blink, trying desperately to keep my tears inside.

"And the *telenovela* is still not over. Don't forget to tune in for the next installment . . ." Luis helps me with my jacket and we slowly walk out of the church, into the darkness of a winter night.

On Avenida Díaz Vélez, at six o'clock, Caballito bursts with activity. The *porteños* return home from work, kids from after-school programs. Mothers busily gather their families together. Only the stores are still open, their lights luring the last evening shoppers like moths to a flame.

Unexpectedly Luis's mood has changed. He's a whiteboard: in a matter of seconds what's written in his eyes disappears entirely, and in the time it's taken us to walk through the nave and make the sign of the cross, mirth has replaced sorrow on the blank slate of his heart; he's spotted an old friend.

Just outside the church an elderly man is busy rinsing and wiping off his portable bar. The black-and-white letters on the side of a primitive red cart read CAFÉ BANGU. Ten white-and-silver Thermos bottles fit precisely into holes on the top shelf, and a simple plastic basket hangs in front. Empty now, earlier in the day it must have been filled with delicious *medialunas* and *biscochitos*. The man serves stores and offices, passersby and habitués. He's the local Starbucks. "Luisito! *Cuanto tiempo!* I haven't seen you in so long." He brushes away his tears of emotion while smiling at Luis. "*Niño,* I saw you on that commercial on TV. I'm so proud of you. If poor Rossano could have seen you . . . Here, take the last cookie. You look too thin."

"Francesca, meet Señor Bangu, my godfather's closest friend. If anyone wants to hear stories about me as a child, he has tons of things to say." Luis hugs him. "*Mirá!* We are close to the Viejo Correo. You've got to see it. Maybe we'll come back tonight, after the show. Yes! We have to come here to dance. This is where I learned tango, the neighborhood place where everyone knew me and followed my progress." Luis is on a roll, eager to show me his entire world: his childhood, his youth, his family and friends.

"Tío Bangu, do you still dance every night?"

A loud *por supuesto*—naturally—brings laughter to the three of us and I can imagine him all dressed up and perfumed. He's no different from anyone else swelling the *milongas* at night.

"I'll bring Francesca to the Viejo Correo tonight. Make sure to be there, you must dance with her."

We open the door—I want to take a look at this *milonga* before the crowds arrive—and step into the cavernous room. Black-and-white checkered floor, tables dressed in red, countless pictures of tango maestros and famous visitors all over the walls—it's all part of the simple, familiar appearance. This place is less touristy, a more authentic tango club. But right now, with its soundless emptiness and smell of stale cigarettes, it feels more like an abandoned film set.

"You look so sad. What's happening?" Ellie's hand touches me lightly on the shoulder. She's always surprisingly attuned to my moods. I shake my head, refusing to believe the words I'm reading.

Today I came home from an emotional day with Luis in Caballito to find another insane e-mail from George. Like a maniac, he simultaneously begs for forgiveness and attacks me for having been the one who was always unavailable. "Too many written words filled your days and months, they took you away from me . . ." Is that an excuse for something else, or is he trying to justify his own behavior?

"You became distant and didn't need me," he adds in his

delirious prose. Suddenly I've become the ugly wife, keeping him at a distance, "having an affair, obviously not the first one nor the last."

It hurts. I don't recognize my husband in these harsh accusations. It's as if he's being fed data by someone else. Maybe I'm paranoid, but I sense Isabel behind all of this nonsense. George has never been one to put his feelings on paper, not even during our brief courtship. His most poetic moments reach their creative apex on my birthday, when he chooses the *right* Hallmark card—precooked by some great thinker in Kansas City.

"I'm disappointed in your behavior, you should always remember who you are and the family you represent." The family! I'm so tired of being reminded of who they are and how they think I should conduct myself.

I read on, trapped in the turmoil of my own thoughts and resolutions. A giant engine has been put in motion and there is nothing I can do to stop it. My work has helped me find freedom and now I have no one to rely on but myself. I feel different. I *am* different. Life dealt me an unexpected hand of cards the moment I arrived in Baires, and I played them. Now I have to pay the consequences.

To think that it's been only a few months since George and I celebrated our silver anniversary in Cortina d'Ampezzo, where we married twenty-five years ago. It was a big party and our children were delighted to witness our apparent happiness. There were long speeches and countless toasts to our everlasting love. Yet it's been eight long years since we've had a real relationship. In many ways I was comfortable with it. He was the old shoe you're always happy to wear, molded by long use—practical, soft, and giving. Writing, cooking, and traveling the world on assignments seemed enough; it kept me quiet. And my success distracted me, helping me to forget how much I missed the physicality of love, how I needed the joy of being desired and courted, of still feeling young and sexy.

"In less than ten days my comfortable life has imploded." I fan myself with the *Clarín,* the best use for the paper that inspired George's rabid e-mail. In our pint-sized apartment the air is suffocating and I open the window onto the noisy evening and Abasto's street life. *Clop, cloppety, clop,* a horse-drawn cart slowly navigates the traffic, crossing Corrientes, carrying a full load of fruit and vegetables. Amused, I follow its anachronistic proceeding through the traffic.

"Hot flashes? Already?" Reality rudely brings me back to the present. Fanning myself, I collapse onto the sofa, longing for my favorite New York armchair, the one I use when I'm editing my articles. It's a cocoon, a needed embrace when I'm at my most vulnerable.

"I'd say that what you're experiencing is just plain old frustration. Everything is much clearer after what you've told me about George over the past few days. I'm sure Isabel must be behind all of this and George is being played by her. She has a husband, doesn't she?"

Ellie's calm reassurance is exactly what I need. But I don't know anything about Isabel's life. I'm aware that she's extraordinarily rich and that she wants both of my men. Why did she have to get in my way? She's undoubtedly thinking exactly the same thing about me. Is she as monstrous inside as she is on the outside? And what does she have to offer that I don't have? After all, George has given me up for her.

"You need more information." Ellie has a will of steel under her blond sweetness and I know she won't relent until she has the answers to her questions. She dials Sarah's number and I grab the phone. I have to know.

Sarah actually admires and respects Isabel's strength and busi-

ness acumen. "Isabel's husband? Oh poor dear, Orville is practically dead, for all intents and purposes. He's suffered from
Alzheimer's for many years and is now in the last stages of the
disease. Nothing more can be done. Isabel has led her own life for
the last decade. He's the one with the money, but she is extraordinarily clever and has taken the chairmanship of the holding company, running everything competently and shrewdly."

"When would you say Orville was diagnosed? Eight years
ago?" I wonder if Isabel met George at that time. A needy woman
in her fifties, a younger man. Do I see any parallels here? I smile
inwardly. "Sarah, you are an angel. It's always important to collect
your facts before starting a fight. And that's precisely what I sense:
I'm about to be sucked into something bigger than me and my
will. Let's see if I have the desire and tenacity to fight for a marriage I'm suddenly not so sure I want."

"Francesca, I'm sorry. And Roberto?"

"Roberto is a present but not a future, I think. I have no idea.
As for Isabel and Roberto, well, that's a totally different situation.
It would be my bad karma to cross her path twice."

Subject: none
Date: 6/20/2008 09:01:02 A.M. Eastern Standard Time
From: Francesca.Rivabuona@aol.com
To: George.Farrington@aol.com

George! So you have the gall to be upset and—I
quote—*worried* because of my well-publicized dinner with
Roberto Hellzinker? How dare you say anything when it's
now clear that—unbeknownst to me—you've been traveling all over the world with that woman, Isabel Alexanders?

And, since I don't recall you subscribing to any Argentinean publications, may I ask who tipped you off so quickly to that the *Clarín* article?

You should remember that we had a pact. A few years ago you chose to claim only culinary rights over me, relinquishing all other prerogatives. It's my privilege not to report to you if I choose to indulge in the sexual satisfaction you have denied me. For too long, I should add.

Let's say that, until further discussion, you'll keep only your *Matriciana* privileges. And that's it for the moment. I know that you have tried to call me several times, but I don't feel like talking to you.

In a few days I'll be in New York—and when I am, we'll sit down to have a civilized conversation. F.

"Oh Ellie, what a mess I've got myself into. How come you were immune to Argentina?" I've just hit SEND and now I gawk at the screen, mesmerized. I can't believe how harsh I can be.

"First George, then Roberto, and now Isabel." On the other side of the world, in New York, everything seemed so easy.

It's time for a Refrescal, my favorite local candy, a real breath of fresh air. Wrapped in red-and-white paper with a quirky penguin on it, these *pastillas* are a bit of whimsy that might help lift my mood. But the frightening question remains: What next?

"No matter how worried you are, you are glowing from within. I think you needed it. Sex is the best dermatologist. *Sex each day keeps the doctor away,* as Mae West once said," Ellie states with scientific assurance. "Many experts agree on this. It's estrogen, my dear. Estrogen is responsible for good hair and good skin. Maybe it has the same effect as a sauna!" Ellie cocks her head, reformulating her last statement. "Well, only if both of you display some aerobic energy during your, well, your encounters . . ."

"How could I ever survive Buenos Aires without you?" I hug her.

"I feel more and more neglected right now," she adds, half-jokingly. "Everyone around me is living the drama of love, passion, and desperation: you, Luis, and Analia have all made me the repository for your confessions and your crises. And me? I'm stuck at home, trying to make do with tango and its *letras,* those desperate words of abandonment, excessive love, treachery, and tragedy. I wish I had a lover, I wish I had ten pairs of new shoes . . ."

Corrida

(A Run)

La noche que me quieras
desde el azul del cielo,
las estrellas celosas
nos mirarán pasar
Y un rayo misterioso
Hará nido en tu pelo,
Luciérnaga curiosa que vera . . . que eres .
  mi consuelo.

"El Día que me Quieras"

I've never been afraid of nakedness, preferring to make love in full light, enjoying not just the tactile pleasures but also the excitement of seeing and being seen. But now it's different. Having been starved of sex for so long, I am suddenly self-conscious, worried about my looks. I'm afraid of being ugly, of not measuring up to the beauty and youth of Roberto's wife and his lovers, if indeed, as I suspect, he has stacks of them.

I jump out of Roberto's gigantic bed, wrapping the sheets around me and trailing them to the bathroom as regally as Christine in *The Phantom of the Opera*. I close the door and check my tummy in the mirror, and then slowly turn around and twist my neck to see my back better. My eyes start right at the top, appraising my shoulders and the muscles crisscrossing the torso, and go all the way down to my behind. If I hold my breath and keep everything in, it really looks as if I am—hmm!—a well-kept forty? Forty-five? I stand in profile and turn to the front, checking my arms and that damned soft spot under the armpit that tends to jitterbug unless I keep it under control with lots of exercise. No, for the moment it's fine. Phew! I even have a *waist*. Those hard hours of working out have paid off; I didn't sweat for nothing! But tell me: Why don't men ever fret about their looks?

"What are you doing in here?" Roberto's hands grab my buttocks, weighing them. His fingers start probing. I pivot away from the mirror to look at him, squeaking in surprise, embarrassed at having been caught unawares.

"Let's take a shower," he whispers, straightening my shoulders, placing me against his body. We are like two pieces of a puzzle, one harmonic design. His hands keep moving slowly over my skin. Stopping here and there to tease, he plays with my back and runs his fingers in front to press my waist, my belly. I am immediately aroused; I can feel his excitement, I see it too. He's flying high in a room where everything has been planned with seduction in mind.

Roberto pushes a few buttons in the luxurious bathroom and a white cloud of steam hisses softly around me, shrouding his features. Millions of particles of water fall on us like opalescent pearls as he guides me to the marble bench spread with a big towel. I can't see him completely but I imagine his eyes, his smile when I feel his hands touch my legs and reach up in between the thighs. His fingers fill me slowly, exploring with the assurance of ownership. I rise, resting on my elbows, seeking out his eyes, his mouth, wanting his kisses. From within the soft mist I take hold of him, circling his penis with my fingers, tracing the outline of his erection, until I can guide him inside.

But Roberto torments me. He wants us to take our time, to play with each other's bodies in a game where every ruse is permissible, every fantasy is right.

He's turned me on my tummy, pinning me with his weight. One hand on my shoulder, the other massages my buttocks. Deep, calm strokes to make me relax. He presses deeper and deeper, until I find myself arching like a cat, unable to control my lust. I want him. I'm open, ready.

Roberto knows how to touch the keys that make me jump like a live wire; he has an uncanny instinct for what makes me tick. I've never had a lover so physically attuned to me and my wishes. He holds back his own pleasure in order to take me to the highest level of ecstasy. Only then does he allow himself to come.

The steam has ebbed away together with my screams of pleasure. Roberto pushes a few more buttons in his state-of-the-art, sybaritic palace of a bathroom and the apartment is filled with notes and lyrics that would make a nun surrender to any lewd proposal. "'El amanecer' is my favorite tango. Listen . . ."

Exhausted but gratified, I sink into a comfortable wicker armchair, covered in white cloth. Roberto fills two glasses of chilled Krug champagne from a silver container. Now, that's *my* favorite.

"Breakfast! This is a great bottle, 1947. A good year." He sips from his crystal flute, his eyes closed.

"Hmm, older than me and still bubbly."

But there is more. "Want a hit?" I watch him take a miniature pouch from a drawer, calculate the precise quantity of grass, and compress it tidily with the help of a sharp silver blade. I've never seen anyone roll a joint so fast! After all, he is a surgeon. And in the last few days he has certainly proven to me that he knows how to use his hands.

"We have all the time in the world before you go to your classes. And I'm taking the entire day off." Roberto lights the joint, inhales dreamily, and passes it over. A steady rain drums monotonously on the air-conditioner box outside the window. I'm beginning to wonder if I'll ever see the Río de la Plata under a good sun and a blue sky. The early morning light has turned a peculiar shade of yellow and lends the clouds an apocalyptic hue. I am not used to *porro,* and the first puffs send me into a fabulous state of suspended consciousness. I smile lethargically and stretch out on my chair, until Roberto picks me up and carries me back into the bedroom. Who am I to protest? A thrill runs down my spine, *pelle d'oca*—goose bumps—cover my arms; I can't remain indifferent when he touches me. I've become a transformer and the only thing he needs to do is push a button. Any button, and electricity hits my body!

Porro has loosened my tongue and I can hear myself talking. I feel like I'm in one of those television programs where the audio is out of synch with the visual frame: lips moving, sound following lazily. My brain sends orders that are executed only a few seconds later. And I don't care.

I look down at a verbose Francesca as if from a higher floor. I see myself snuggle into Roberto's arms, watch my hands move greedily all over him, check to see if my sex appeal is still working. Roberto turns toward me and pins my legs down, mounting me with a sort of frantic rage, as if he needs to disappear within me. It hurts; he reaches deep inside, pushing with violence. At first I tense, about to cry out to make him stop, but then I let go. I want him to. I need his fury, this sense of totally belonging to him, having him take me as if he possesses me. Am I some kind of masochist who equates pain with pleasure? Slowly Roberto calms down, he begins moving in and out in a different, gentler way. Suddenly he pauses.

"Oh God, what are you doing to me?" His eyes widen as my inner muscles pump steadily in and out, grabbing him, sucking him, and then letting go. I can feel my inside stretch and release all the way up to that magic point, the repository of sensual gratification.

"Francesca?"

"Mi amor . . . ?"

I look at him, all flushed, excited. I'm prepared to open my arms to his body, which will soon convulse with the spasms of his orgasm.

"You can use it, and *how* . . ." Roberto's voice is just a thin whisper in my ears. He has collapsed over me, wiped out. "I've never experienced anything like this . . . You must be one of the few people aware of that muscle. How did you learn to use it?" He closes his eyes.

I chuckle. Me, a modern Mata Hari.

"It's as if you were trained to give pleasure. Making love to you is full of surprises." The wonder in Roberto's eyes amuses me.

"Years ago, after a particularly steamy night, I learned one of life's lessons: *When you make love to a lady, treat her like a whore, but when you make love to a whore, treat her like a lady.* My boyfriend told me and I've never forgotten it."

In the aftermath of love, our hips join in the sculptural stillness of graceful curves. Filled with perfect joy, I sigh and let myself go.

Suddenly I'm worried. "What should I do about Isabel?" I'm living the profligate life without thinking about tomorrow's consequences. And I'm afraid that I'm going to have to deal with a woman whose strength and connections are certainly more powerful than mine.

"For the moment, let it be. I'm not in the best situation either; Isabel can be vindictive, but hopefully my lawyers are on to her. I'd never let myself get locked into a contract with some-one whose goodwill depends on my sexual performance." Arms crossed behind his neck, Roberto gazes up at the white ceiling.

He changes the subject. "This was good stuff. I do it only once in a while, when I need to relax completely. I like it that we did it together." He turns on his elbow, brushing the tip of my nose with a kiss. "Has anyone told you how special you are? How did I live without you until now?"

"Easily, with your horses and your clinics and your lovers and your wife. How come you have no children?" In my blissful state, I couldn't care less what I say.

"Ana María didn't want them. She always put it off to the following month, the next year. Too afraid of ruining her body, her perfect abdomen. As for horses? You have to admit that those blessed creatures never have too many questions and never talk back. If they do, you can always teach them a lesson with the whip and spurs!"

"That was a *seriously* un-PC answer!" I look at him indignantly.

"You asked for it. And anyway, you are the one with an *esprit mal tourné,* as they say in France. You took my phrase in the wrong way. I had no intention of equating polo horses with women, it was solely your interpretation." Roberto's face closes up and I start to worry. "When do you have to go back to New York?" He hugs me tight.

"I am leaving four days from now . . ." My words are a broken, miserable whimper. Up till now I haven't considered the idea of actually going back to New York. Or if I did, I immediately dis-missed the thought. Now that Roberto has spoken those words, the calendar pops up under my eyes as if on a gigantic screen: only Thursday, Friday, Saturday are left, and then, on Sunday night, my flight home.

"Oh no! I'm playing in a polo match in Córdoba. It's a benefit I committed to a long time ago. I can't let my team down. I'm leaving early Friday morning." Genuinely distressed, Roberto pushes me away from him, frowning, but I drag him against my breasts, trembling. That joint has doubled all my sensations, and suddenly our sultry morning has turned gloomy. A frosty hand has grabbed my heart. Roberto calms me with kisses, wraps me in his warmth.

"I'm never like this. I don't cry, I don't make scenes. I'm sorry. It was stupid of me, but the idea of facing George and his years of lies is so hard." I can't possibly tell Roberto that I find going back to life without him unimaginable—or that I will miss him. I'm surprised by the speed at which our relationship has evolved.

I free my discarded trousers and sweater from under an armchair, where they lie confused with a pile of books and magazines. "How on earth did they end up there?" That *porro* must have been strong! I don't remember much. I look at him, searching for an answer.

"What do you expect me to say? That you make love like a *puttana?*" Roberto, sitting in bed with his legs crossed, shakes his head. "Should I pay you?" His smile softens the provocative harshness of his words.

"Yes! Tonight you'll take me to dinner and will order the most expensive bottle of wine. Not only that, but afterward we'll go to the *milonga* and you'll dance with me for the entire night. I want everyone there to envy me, to ask themselves what I've done to have you all for myself."

"Ha! Is this how to share an apartment with a friend? I haven't seen you forever." Ellie lowers a copy of *Gente,* fortunately an old edition, with photos of someone else's problems. Her glasses slip over her nose and stop just on the tip. She gives me the once-over, annoyed. "So much for spending time together in Buenos Aires!"

She's right. I'm guilty of abandoning her for an entire night as I disappeared from the *milonga* without even kissing her goodbye, but I don't think I owe anyone anything right now. I've turned into the most selfish person on earth. From now on it's going to be me, me, me!

"Ellie! Right now Roberto and the hours spent with him are my only recipe for sanity. I don't intend to give it up. Plus, I'm leaving in a few days." I haven't thrown myself into full-blown adultery and wrecked my marriage only to get embroiled in more duties and commitments. "And you have no idea what happened." I'm still shaken, remembering the blinding flashes the minute I walked out of Roberto's apartment. I now know what it means to live in the public eye. Only I never wanted it to happen and I feel trapped.

"Francesca! Don't tell me. Are they following you and Roberto?" Ellie is aghast.

"I just know that I thought I'd entered another world. Roberto tried to shield me, but there was nothing he could do."

They'd crowded around us: "Does your wife, Ana María, know? Is George aware of the fact that you've spent the night with another man?" The paparazzi kept shouting impertinent questions, all the while clicking away. It was one of the most awful moments of my life. Everything I'd built during those years of marriage was going up in smoke before my eyes. I plastered my best fake smile and quickly disappeared into Roberto's car.

"The damage is done, though. Isabel, and thus George, will know within hours. Who would have imagined that doctors were so famous in a country like Argentina?"

"Well, of course Roberto is famous, but the main story here is Ana María. She draws all this attention, I think. But how do they know George's name?"

Great! The very first time I play away, and I make headlines. How's that for luck? Buenos Aires feels like another planet, where anything is possible. Dreams and nightmares become reality. I'm letting everything go: George, my New York life, even my own children now seem like vague characters in a foreign soap opera. I should snap out of this. I'm definitely treading in dangerous waters. From now on, my life and my future will depend on the way I handle myself.

"You sound as cool as a cucumber. Are you sure you're feeling well?" Ellie's loving voice is like a balm. "Sorry, I shouldn't have nagged before, but last night the apartment felt so lonely when I came back from the Viejo Correo. You'd left before me and I'd assumed . . ."

It had been Ellie's triumphal night and afterward I hadn't been there for her, to congratulate her, to celebrate her success. I feel guilty.

"What an honor when Copello invited you to dance in front of everyone. I couldn't believe my ears when he chose you."

"Imagine! *Me!*" Ellie is still flushed when she thinks about it.

It had been a magical evening. Everyone had gathered at the Viejo Correo, the neighborhood *milonga* Luis had taken me to earlier in the day. Its simple interior and cozy feel made it an unusual place for the aristocracy of tango to gather; but that night Yoli was being celebrated: seventy years old and still going. She'd chosen the old club, where she'd taken her first steps and where now everyone had come to fête her. Walter, César, Mariela, Pancho, Maxi, and María, and many of the best dancers in town—old and young— came to pay homage to the doyenne of tango.

Talk about intimidating! The tango stars laughed and joked, keeping strictly to themselves, of course, bunched together in a corner not far from the music booth, like the popular table in a school cafeteria. I sat with Roberto, Luis, Analia, and Ellie, close to the Olympus of tango, relaxed, happy to look around and use my new knowledge of steps and rules, checking the familiar characters who, night after night, crowd the *milongas*.

Dancing here is like going to war. I need my gear—black skirt and strapless top—and my weapons—my new Comme il Faut stilettos—and then I simply aim.

"Straight to the eyes: *Boom!* Those guys—the *tangueros*—can be yours, one after the other, the rules are foolproof." Ellie pushed my elbow, egging me on.

Opposite me, across the dance floor and against the wall, sat scores of single men, clustered in groups of two or three. Imperturbable and unhurried, they exchanged knowing glances while surveying the dancing couples.

I focused briefly on a really fat man with a flowing mane of white hair, forgetting that by doing so I was actually asking him to invite me. Sure enough, a downright explicit wink shot back at me through the crowd: an unmistakable request. What to do? I am Italian and I know never to make a man lose face in a place like Argentina. Cursing inwardly, I nodded a polite yes and got back a head tilt with which my *caballero* summoned me to the dance floor. *El cabeceo* at its best! Desperate, I got up and joined him, prepared to make the best of things. I smiled and settled into his arms.

My body, draped over his large belly, immediately managed to assume that elusive, tilted position I'd spent a week trying unsuccessfully to learn. Pushed by his abdomen, my legs were placed at the perfect angle, I was comfortable. When "Uno," a poignant tango from the 1940s, rolled down from the DJ booth, we moved, or, rather, my partner led me along the line of dance (the requisite path one has to follow to avoid *milonga* traffic jam) with unexpected lightness and musicality. I relaxed and instinctively answered his requests, following the flow of his steps.

"*Pero cómo bailás linda.* How well you dance." A *maestro bandoneonista,* he made me feel each of the notes with the simple pressure of his hand around my back and deftly transported me into the depths of the music, translating those notes with the fluidity of his moves. When I returned to our table, I was flushed with the aftermath of dancing. Had I just touched the essence of tango? Ellie squeezed my arm, nodding knowingly, and Roberto, unfazed by everyone's stares, kissed me hard on the mouth.

At about half past midnight, the club's manager, Diego, stood up to huge applause and raucous screams.

"Tonight we have the honor of celebrating Yoli's birthday. She's reached the Fantastic Seventies. Let's all toast her, our beloved teacher and friend, and wish for ourselves the looks and stamina she still enjoys."

Yoli—hair dyed black to match the color of the velvet that enfolded her body—left her chair and walked like an empress to the center of the room. A single cone of light shone on her strong lineaments and picked out her red lips. She posed and smiled to the audience as she raised her arms in a dramatic gesture.

"*La Diva!*" Luis whispered, admiring her.

"You wish you were her," I teased him, amused by the way his eyes scanned her every movement, every detail of her dress.

"And now the birthday dance! *El baile de cumpleaños!*" Diego's deference for Yoli's skills showed clearly in his broad smile.

Out of nowhere a long line of well-wishers had formed, curving and snaking almost to the entrance of the *milonga.* All the famous dancers, men and women, and the most popular *tangueros* waited to perform the typical celebration. "Felicia," a fast, light tango *milonguero,* brought everyone to their feet.

"What are they doing?" I turned to Luis, but he was already gone, in line with all the others, joking with César and Mariela, waiting for his turn.

Ellie shushed me. "This is one of the most wonderful traditions. Look!"

One after the other—for the space of two or three musical phrases each—the dancers took their turn with Yoli, who playfully adjusted to fit the arms of each of her admirers. Her feet never left the floor, as if she were polishing it to a glaze with her musicality. I was transfixed.

Luis's turn arrived—he was the last—and Yoli smiled, her left arm rising gracefully behind his right shoulder, slowly circling his neck, resting close to his cheek. The first tango had segued into a dramatic one, just in time for him to lead her into a *boleo* and a *llevada*. They ended in a striking pose, her body against his, their two profiles touching, her legs in a perfect half-split.

The room exploded in frenetic applause. "*Eso!* That was it!" The enthusiasm overwhelmed me, capturing my soul, once and forever. As if I needed encouragement.

"Her legs still have the strength and the velocity of a whip. Did you see how she almost touched her shoulder with her foot? Will I ever be able to do anything like that?" Ellie shook her head in wonderment.

Diego returned to the center of the room with the microphone, his words drowned by the noise of the cheering crowd.

"Tonight we also have the great fortune of having with us the most famous dancers in the world. One of them, Carlos Copello, will perform. He didn't bring his *pareja*—his partner—so he will invite two of his students to perform with him." The sweat running down Diego's forehead drenched his sideburns, turning his pink shirt a deeper shade of red.

Copello—sleek hair à la Rodolfo Valentino, eyes as mysterious and shadowy as Hades—wore a black shirt and pin-striped trousers. He walked slowly to the dance floor and, pivoting with his usual cool style, rested his eyes on Analia.

"I will open my dance with Analia, a great dancer, a fabulous performer. You should all know that she's just been cast in a Broadway show and that she's moving to New York for several months. We look forward to seeing her on another stage." He bowed and took her into his arms.

"I can't take my eyes off them. *This* is dancing." Luis looked at Analia with joy and pride. *"Eso! Eso!"* he shouted. Ellie and I stood close to each other, holding our breath before such bravura. My hand flew to my heart, as if to control its beating.

"This is our Analia, shining like the star she is." Ellie shared a smile with me.

"I'll never forget the first time I saw her. She was sixteen and had just won the International Tango Festival. She was incredible." Luis's eyes glisten.

"And now let me invite a student of mine to dance. She's not a professional, but her skills and love for tango have placed her in a special position. Ellie! Will you join me?"

"Who?" Ellie was nonplussed. She looked around in disbelief, as if she wondered whether there might be another Ellie in the room. Carlos kept smiling, moving toward her, his hand extended in an invitation she couldn't possibly refuse. I was as stupefied as she was. The blood started racing in my veins, as if I were the one on whom such honor had been bestowed.

Trembling, Ellie walked over to Carlos and looked imploringly at him. "Not me. Why me?"

"Tranquila!" he murmured. "You can do it." He placed her in front of him and waited for the music to begin.

¡Qué saben los pitucos, lamidos y sushetas!
¡Qué saben lo que es tango,
Qué saben de compas!

What do the stuck-up,
The emaciated and the fops know,
What do they know of tango,
What do they know about rhythm?

As the familiar notes of "Así se baila el tango" sounded, the entire room roared with frenetic applause. Slowly, dramatically, Carlos lifted his left arm, waiting for Ellie to accept his formal invitation by joining her hand to his. His fingers took firm control of her back; with a flourish Ellie's left arm circled his shoulders and she waited. Carlos's feet glided on the floor, propelling Ellie backward, her back arched and her legs extended behind, reaching for an impossible extra length. She surrendered to his power, lowering her eyelashes, feeling his orders, dancing only for him.

"*Eso!*" Analia, Luis, and I shouted in unison when the music ended. "Indeed, *así se baila el tango!* That's how tango is danced!" We hugged one another, sharing our happiness at our friend's success.

When the ovation finally died down, Ellie walked back to our table in a daze. She couldn't see where she was going. About to lose her balance, she had to sustain herself by grabbing Luis's hand, tripping on the chair he was offering her.

"You were amazing! No one could take their eyes off you. I'm so proud to be your friend. You made us dream," I kept repeating like a broken record, hugging Ellie, jumping up and down.

"Really?" Ellie lit up. Those four long minutes crowned her many years of studying. Precision and control over her movements had enabled her to follow Carlos's complex, demanding orders.

"For a teacher, it's very important to show the level his students can attain. You made me hope that one day I, too, will be able to dance like you did." I'm in awe and just a tiny bit envious.

"Look at her! Ellie, my own creature. I'm so proud of her." Tears of joy—the rewards for having been a relentlessly despotic teacher—shone behind Luis's glasses. The memory of year after year of tedious repetition brought a sparkle to his eyes.

Quebrada

(Breaking Up)

*E*ven more than usual I feel as if I've been catapulted into an Argentinean *telenovela*. Today I heard from Analia, and things are definitely not going well for her. Common sense would suggest that she stop this sick, hurtful relationship, but, absorbed by passion, she continues to hold on to a frail thread of hope.

Late morning, her jazz class canceled, the bus connections surprisingly fast—Analia had decided to surprise Luis with a home-cooked lunch. Loaded with supermarket bags, she walked up the stairs to his apartment in Boedo. Playing housewife relieves her anxiety and cooking for Luis is rewarding; it quashes any fears she has for their future. No matter what she prepares, a delighted smile greets her efforts.

"Maybe it will make him click again. Maybe the party at Francesca's didn't mean anything," was her mantra, rushing up the last steps.

Oh, if I could just teach Analia a few things about the questionable power of food over sex. I could definitely provide her some good insight.

"Eleven eleven a.m. A wish! A wish! Oh God, have him love me. Make him realize I'm the One." A look at her watch started the litany from her childhood, the silly game she's always played with her cousins. Only, this time she wanted to believe in it. "He'll marry me, I'll have his kids."

The door was unlocked. Turning the handle with one hand, she kicked it open with her right foot and shoved a heavy bag inside with decisive vigor. As elegant as she is when dancing, Analia is impulsive and boisterous in her everyday life. A loud thump and cans, sacks of flour and sugar, meat and vegetables scattered on the floor. She threw her backpack on the sofa and turned to go into the kitchen.

The sudden stillness surprised her; she stood motionless, listening to its deafening silence. There had been music, noise when she'd opened the door. Now an uneasy quiet pervaded the apartment. She stopped and listened. She frowned. And she suddenly knew.

Luis—hurriedly putting on an old shirt—materialized in the dark corridor.

He gawked at her, frozen; he looked pained. He reached out to grab her shoulders, to touch her.

"I still wasn't sure what was going on. I simply concentrated on his arms—those arms which had held me only nights ago. Francesca, why is this happening to me?" Her loud sobbing drowns her words as I press the phone to my ear.

"I'm so sorry." Luis spared only this line.

Analia's hand rushed to her mouth to stifle a silent scream rising from within. A blue T-shirt outlining each muscle of his torso, his lips turned down in an ironic smirk, Oliviero emerged, hands inside his jeans pockets, staring at her.

"I see no point in staying for a drink now. Bye! See you around . . ." Calmly he kissed Luis on the lips, eyeing her all the while.

The door closed gently behind him, but cracked open again, a few seconds later.

"Well, it couldn't be more theatrical than this." His laughter echoed behind him.

"Luis was white as a sheet, so much sadness in his eyes." Analia cries quietly.

I try to find the right words to comfort her, but it's clear to me that their dream is finished. Luis will go back to his routine, his gay life, his adventures; what he had for a short time—normalcy—eludes him once again. Tempered by a lifetime of painful losses and deaths, he is familiar with the feeling of being jilted, left behind. All the people he loves seem to disappear, somehow, somewhere. But now he's the one inflicting pain, deserting another human being, hurting a loved one. Analia will fade away from him; for Luis there is no return.

She stood in the corridor for what seemed like an eternity, motionless, gripping Luis, sobbing silently, listening to the staccato beats of his heart, the bitter notes of their forthcoming separation.

Volcada

(Knocked Down)

¡Decí por Dios qué me has dao
Que estoy tan cambiao,
No sé más quién soy!

"Malevaje"

I'm late for school. I run across Corrientes, holding on to my jar of *dulce de leche,* my lunch. Somehow, instead of becoming the fattest woman in the world, I am losing weight; it's astonishing. Who knows what's happening to my blood sugar levels? If, as a result of the George-Isabel-Roberto predicament, I decide to cut my veins, it may well be that only glucose will gush out of them, courtesy of my new diet. Unfortunately all this sweetness sits in my stomach for hours and it feels perpetually like an inflated balloon.

Today Luis teaches the second part of the class: two long hours dedicated to *giros,* turns, and grapevines. Unshaven and sloppily dressed, he surprises me, used as I am to his impeccable appearance. His eyes are tired and he stays aloof the whole time.

I don't care. I've reached a breaking point and everything is difficult. For this reason, if no other, I'm glad that my classes end on Saturday. My brain has just enough room left to absorb Luis's corrections. If I keep on like this I'm going to confuse my entire body; I can't even tell my left foot from my right. Ellie and Analia say that it's normal and one just has to be patient, but I simply can't process his orders.

"When I watch people dancing I want to *see* the song they dance. Follow the notes, let me *see* them," Luis insists, looking straight at me, singling me out.

I can't stand it when he is more feminine than I am! I hate it when he gets on his tippy toes and starts showing the class how we—the women—are supposed to dance. His *ochos* are perfect and sexy, his legs snake sensuously on the wooden floor, and he looks at his temporary partner as if he's the most gorgeous creature in the world. A feeling of inadequacy has set up camp inside my head—and it seems it's here to stay. I have to remind myself of everything I've accomplished, and that change is possible, but not overnight. So I breathe slowly for a couple of minutes, mustering the strength to continue.

But when Luis barks a "don't wobble" at me, I burst into tears, horrifying him. I'm emotionally exhausted. And, on top of it all, I'm convinced someone followed me here today. A woman— seated on a bench at the end of the studio—never stops looking at me and, paranoid as I am, I suspect that I might have seen her before. There's something peculiar about her.

"So much for a discreet job. I'd never hire her." I'm surprised to hear myself speaking out loud. At the end of class, in the crowded but silent studio, my words are as strange as ski boots on a dance floor.

"What?" Luis puts on his heavy sweater and carefully wraps his signature striped scarf around his neck. Long and rainbow-colored, it reminds me of the seventies. I'd never be caught dead wearing that look. Might be retro groovy nowadays, but for me it's too close to home.

"Isabel will need all the facts she can get in order to destroy me. And I know she'll put her hands on them. After all, I've been completely careless about my relationship with Roberto. Even the blind would have seen it. And now, with the *Clarín* article and someone spying on me . . ." I adjust his scarf and tie it better, aligning the two ends. "There!"

Luis glares at the woman, horrified. "Let's go have a drink. We both need it."

What will be next? Will *Gente* come out with a line about my secret encounters with a tango dancer?

I've really begun to look forward to these tête-à-tête encounters. We are so similar and even if we've just barely met, we open up with each other. With Luis there was an immediate understanding, no shame in discussing our weaknesses. My new passion for tango is changing the way I look at my relationships and I've begun to see things with a different perspective. My own insecurities are mirrored by the tango learning process; I feel that the more I can discuss my problems with him, the easier it will be for me to master this dance and my personal problems.

"Francesca, stop worrying about everything all the time. Or at least choose your main concern. Certainly it can't be tango. You started learning it less than two weeks ago. What do you expect? Back in New York I'll teach you all I can. Don't worry! I'll make you perfect."

Soothing words. I wish he could say the same about my other problems. My life and future are in jeopardy, and yet I'm ecstatic about his promise of achieving tango proficiency. What's happened to me? Where are my priorities?

I used to value my sense of practicality, of always being in touch with reality. Now I am as fickle as they come. I shake my head, hoping to bring order to my brain.

"Luis, why do you look so dejected today? Some existential crisis I should be aware of? Are you allowing yourself to be adored by your new lover?" I smile at my dispirited friend.

Everything is going wrong. First with Analia and now with Oliviero. Luis is dying to unload his problems on me. And he's right to be worried. I've even heard rumors about Oliviero and Valerio.

"All right, yes: I am a diva! And I am *not* going to accept his behavior . . ." Luis pounds his fist on the bar table. I jump up, surprised. I motion the waiter: more *conitos* for me and two strong coffees to accompany another round of revelations.

"Imagine: he doesn't call me unless I call him. Do I have to be the one who nurtures all relationships? And he criticizes all my decisions. He wants me to stay here and give up my life in New York. He's accused me of being immature and too young. Fuck it! I don't need him."

Darkness has shadowed his eyes and he stares into the distance, searching for an entirely different world above my head. I—instinctively—turn around to discover what it is he's staring at. It's Luis's most disturbing habit.

"I am not going to accept any abuse. From anyone! I've had enough."

"Stop this nonsense, Luis. Stop it immediately. After what you've already gone through with Valerio, you must be very careful if Oliviero is as powerful as they say. Or you'll have made two enemies for life."

Has he thought about Analia? I don't want him to hurt her anymore, but he seems too involved in his own problems to care about her.

"Why do my relationships die within a few days? Why?"

The reality is that men are afraid of Luis. He intimidates them with his looks, intelligence, and especially the sex appeal he flaunts so openly. It takes a very brave guy to have the courage to start an affair with someone as threatening as him.

"Threatening?" Luis pretends not to understand what I mean. His flirtatious side is already playing tricks with me.

"There! You're doing it right now. You *know* what I mean. Didn't you confess that you are both sexes under the same skin? Well, make an effort and try to summon the skills of each one if you want to hold on to a lover. After you've won your place in someone's heart with your beauty and sex appeal, you must secure it with a tiny bit more unselfishness. In a couple there is no space for two divas . . ."

Whoa, I'm tough. But I know I'm right, and if I have to play psychologist for a while, at least I'll tell him what I see as the truth. Luis gets completely involved with whoever is his latest passion, whether it's a student or a friend. As fiercely protective as he is of his important relationships, he's a sucker for the new kid on the block.

I watch him and decide to let him talk. Once again the stage is his and I put aside my own problems.

"What are you going to do about Oliviero?" I steer him into the present, though it's not clear why I'm involving myself in this story. I've already taken on too much by trying to help Analia *out* of it.

"*Sarna con gusto no pica.* If I love what I am doing, no matter how hard it is, it seems easy. The same with men. If my relationship with him is bringing me only problems, then I shouldn't continue it. I can't go on calling him without getting an answer." Luis waves to the waiter for more coffee.

"Last night I made dinner for Oliviero at home and he sat on the sofa, looking at me, without even raising a hand to help me. At the beginning I didn't pay attention, but then it started to annoy me. I served a perfect Chinese meal, homemade. And afterward, without saying a thing, he practically raped me. It was brutish. But the thing is, I liked it."

"Well, what can I say? What a mess. I really advise you to stay away from brutality—you never know where it might end. I hope he wasn't violent." Although I know Luis is street smart, I'm uneasy listening to his story.

"He slapped me." Embarrassing, yes, but there's something else behind his words. He looks as if he wants me to guess the truth. He needs to confess it.

"So?"

". . . it turned me on! For a moment I felt all hot inside and submissive. It was a weird kind of pleasure. My stomach got all knotted and I wanted him to make love to me, then and there."

"And?"

"And he did. We did." For the first time I see Luis blush and I'm amazed that he's telling me his most intimate secrets. Or are these real secrets? Am I the privileged one—or just one of many?

"Luis, is Oliviero's age a factor in your attraction to him? Are you looking for a much older boyfriend?"

"I've asked myself the same question. I'm Argentinean and we all dabble in psychology a little bit, right? The answer to that is that I'm not sure. I feel old myself; I may be only thirty, but it's as if I were sixty. I prefer the company of older people—like you, for instance."

"Ah! Yes, of course. The cruelty of youth," I joke. For a while I'd forgotten how ancient I am.

I don't know what to say anymore. Oliviero sounds like bad news, but it's been only two days—and how can anyone decide where a relationship is going after forty-eight hours and a few fucks?

Analia is something else. Too young to understand how to manage Luis. Will she find the happiness she deserves? Can she forget Luis? I look down at my empty cup, tracing lines on the coffee stains with my spoon. Hoping to read the future, looking for a sign.

Speaking of which, what will happen to Roberto and me when I return to the States? And George? A scandal is a scandal. No matter who's right, I know I'll have to suffer the consequences of my behavior and I fear my friends' reaction. Will they immediately build a protective fence between their husbands and me, the sorceress, the adulteress? And George's family, the kids? I don't even want to think about them.

We both get up without saying anything else. Luis has retreated inside himself, but he takes my arm under his and squeezes it. He's so extraordinarily handsome, with his high cheekbones, his black curls—those *rulos* he hates so much—and the infinite sadness that fills his eyes.

"And Roberto? Tell me all about Roberto . . ."

Gancho

(A Hook)

Subject: Re: photos
Date: 6/20/2008 11:01:02 A.M. Eastern Standard Time
From: Francesca.Rivabuona@aol.com
To: George.Farrington@aol.com

George. Please, do not make things more difficult than they really are. Let's keep Isabel out of the picture until you and I have decided what to do with our lives. It's quite clear that we are at a point of no return, precipitated by Mrs. Alexanders's keen interest in my actions.

Yes, *Gente* came out today, and no, I still haven't seen it. I congratulate you in having beaten me to the newsstand. For someone who is in New York (or is it still Europe?) it's quite an accomplishment.

After breakfast I'll go and buy one, out of curiosity. The truth is, it shouldn't concern you much, given that we—long ago—agreed to forsake an active sex life. But now that I know of your relationship with Isabel, I can see the matter has changed.

Don't worry, I won't create problems. Just leave me alone. It's the only thing I'm asking of you, for the sake of our families. A bit of dignity will save a lot of headaches and our children will be grateful if we spare them embarrassment. We need to agree on how to tell them.

Soon I'll be back in New York. See you then.
Ciao
Francesca

A few blows in cyberspace and my marriage is over: a sterilized, technical demise.

I have no idea what to do next. Isabel is capable of anything and I pity my husband, who has become a spineless puppet in her hands. But, as the twins would say, whatever floats his boat. Worse, though, what if *that* someone sends preemptive information to our children?

My nights with Roberto are an undeniable fact. I have no excuses and it'll be difficult to explain my behavior. Will I have to confess the most intimate details of my marriage to the kids? I don't think I'll resort to that.

Crying, I realize that the future doesn't offer me many options right now: I can't count on Roberto because I just met him, and it would be too much to ask of him. And I'd never have expected to hurt so much for George.

"Ellie, help!"

"Francesca! What can I do? I don't know what to say. Would you like me to run to the newsstand?"

Ellie's warm hug is my only consolation. She's a good friend who doesn't judge my wrongdoing. But am I really at fault? At this precise moment I'm incapable of even feeling guilty.

I wear my jacket over my sweatpants and move toward the door. "If you're ready, I'd love to go with you. I've got to see with my own eyes what it's all about. It must be pretty awful."

We walk downstairs and push the door open onto a rainy day; I don't have an umbrella but I really don't care if I get wet. I want to die! A slow, sniffling death accompanied by deep coughing and convulsions? A modern Violetta in Buenos Aires, doubled up on our sofa, wearing my new frilly white blouse. Nah! That's not me. I'm a fighter and I'm headed straight into battle.

And to think that our last night—barely two days ago—was so romantic. The *milonga* where I danced for hours, mostly with Roberto, held in his arms, my head on his chest, my eyes shut, to capture each note. A sensual ecstasy I couldn't have imagined just two weeks ago.

The *sudestada,* the southeast wind, is wreaking havoc all over the city. Umbrellas dot Avenida Corrientes like a crazy pointillist picture, huge black shadows yanked into shreds of fabric and metal ribs. And the *sudestada* blows through my heart as well.

I flip through the pages in search of The Pictures, while the rain trickles down from the tin roof of the newsstand into my collar.

"*Oddio mio!* No!"

"Francesca, they caught your Walk of Shame. This is pretty terrible. I'm so sorry. At least you look gorgeous!" Ellie's eyes characteristically jump out of their sockets. We join our heads together, in an effort to see every detail and to avoid total drenching.

"Okay, not much we can do here. Let's go home and take a better look." Ellie grabs several copies. "They may come in handy later on."

"Yeah, sure . . . for my grandchildren! To see what kind of a liberated *puttana* their grandmother was." I have to admit it: I'm in total shock. I would never have expected such an outcome. New proof, if I ever need it, that God's avenging sword was definitely as swift as I feared. Thou shall not covet thy neighbor's wife. Or husband, in this case. But what about dear George? Is God so macho that George gets to escape punishment?

On our way back, just a block, we stop to loot the bakery: *medialunas de grasa,* my favorite, and all kinds of *biscochitos*. I buy as many as I can put my hands on.

Suddenly I feel like I have to cook. I have to make something in order to exorcise all these negative events, to free the tension bottled inside me. I stop at the local store to get what I need.

"Are you mad?" Ellie looks at me as if I've gone berserk.

"Cooking is better than going to a psychoanalyst and baking is better than Prozac. I need to cook, otherwise I'll go crazy." I fill the supermarket basket with chicken, ricotta, herbs; I grab some eggplants, their rich purple counterbalanced by the pale green of the celery stalks nearby. Sicilian caponata! It's exactly what the doctor ordered. Now for some black olives and capers, parsley, and a few anchovies. Preparing the meal will fill my morning until I go to my tango classes. I'm sure I can round up Luis and some others later for dinner.

"You are insane!" Ellie listens to the list of dishes I'm going to prepare tonight. "Well, while you're at it, why don't you make your famous lemon cake with the sorbet? I'd love to taste it . . ."

Back home, I dump everything on the kitchen table and rush to look at the magazine. There I am. Two entire spreads—four pages—with an English title and its Spanish translation: "The Walk of Shame. *El camino de la verguenza.*" In the first photo it's four a.m., straight from the *milonga*. My hair is neat, I'm all dressed up, and my makeup is more or less perfect. Roberto has his arms around me, smiling.

How did they get these pictures? I didn't see the paparazzi. I didn't see the flashes. Unless . . . at the crossroads in front of Roberto's loft, there's a tall lamp he likes because it adds extra security to the place. I'm not sure he'll be so happy about it now.

"Your Jimmy Choo boots are very photogenic." Ellie can't resist one of her wisecracks. "Next time you spend the night with Mr. Doctor, I'll give you some of my jewelry. You are the best walking advertisement anyone could hope for!"

In the next picture I'm coming out of the building, in the morning.

"Okay, okay, I didn't really have time to comb it . . ." My hair's all over the place, my dancing shoes protrude from my handbag, and I'm not wearing even a hint of makeup.

"But you must admit that you look rested and happy, even if a bit surprised." Ellie giggles again.

My mouth is open in a stupefied *Oh!* and my eyes are shut under the glaring lights.

"Of course, they use flash in the morning and natural light at night. How sophisticated . . . I certainly look startled and Roberto, too. I'm sure it's been a shock for him, just as much as for me." Suddenly my phone rings and it's him: apologetic, worried about me and my reaction.

"There's not much I can do about it. George has already sent me an e-mail and by now Isabel must be grinning her siliconed smile! One day she'll pay for this. Don't worry." I start sobbing. If only Clarissa knew how my life has been overturned because of her assignment. "Roberto, go back to your work. You're not responsible. I appreciate your concern, but it doesn't solve anything. See you tonight, if you have time. I'm going to cook—and I'll feed whoever wants to come." I open one of the kitchen drawers and take out another of my Argentinean secret weapons: a *Tita de Terrabusi,* a chocolate-covered biscuit. When in doubt, binge!

"*Que sarnosa!* What a disgusting person!" Luis is the next person to ring me. No one has any doubt who's behind all of this. "What will you do? Is there anything I can do to help?" His tender voice reaches my heart; once again I burst into loud sobbing while Ellie strokes my hair.

"You need to cry. Go ahead, unload. But remember, you have many friends here now and we love you." Luis is going to meet us for lunch and is already on his way to the apartment to be with me.

The phone is ringing off the hook: Analia is very impressed—

she's never known anyone who would make the pages of *Gente*—
and Sarah is furious.

"There must be a way to stop this. She has overstepped all
boundaries. I would never have predicted such behavior from her.
What they say about Isabel is true: she doesn't stop for anything.
Oh, Francesca, I'm so sorry. I wish I'd never taken you to Clínica
Pluribus." Sarah's sense of responsibility eats away at her. But who
would ever have expected self-possessed, conservative Francesca
to behave like this?

It's not just suffering: it's humiliation and sadness, confusion
and a debilitating sense of incompetence. I'm a paper boat thrown
in the middle of the ocean; I've let myself go without considering
any of the possible consequences. But what makes me furious is to
have been played by Isabel, to have dealt her the hand she needed
to win the game. My very first transgression allowed her to get a
stronger hold on her lover, my husband.

I hope her triumphant sneer will soon unstitch her carefully
patched muzzle. With her silly blond ringlets, she looks like a
cocker spaniel on acid!

"I'd love to confront her, but then I'm afraid to lose the little
dignity I have left. Is she at the same hotel?" I furiously consider
what I could do to provoke an explanation from her. Face to face.

"What will happen to your marriage? Can't you have it
annulled by the Sacra Rota? After all, your family knows everyone
in the Vatican." Ellie knows my parents took good care of Sarah
when she separated from her first husband and were able to guide
her successfully through a difficult annulment process.

"No way! I'd never do anything like that. I had three children
with him. It would be the height of hypocrisy and a total denial of
our love for each other—past, it seems! We've shared some great
moments." Why can't I stop crying? Anyone might now mistake
me for the Iguazu Falls.

"I could go to the Faena and grab her by her fur turban, undoing her carefully cemented blond hair. I could slap her! I could . . . I could . . ." Unfortunately there's nothing I can do. And if I actually had the courage to confront her, I'd lose credibility in my own eyes. Let her keep plotting, a spider in her own web. George is all hers, if she wants him so much. She'll no doubt have him for supper!

It's better if I cook and ignore the phone. The only person who should have called, hasn't. George. Twenty-five years of marriage and he doesn't have the guts to ask me directly what has happened? E-mail is cowardice. He was supposed to be my best friend, my companion, my partner for life. Then again, I'm guilty here too!

I strip the bulging eggplants, cut them into small cubes, and fry them with the lithe, perky celery. I've got a thick, spicy sauce, studded with gorgeously ripe tomatoes, fleshy black olives, and nubbin capers. George—once upon a time—would have been panting for it.

"What are you doing with vinegar and sugar?" Ellie watches me like a hawk while I sauté the onions.

"*Cara mia!* That's the secret of caponata . . . I guess you need a Sicilian grandmother." It's foolproof: cooking always manages to make me smile. I feel better, calmer already. What will be, will be.

For the moment, a tantalizing smell wafts through the apartment, reassuring me.

"You are a maniac. Look at you, you've already filled the kitchen with enough food for a week. Who's coming tonight?" Ellie can't believe her eyes as she sees me systematically put together all kinds of dishes. The chicken has already been reduced to narrow, regular strips and rolled with my secret concoction of ricotta and herbs; now it simmers on a low flame.

"It doesn't matter. Anyone is welcome. Roberto and Sarah, Luis, Analia, who needs more?"

The doorbell rings while I'm putting together my dance kit. It'll be Luis. We'll have a bite together before going to the *escuela*. Should I call and say that I'm sick? Should I go? I'm not sure I want to be barked at for hours, while I feel like dying inside.

"What are you doing here?" A handsome man towers at the door, water dripping from his green Burberry. And it's not Luis.

"Are you going to invite me in?" Roberto smiles and holds his arms out to me. His kisses quickly move over my forehead, my cheeks, my mouth. *"Fatiga de los adoquines:* you're worn out! That's the doctor's diagnosis. There's a cure, and the prognosis is absolutely benign."

I'm perplexed. Maybe he's here to have lunch as well?

"Grab your makeup and your overnight things and come with me. Shush! Don't ask too many questions. You'll see." He puts a finger over my lips and leads me to the bedroom. "No dancing today. No classes. Ellie, you can tell the teachers that this woman here needs some rest. The doctor is in charge now." He goes to the bathroom and starts gathering some of my stuff.

"Esperá! Wait! What do you mean?"

"Do you trust me? Yes? Okay, then just do as I tell you. Pack a small bag with whatever you need: lipstick—any pills?— foundation, powder . . . You're the woman here. No dresses. No clothes. Jeans will do. Don't worry." He smiles his gentle, funny smile. He's nothing but love and tenderness. And, yes, all right: I'll do whatever he wants me to. Maybe we're off to his loft. I don't need clothes there, obviously! And what a relief not to have to go to my class. I'm such a stupidly disciplined person; I would have gone for the sole reason that I had committed to it. But now the idea of relaxing my body and soul, even for just one afternoon—oh!

Ellie stands by the door, watching me put together a few things, and looking puzzled. She puts her hand on Roberto's shoulder and presses it down as hard as she can. She has to get on her tiptoes to be able to reach him.

"You're not going to hurt her any more than this, yeah? She doesn't deserve what's happening. Please?"

"Don't worry. I'll take good care of her."

As we run out the door I shout instructions to Ellie about how to finish the meal I had begun. Downstairs, the driver opens the door and I slide into the luxury of Roberto's opulent Mercedes. On my side of the seat there is a huge charcoal-gray cashmere scarf.

"For you. You mustn't get cold." Roberto wraps it around my shoulders, as if I were the most precious person in the world. He's capable of gestures I'd never have imagined when I first met him. His macho looks, his polo playing—it all sets up a false impression of him.

"Al aeroparque?" The driver smiles, looking at me in the mirror while addressing Roberto.

"Sí enseguida, por favor." Roberto is busy on the phone with his secretary, canceling appointments and moving everything to the following week. Where is he taking me? The airport? I shiver with the thrill of expectation. \

We cross Palermo, skirt the park, and leave behind the honking traffic that paralyzes the city at all hours. Strange—this is not the direction to Ezeiza, the airport where I arrived. I rummage inside my bag, making sure I have my passport.

"You won't need a passport . . ." Roberto teases, explaining nothing. He nods with satisfaction: the shawl looks good on me. I am still shell-shocked by the *Gente* article, incapable of expressing my feelings, and I let go. My head drops against his shoulder. I'm tired; I want to close my eyes and sleep for hours, days, maybe an entire month!

We breeze down a narrow two-way road, flanked by tall trees

and empty fields, bypassing a sign for the major Aeroparque Jorge Newbery, and continue straight ahead, on what feels like a country road, until we stop in front of a low building.

I blink twice as the pilot of a silver G5, a dazzling Gulfstream, comes out to greet me. He smiles when I sink into a seat of sumptuous cream leather. I turn to Roberto for explanations. Could this be his plane?

"Let's say that it belongs to the company . . ."

"But then you *are* the company!"

A whispered conversation with the pilot and then Roberto falls silent. He goes to the window just in time to catch the sight of another private jet already in the air, its nose straight up and climbing. "That was our Isabel taking off for New York!" He indicates the outgoing plane. "No immediate confrontation for you."

"One less decision to make, I guess . . ." Roberto slips playfully under the shawl. "Everything will be fine, don't worry," he reassures me, and immediately I relax. The plane takes off and I don't even realize it. We sail smoothly upward, and nestled in his arms, his mouth close to mine, his scent already a touchstone for me, I am lulled into a deep sleep.

When I wake up Roberto is on the phone, but his eyes are on me. He blows a kiss from his desk.

"About to land." He motions silently. How long did I sleep? The sun is two thirds of the way through its daily trip, and the sky above the dark clouds is taking on a deep russet streaked with gold. I never wear watches and I don't know if I've slept for hours or only minutes.

The plane angles downward; the engines roar and we pierce the blackness underneath us, appearing and disappearing in between clouds, reemerging several feet lower above a countryside still green despite the season. From above, it reminds me of central Italy: Tuscany, Umbria, or maybe even Le Marche. Rows and rows of disciplined vines zigzag the hills, bare now in winter, but in autumn the source of the Argentinean wine I have learned to appreciate so much.

"Roberto! Where are we?" In all this immensity there are no cities in sight, only nature and a landing strip that seems to end nowhere.

The plane makes a sharp turn, the right wing swerves down under our seats, and the infinite panorama appears from underneath.

"You'll see . . ." I can't get anything out of this guy!

A green Range Rover waits for us and less than five minutes later we wind up a road along a marvel of landscape artistry where all the local plants have been mixed with specimens brought in from every state in South America.

"This garden never shows its true beauty in winter. But in October you'll go crazy here." Roberto rattles off the names of the tall trees like a pro. "Gardening was my mother's greatest pleasure and this was one of her projects. She designed this property for a family friend. Look around. Enjoy the vista, and as soon as we're there, you'll understand everything." His laughter is contagious. I wrap my shawl around me and try to stifle a nagging thought: I brought only my toothbrush. What does he expect me to do if we're visiting some friends?

The house, a low, contemporary building, sits on a high plateau, its glass walls open to the valley and a 360-degree, bird's-eye view—as if we were still flying over the tall trees we admired on our way up. Glossy, oversized modern sculptures dot the courtyard and the steps to the front entrance. The sunset paints the house with a deep coppery shimmer.

"Impressive; they remind me of Beverly Peppers."

"Maybe because they are Beverly Peppers!" We walk past an

enormous kind of egg yolk in the middle of the back terrace. "And that's a Moore."

No one is coming out to greet us. I'm perplexed.

"We are in the Mendoza region. Welcome to La Soledad!" Roberto takes my hand and leads me inside, past the main entrance and straight into a huge, magnificent room transformed by a collection of antique bird cages into something magical, a game of micro-architecture, a romantic dreamer's fragile chimera.

Roberto turns to me with the same expression the twins have when they want my approval. "I'm considering buying it. What do you think?" He pulls me toward the bedroom.

It's almost an entire house on its own. A glass wall (pity the one who has to wash it!) is the only thing that stands between us and the lush greenery outdoors. The sunset streams in, suffusing everything with a warm coral blush.

Roberto pushes open a sliding door, happiness spread across his handsome features, lighting up his eyes. I love the way his eyebrows lift mischievously. In fact, I like all his gestures. It's as if I've known him for years. How many days have we been together? And already I can't imagine separating from him. Dangerous, dangerous thoughts I should never indulge.

"You might need these, tonight and tomorrow . . ." He points at some empty suitcases: as if by enchantment, everything is already tidied up and hung in the walk-in closet, itself double the size of my Buenos Aires bedroom. Luxurious underwear fills the drawers to the rim and an embroidered silk robe is carefully laid over the back of an armchair.

"Something you might want to use tonight." Roberto triumphantly pulls a dark gray dress from one of the closets. "It's a Manuel Lamarca, an Argentinean designer."

Either he is a frustrated personal shopper or he is a closeted gay! My mind flashes back to all those exquisite shoes, exactly my size, in extraordinary combinations of color and texture. Incredible as it seems, Roberto has bought me an entire wardrobe, which he calls a twenty-four-hour kit, but I doubt I'll want to change very often in this short period of time. He's thought of *everything,* including riding clothes for tomorrow's morning visit to the countryside. In this area, horses are everywhere, like taxis in New York.

It turns out that the house and the gardens belonged to Alvaro de Peralta, the richest man in Argentina. He died and left the estate with the written hope that Roberto would use it and love it the same way.

"Don Alvaro was so madly in love with my mother that he never married. They were very close until her death. Not one day went by without the two of them talking to each other. My mother died last October and he followed her a few months later, in March."

So, there's old-world romance contained within these walls. A kind of melancholy, the emptiness of riches that couldn't get Don Alvaro what he really wanted from life.

"I've never been here with any woman, not even Ana María. I just wanted to let you know, in case . . ." He looks straight into my eyes.

"I feel like Goldilocks. I mean, I've just wandered into a fairy tale where everything is prepared for me and it's all just right." I touch the dress, admiring the beauty of the imported fabric, a voile of cashmere with a tinge of red as well, infinitesimal dots woven in by the hand of the best artisans in Italy.

"I wanted to see your legs . . ."

"This is too much, Roberto."

"No one will recognize you here and it's such a small place that you'll feel safe. So get ready. Put on your new jeans and sweater, and I'll take you around." Roberto kisses my lips lightly, keeping me close to him. I love the smell of his breath. It's always fresh, I want to draw it into myself, and I find myself looking at his mouth, wanting to kiss him. It's a strange sensation of almost wanting to rape him with my tongue; I need to explore him, to drink in his taste.

"Who helped you choose these clothes for me? And the ten pairs of shoes last week?" My usual curiosity gets the upper hand.

"*Nadie!* No one! I always loved to buy things for my mother, Ana María, my girlfriends. With you it's so easy: I know your body and you fit into everything. It wasn't really a big risk. Besides, you needed a boost, right?"

Oh yes, I've needed a boost for many years and never realized it. At least for the moment, I thank God for Clarissa and her article, for tango, for my daily breakfasts in Abasto with Ellie, and for this man who's nothing short of unbelievable.

"Ellie! I'm in the car, coming home; I'll be there in ten minutes. You're not going to the airport for another couple of hours, right?" I wish I could fly over the traffic and land at our doorstep, to rush up and hug Ellie. I have too many things to tell her: the plane, the house, the horses, the valley, the winery, and . . . Ah! The letting go of the morning after.

"Have you already packed? We need some quality time together." The phone in one hand, I search in my bag for the gift I bought her at the winery: two extraordinary-looking pieces of local stone, a geological marvel she can set in her own design. A pair of earrings, maybe? Something special to remind her that life can bring surprises, even when you least expect them. Only yesterday I was ready to bang my head against the wall and today I'm triumphantly remembering my twenty-four hours with Roberto. A day, a night I'll never forget, no matter how our story ends.

"Feels like you've been gone for a year. Look at you! A serious case of the cat who ate the canary . . . And this?" As soon as I walk through the door, Ellie hugs me, touching my shawl in disbelief.

I need to unload, I have to tell her all that happened to me. Will she believe me?

Dinner at the *estancia*. The house chef, stocky Ramona, had prepared a feast in the kitchen and our table was set in front of an immense fireplace. Antique copper pots and nineteenth-century wooden tools decorated the walls.

"These *ñoquis con tuco* are as light as my *gnocchi al pomodoro*. What a low blow to my pride." Brandishing the fork in my hand, I closed my eyes, the better to enjoy the pure perfection of the food I was savoring. "I'm going to have to come back with some excuse—maybe an article?—to eat here again." I had filled my plate with *humita,* and Ramona, hands on her wide hips, watched me eat, delighted at the way I inhaled the delicate corn dish.

"You need no excuses to come here." Roberto stared seriously into my eyes, and my heart jumped a bit. It was almost as if he were imploring me. "With all that's happening between George and Isabel, you might want to spend more time in Argentina." He must know more than he's letting on.

"Listen! Men like this don't exist; unless he's fake or has come down from another planet, maybe the moon," Ellie interrupts me. "I'm sorry, Francesca, but now I'm convinced that your stories are science fiction! At the very least, Roberto should have bad breath or acne; *something* wrong, for goodness' sake. Otherwise I can't believe he's human; they don't come like this. Trust me." Ellie bends over the sofa, indignantly waving her finger in front of my eyes. "I'm not a jealous person in general, but this is too much! Where have you been, Fantasyland? We should talk to Ana María. Let's ask her why she left him and eloped with that actor."

Well, Ellie has a point, of course. Like her, I can't quite believe what's happening to me, but, hey! I leave tomorrow and who knows what will happen? Or even whether I'll ever see him again. Carpe diem, as the Romans said, and who am I to ignore their enlightened suggestion? Seize the day, indeed.

"Ellie, when I compare the past few days with Roberto to the last few years with my husband, there's no contest. Can you imagine being married to someone whose erotic vocabulary is reserved solely for the food I cook? *I yearn for your food, it makes me dizzy with lust.* The night before I left for Buenos Aires, George had the nerve to say that. He lusts after my gnocchi as if they were sexy supermodels." George's desire for gourmet erotica suddenly feels so foreign, many light-years away from my recent experience in Argentina.

My days and nights with Roberto were an erotic fantasy worthy of the best bodice ripper; his sexual appetite is endless and my response always more than enthusiastic. The old phrase—*it takes two to tango*—was coined for us.

There was a reason, of course, for those drawers that overflowed with expensive lingerie. Am I still blushing, just thinking about it? Well, I certainly turned crimson during my flight back, reflecting on our special night. George and I had a great sexual entente for many years but, even when the spark was on, it never ignited the fire that consumed me in just a week with Roberto.

"Are you going to do something for me tonight?" After dinner—empty coffee cups in front of us—Roberto leaned across the white lace tablecloth, reaching for my breasts. He cupped them, sliding his thumbs over my nipples.

"Roberto!" I pulled away rapidly, and looked around to make sure that the staff hadn't noticed. "Thank God they don't understand English. You should behave."

It's infuriating to have become so eager and responsive to anything he does or says. I protest, but mine are just vain, meaningless words. What really happens is that at the first touch of his hands, I become a high-tension cable. There is a direct, magic communication between his touch and my body. A lightning-fast burst of fire erupts and obliterates any rational behavior.

I couldn't say anything; I couldn't eat, I just glanced at him, dissolving inside under the heat of my excitement. I was ready and willing to submit to whatever he wanted me to do for him and with him.

He took my hand and pulled me up from the chair. Talk about feeling disembodied! I wasn't sure I still had a pair of legs. The imposing door leading to our quarters—very far away from the center of the house—shut behind us with a loud *clack!* and we were alone, isolated from the outside world. There I was, eagerly anticipating yet another night of sex.

Roberto cornered me against a wall and started to undress me rapidly. He rolled up my cashmere sweater, exposing my breasts, awakened by his desire. A man's erection must feel the way my nipples do when I'm with him—painful, and disturbingly revealing.

I tried to unfasten my jeans, but he was already pushing them down, almost tearing them. My panties followed suit. I wanted him, badly, I wished for his hands to touch me, for him to fill me.

"Tonight you'll have to wait," he teased. He bent to suck me all over and slid down my body, kissing every inch of my skin. His hands probed, opened, assailed me, and I answered, hungrily feeling him, fondling him.

"You are going to wear this for me." Roberto opened a drawer and took out a frail, lacy bunch of black fabric. "I'll be back in a few minutes and I want to find you ready . . ."

Trembling, I put on the sexy balconette bra, so delicate I was afraid my fingers would tear through it.

I checked the panties in disbelief: *peek-a-boo!* Black and silvery fishnet and lace, they teased and hugged, leaving little to the imagination. An embroidered satin garter belt came with them. Had I ever worn anything as provocative as this? To think that only a few days ago I had planned on buying sexy new underwear. I quickly chased away the image of me seated in front of the computer in my unflattering New York uniform: exercise pants and oversized T-shirt. Thank God Roberto has never seen me like that!

But yes, definitely—I was in for all that was offered to me.

While I was anxiously checking my image Roberto slipped in behind me, his silver hair wet, a white towel wrapped around his hips. His eyes pored over my body, concentrating on my breasts, my belly, my ass. A burning sensation took hold of me and I blushed. I brought my arms up, as if I wanted to cover what was so cleverly exposed by his choice of lingerie.

His fingers trailed over my back, across my shoulders, played softly with my thin lace straps. He pushed aside the fabric on my left breast and his index finger snuck inside. He stopped and looked at me. He brought his finger to his lips and wet it, then slowly touched my nipple again, the wetness turning into erection, the erection transforming into heat. A liquid sensation of warmth rushed down like lava between my legs; I thought I was going to faint. That secret area took on a life of its own: it ebbed and flowed like a sea anemone under the somnolent rhythm of the ocean waves.

His hands on my waist, measuring it, pressing his fingertips together as if he were tying a ring around it. "Wear these for me." He pointed to a pair of black high-heeled shoes on the floor, near the bed. "Walk for me, dance for me," Roberto ordered.

A perverse desire to excite him engulfed me. Look, don't touch! I wanted to provoke him, make him want me, agonize for me. *A bit ridiculous at my age?* Warning messages flashed down from my brain, but I silenced them.

I started walking as I knew how to, as I'd seen in all the movies—underwear and seduction, Sofia and Marcello, Kim and Mickey. I lived my Helmut Newton fantasy, recording my own black-and-white pleasure.

I don't even remember the name of the tango he played, but the notes accompanied my movements as I walked and bent, pivoted and glared provocatively at Roberto, until it was all too much, for him and for me. Till I had to stop in front of him and allow him to play with the panties and the garter, lift the fabric, probe, search, enter.

"And now this . . ." He took up a black satin mask from its place on the bedside table. "You will wear it and be ready, available to surrender to everything I want to do with you. You won't know, you won't see, you'll only feel . . ." His voice raucous with excitement, Roberto took me into his arms and lifted me up, depositing me on the chaise longue at the end of the bed. I knelt and he pushed my upper body onto the bed.

"Have you ever done it?" Roberto whispered, already lowering my panties. The heat that emanated from his body pervaded me and a huge surge of excitement rushed through my entire being. I waited.

"Have you done it before?" he repeated urgently.

"No." I shook my head, overwhelmed by fear and a strange longing for the unknown. I had always refused to do it, it just never seemed right before . . .

"Relax." Roberto stroked me, bringing me to the verge of an orgasm I couldn't, didn't want to restrain. "Don't! Don't come." It was an order and I submitted, waves of lust running all through my body. I had no idea how I was going to control my inner reactions.

"Now"—his hands grabbed my waist, his body heavy against mine, and he penetrated me—"relax." An incredible pain shot through my entire being. I tensed and finally let go, sobbing, crying out loud, until I came like never before, consumed by the endless pulsing of my entire body.

I must briefly have lost consciousness, because when I woke up I was in Roberto's arms, and he was kissing me, moving away the mask, lightly passing his fingers over my eyes, my cheekbones, my neck.

Now, in our apartment in Abasto, I shake my head, trying to banish those memories, and I blush again, incapable of controlling my reactions. Ellie looks at me inquisitively, her hands on her hips.

"Hmm . . . you're holding out on me."

Giro

(A Turn)

Tengo miedo del encuentro
con el pasado que vuelve
a enfrentarse con mi vida . . .
Tengo miedo de las noches
Que, pobladas de recuerdos,
Encadenan mi soñar . . .

"Volver"

*T*he irrevocability of all that's happened weighs on me. What am I going to do here without Ellie, in an empty apartment? For another twenty-four long hours? Her reassuring presence, her friendship was such an unexpected gift.

Contemplating my return to New York, I feel at odds: Should I let things go their natural way, or should I fight to save my marriage? It's hard to believe that I've destroyed so much in so little time: twenty-five years of marriage gone in the space of two weeks.

And with Ellie off to New York, the sudden hollowness of my life is even more staggering. I have no more tears. I cried yesterday, I cried today in the plane coming back from Mendoza, and I cried a few minutes ago, when she left for the airport.

"Be strong, be brave. Only twenty-four hours and you'll be back in New York. Remember, I'll be there for you anytime you need me." Ellie dried her eyes with the palm of her hand, searching in vain for a Kleenex.

"If it weren't for you . . ." I kissed her, unable to finish my sentence. I felt choked up, even while tears silently streamed down my cheeks. I helped her downstairs with her bags and stood on the doorstep. I followed the car as it squealed a right onto Corrientes, until I lost sight of its red taillights blinking in the dusky luminescence of a winter evening.

"And you thought I'd leave you alone?" A hand touches my shoulder and I turn around to see Luis standing in the doorway, laughing.

I want to leap in the air and hug him. "What are you doing here?"

"This is a relay! I spent the morning with Ellie and she made me swear I wouldn't let you out of my sight, so guess what? Since we had to have dinner without you last night—by the way, your food was delicious—I decided that tonight will be my treat. The only difference is that, unlike you, I will be there." At first I don't get it, but when I remember my dramatic disappearance only twenty-four hours ago I crack up.

"So, how was dinner? Who came? What did you do?" I completely forgot to ask Ellie about last night. It's a relief to discover that the food turned out all right after all that shopping.

"In the end, it was only Ellie and me, at ten, after the theater. Ah! I forgot. Oliviero showed up quite late." Luis passes his hand through his curls, his chin goes up, and his eyes look somewhere behind me, assuming his usual transfixed expression.

My last evening in B.A. is already looking brighter than it did just a few minutes ago. As we slowly walk upstairs, arm in arm, *la portera* opens her door to peep at us, a pungent scent streaming out of her apartment. She must be frying something. The smell immediately transports me to my childhood and the home of my ever-disapproving aunt. The white hair of this Argentinean lady encases a pointed chin, a beaky nose, and a pair of prurient black eyes.

"*Cómo estás?*" Am I paranoid, or is she checking me out because of the magazines? In the week we've spent here, she's never even spoken to me.

"Mmm! *Qué aroma!*" Luis immediately shields me from the woman's piercing sly look and drags me up one more flight. We close the door and collapse in a fit of laughter. *Tutto il mondo è paese.* It's the same all over the world. Nosy neighbors are everywhere.

"I'll tell you about dinner last night, only if you'll spill the dirt about your trip with Roberto!"

Three ill-matched people around the table, guzzling wine and feasting on another of my Italian dinners.

"Poor Ellie, I don't even know how she coped alone with me and Oliviero. Lots of ruffled feathers! You should have seen her trying to defuse the problems, changing the subject, directing us to discuss anything but our situation. The only thing that went smoothly was your menu: caponata and chicken rolls. We inhaled them!" Luis smiles broadly.

"Going to the *milonga* is what really saved the night for Ellie. Oliviero and I left her at the entrance of Club Gricel and I know she had quite a fabulous evening. Ever since she danced with Copello, they've been clamoring for her."

In the tango world there's nothing like being singled out by a well-known dancer, a maestro. It's an anointment of sorts, which raises the lucky one to semigoddess status. There are congratulations—and often envious words—from the *milonga* crowd. *When I danced with Gavito, Osvaldo, El Negro Copello . . .* Those words, casually inserted in conversation, elicit a sense of reverence among the tango crowd.

"And where did *you* and Oliviero go?" I ask. I plop on the sofa and draw my knees under my body; a glass of wine will ease our way into this last evening in Buenos Aires. Let the risqué broadcast begin: Happy Hour of Truths!

"There is no way that this relationship is going to last, Francesca," Luis burst forth, taking me by surprise. "The sex is great, the guy is good-looking and has a brilliant mind, but he scares me."

I don't like that statement. What does he mean? I don't want the older man to hurt Luis. Although I've known him for only a short while, I feel a maternal desire to protect him. This is the last thing he needs right now: distraction from his routine and from his goals. His relationship with Analia is enough of an emotional strain. And then there is the Valerio factor. If what they say is right, and the two directors did indeed date, then Luis has really put himself in hot water. First Analia and now Oliviero? All because of sex . . .

"Did he hit you again?" I search for telltale signs, but, unless Luis volunteers the details, there is really very little I can get him to reveal.

"That's not the point. The problem with him is that he wants to dominate my mind and my body. I don't particularly behave like a virgin in any of my relationships, but this situation is definitely different."

Luis plays with the hem of my dress. "This is cool!" He snaps out of his reverie, fingering the fabric knowingly and giving me the once-over. "You look great. What happened while you were with Roberto?"

Fifty years old, and turning strawberry red at the least provocation? My world has really been turned upside down. But Luis's laughter flows over me like a sweet balm.

"Tell me about Oliviero," I insist. I'm not ready to start talking about Roberto. *And Analia?* I want to add.

"Oliviero is a two-faced Janus: one day he is the kindest man in the world and the next he's a monster. Maybe it's all the drugs he does. His brain must be fried. Unfortunately, other aspects of our relationship have become extremely seductive—I'd say irresistible—and so I forget the way he treats me . . ."

Oliviero and his youthful looks. How can he do coke and still have the face and the body of someone so much younger? Suddenly I remember his eyes—often dilated, unfocused—and I don't want to see him with Luis anymore. He is bad news.

"He wants me to perform in his next show in Buenos Aires, a musical based on *Doña Flor y sus dos maridos,* the great book by Jorge Amado. It would mean having to spend several more months here and I don't know that I want to do it. I have too many engagements in the States." Luis paces the living room, refilling his glass and looking at me as if asking for my approval. "Plus, I would end up in a dangerously binding situation. And imagine Valerio. First Analia and then Oliviero?"

"Last night, after leaving Ellie at the *milonga,* we walked to his apartment and of course we had a terrible scene. Why can't sex just come easily? I seem to have to go through a lot. I'm about ready to cut off my *pito* and become a monk!"

"Careful with that wine! You're going to spill it if you keep moving around like a lunatic." But I agree with him. Too many unpleasant things happen in the name of sex. Look at me and George. And that voracious Isabel . . . I still have to find proof of my theory, but if they've been together for a while, it would certainly explain why my husband would have lost interest in me.

I agonize over their relationship: When did it begin? My hurt feelings are currently anesthetized by my affair with Roberto, but what about later? I fear my return to New York. How can I possibly go back to my old life after everything that's happened? I shake my head of these thoughts and try to concentrate on Luis and his problems.

"Yesterday Oliviero asked me to have sex with other men, in front of him. And you know what? *Mirá,* it's not that I'm virtuous, in other moments I would have done it no problem, but with Oliviero it's different; I felt like he was asking only to assert even more power over me. So I walked out of the apartment."

"You probably did the right thing. Just be careful. That kind of person can turn on you in an instant. It's only too human; wanting to control other people must be a primeval instinct."

"How smoothly everything goes when there's no sex involved." Luis sighs.

"Yes, but a lot less exciting." I giggle, remembering my last twenty-four hours with Roberto.

"And now: *spill!* What did you do with Roberto? He robbed you like a medieval knight, whisking you away on his galloping Mercedes." He winks.

"Ha! And not only a Mercedes, but also a flying unicorn in the shape of a silver G-Five. Not bad as G-Fives go, actually." I think about all the details I'm *not* going to confess. First and foremost my experience of practically losing my virginity a second time around; although it has helped me to understand Luis better. But I can't possibly confess to him that I had always wondered why so many people secretly prefer to make love like that. Now I know: traumatic for sure. As per pleasure . . . hmmm, the jury is still out.

"This is unbelievable!" Roberto is definitely the greatest romantic I have ever encountered and Luis sits up straight, listening to my expurgated tales with rapt attention. He nods enthusiastically, approving every last detail. Of course I omit

one key scene, but my description of the flight, the private landing strip, the house, and all his fashionable purchases go down
very well with Luis. Especially when it comes to the lingerie
detail . . .

Having lashed out at the highs and lows of our romantic lives,
we make plans for dinner: *parrilla,* nothing sophisticated, just
a simple *bodegón* will do, and that's how I find myself in one of
the most delightful places I have been since I arrived. Leave it to
Luis to understand my craving for simplicity. After at least half
an hour weaving in and out of horrendous traffic, our taxi leaves
us in Pasaje Las Casas, in front of Pan y Teatro, once again back
in Luis's world: Caballito. A dim streetlight makes the restaurant
look like an old country house. An untidy bunch of tall trees and
overgrown bushes clusters at the corner of the street, obscuring
the entrance. I wish I could see it in the summer, bursting with
flowers, sheltering the clients with its luscious shade.

"My treat!" Luis doesn't even wait to be shown to his table.
With the self-assurance of the habitué, he leads me to a cozy corner of the room, moving past big rustic tables and the old upright
piano in the middle of the room. "Here we can talk about everything and you can relax. No one knows you—and no photogra-
phers will *ever* come here."

Mini empanadas crumble in my mouth, releasing the full-
bodied flavor of savory cheese and succulent ragout. Even the
bread—arrayed in many shapes and varieties on a sideboard—
has a unique homemade flavor with the briny savoriness of olives
and the tang of walnuts. I throw myself on the basket of piquant
rosemary-and-onion focaccia as if I hadn't eaten in a week. A bowl
of green chimichurri is already on the table; its aroma hits me at
once with the simplicity of its two basic ingredients—parsley and
garlic—unified by strong, pungent olive oil.

Luis wears a loose, ribbed orange cashmere sweater—the

kind women steal from their boyfriends in order to feel small and protected—and it looks great with his dark complexion and black hair.

"Remember the hospital I showed you on our way to the restaurant? It was there that the first act of my own, personal *telenovela* played out." Luis grabs an enormous piece of bread and slathers it with enough mayonnaise to feed an army of hungry *porteños*. I refuse his offer of a bite and concentrate on his words.

"A few hours after I was born, my father asked to see his child again, only to hear the nurse respond: '*Lo siento*, the baby is dead.' In those days Argentina was plagued with baby theft and my father immediately summoned his comrades. The hospital was cordoned off and, sure enough, a few hours later they found me sleeping peacefully inside a basket on the hospital roof." Luis shakes his head as his right hand clears a few bread crumbs from his mouth. "That's how I started my life: nearly kidnapped!"

He never fails to surprise me. Every time I sit down with him—at a restaurant, a bar, a café, even on the couch of my little apartment—I know he'll reveal a bizarre new tale.

"You and all the mythological heroes, of course. Did I ever doubt that you were special, right from the start? Romulus and Remus—on their way to founding Rome—floated down the Tiber in a basket. And let's not forget Moses! You are in great company, but now you also have a major predicament: What are you going to achieve in life to measure up to your predecessors? Metamorphose into the God of Tango? Right now sweet notes and desperate *letras* swirl around you in a permanent aura," I burst out, and Luis laughs, his head thrown back, happy once more to have gained my full attention.

He's put a spell on me. I want to steal him and take him away. With me. Anywhere, everywhere. I understand why someone would have wanted to take him as a baby. I watch him, surprised by the protective feelings he stirs in me. The flexibility of his lean body: he bends forward on one of his long legs, the other twisted in an odd position under him. His feet—especially when he's concentrated as he is now, reading the menu—perennially beat the time of some soundless inner music, while his glasses lend him a serious professorial look.

It's no wonder people hate to be neglected by him. When Luis focuses his attention on you he makes you feel special, unique. Analia's desperate words come to my mind.

"*Mai più nessuno al mondo, ti amerà così* . . . No one will ever love you so much . . . It's Mina, the Italian singer he adores and listens to obsessively. Francesca, it's a curse," she admits. "I wish he sang it for me." Each time Luis sings those romantic *letras* in her ear, words of true love they both cherish, she desperately believes he's dedicating them to her.

Of course, Luis is too straightforward to be deceptive; he just doesn't understand what tragic confusion he creates. And Analia is right, Luis easily becomes restless—he gazes around in his uniquely hard way. As he hunts, he strides—feet slightly apart—determined to find a mate.

"I am actually looking forward to going back home. I need the sun, I need warmth. This has been the coldest winter ever in Buenos Aires, and you had to be here for it. We must go to the beach as soon as we're both back in New York."

Luis's words startle me out of my reverie.

"How do you survive in the States then?" I dig into the Argentinean equivalent of a great *parmigiana di melanzane*. I think of Naples, Positano, Ischia, all those small towns and villages whose poor inhabitants immigrated to Argentina. The dish I'm savoring is exactly the same as in Campania. The mozzarella melts in my mouth along with the sweetness of faultless tomatoes and eggplants.

"Well, New York has given me the chance to care for my family." The smile is gone, and once again deep sadness has taken over.

"I had to help my family. My success in the States allowed me to pay for my nephews' studies, to help my sister get her nursing degree." Luis has stopped eating, and his knuckles are white as he clutches fork and knife without realizing it.

Two elderly musicians—a pianist and a violinist—regale us with old tangos from the twenties. A sound that reminds me of the old street organs: metallic, jarring notes that filled Buenos Aires at the beginning of the century. D'Arienzo, Canaro, Calò, musicians who gave us those first immortal successes.

"But your father?" At times it's embarrassing to have been brought up as comfortably as I was, knowing nothing of life's struggle. But Luis is one of those people who is never envious, who concentrates solely on bettering himself, leaving behind all of his bad memories.

"He died soon after my mother."

"*Oddio!* No one would ever believe it was a true story."

Poor kid. I listen to his story, the eternal chronicle of love and rejection. And, in his case, of difficult choices and wishes. "Because of my dissatisfaction and my frustrations, I always hurt."

"Don't bite your nails . . ." I hit his fingers impatiently.

"My conscience is constantly assaulted by a myriad of questions; they torment me, they won't leave me alone. I fan them away and yet, I tire of the constant fight, I want permission to dream. I want to be happy; I want a lasting relationship with no bitter end. Is that too much to ask?" Luis slides down on the chair. His eyes are closed, his soul wide open.

"I want to be *normal,* I want a family, my own kids . . ."

"Have you ever been in love?" I scrutinize him, already so dear to me.

"Yes, once. Only once. Everyone else was just a passing thing.

He was Italian. But it's all finished." Luis covers his eyes with his hands. "He's gone and I'm still thinking about him, asking myself what went wrong. Even now, when I open my e-mail, just the possibility of seeing his name makes my heart beat faster. It's a rush, but it's different from when I'm dancing or running. It's still unbearably painful."

"What went wrong?"

"Who knows? We were happy but one day he woke up and asked me to leave . . ." The simple act of sipping his wine helps him to hide a new, insidious rush of tears.

"What about Analia? You must be kind to her. It's the least you can do after letting her down the way you did. Thank God it all lasted less than a week."

"I think my heart doesn't agree with my brain. It must be some kind of hot-sync problem: that particular file, the file of rationality, has never been stored in my heart. Even though my head wants Analia, my heart won't agree. It would never have worked out."

I try my best to console him. I can only hug him as I do when my children hurt. God, I miss them so much. I haven't spoken to them in days and we've only been in touch by e-mail. What kind of a mother am I? It's as if all the compressed, pent-up frustrations of the past years suddenly exploded when I arrived in B.A., reducing me to a state of dangerous negligence.

"Enough of this! It's your last night here. No more talk of sadness. I promised you an evening at the Viejo Correo—this time it'll be relaxed and less scary, without the august presence of the Gods of Tango." Luis's sudden mirth shakes me from my reverie. He helps me on with my jacket, smiling, knowing full well that I'm excited at the idea of having him all to myself at the *milonga*.

Once there, my *Luis, I can't dance with these boots!* elicits a quick scolding look and an impatient *Don't you know that you have to carry your shoes with you at all times?* I feel guilty, but my unexpected flight to the Mendoza region—not to mention the dissolution of my marriage and my fears about my return to New York—are all pretty good excuses for forgetfulness.

"All right, don't worry. *Espera.*" Without adding another word, Luis disappears and I'm left alone with a bottle of *sidra,* the famous *champagne de los pobres* he adores. We've come full circle.

Today Ellie isn't with me and I'm left to myself and my own discoveries. Will I have a good evening? Will I score lots of invitations?

"No, *disculpe,* I don't have my dancing shoes . . . *No tengo zapatos* . . ." I have to repeat several times, shaking my head and smiling at those kind *tangueros* who invite me to dance. I hope I'm not ruining my chances for future invitations.

A husky voice interrupts my thoughts. "*Hola! Cómo estás?*" I look up to meet the dazzling smile of a remarkable young woman, whose looks combine a sure femininity with a peculiar harshness—I can't quite put my finger on what makes her so striking.

"Would you like to try these?" A pair of high-heeled black shoes dangles from the long red nails of a soft hand. The lower notes of her voice once again strike me as not quite matching the sensuous looks she flaunts. "These are a forty, should fit . . ."

"How do you know?" I look at her in surprise.

"*Bueno, soy Tamara, amiga de Luis* . . ." She whispers as sweetly as if she were reciting poetry. "I always carry another pair of shoes. Just in case." Tamara? Who's Tamara? I jump up, looking for Luis, and there he is, tickled by my reaction, delighted that his friend has surprised me.

Tamara might as well have been funneled into her crimson jersey dress—it leaves *nothing* to the imagination. Flaming red hair cascades on her shoulders in artistically composed curls; at second sight, I notice that heavy makeup covers a less-than-perfect complexion. There's a hint of dark shadow on her cheeks . . . Big golden eyes flutter their long lashes at me expectantly, and—as she bends—long diamond earrings sway provocatively over her shoulders.

"*Gracias, mil gracias,*" I stammer, confused. I try on the shoes, my head racing with thousands of questions. Now I get it: a drag queen! I look up at Luis and burst into frenetic laughter, immediately infecting him. Tamara stands up, grinning at the two of us. But her shoes fit perfectly and I'm ready, happy that my night has been saved.

"So, what did you think of Hernán-Tamara? She's a famous TV personality and the only transvestite you'll ever find in a *milonga*. At least for the time being." Luis revels in the hilarity of the situation.

"This is the first time in my life that I've borrowed from a drag queen. It's supposed to be the other way around!" I'm already happily folded in his arms, navigating the room. "You must tell me more."

I can't believe I'm the same Francesca who only a week ago sat terrified and intimidated in a corner. Now I'm here, borrowing shoes from a drag queen and having *a conversation* as I dance!

Tango's close embrace can produce miracles—fleeting pleasures that last the few minutes it takes to dance a song. There is the clean scent of a starched shirt, the subtle fragrance of a great aftershave, a firm lead that allows the woman to express herself. When I relax and close my eyes, I know I'm closer to the secret of this dance: it's like jumping on a boat and allowing the wind to fill the sail at full strength.

Luis can make anyone believe that they are a superb dancer. My cheek against his, the tip of my nose lost in his curls, I let myself go, transported by the music. Every tango plays only for me, the *bandoneón* dedicates each note to me, Francesca. It makes me shiver and cry inside. Dancing with Luis—in my best moments of course, when my body remembers all the instructions—is like being under a magic spell that envelops only the two of us, and separates us from the whole world. I allow myself to be conquered by the sensuality of the movements and follow the music transmitted by his body.

"Thank you! Your shoes saved me." At the end of the dance I take Tamara's hand in mine and she smiles back at me shyly.

"*Por favor . . .*" She shrugs.

Amague

(A Fake)

Tú canción
tiene el frío del último encuentro.
Tú canción
se hace amarga en la sal del recuerdo.
Yo no sé
Si tu voz es la flor de una pena . . .

"Malena"

It's Sunday afternoon and I'm in the car on the way to Ezeiza, the international airport. I've been crying—more or less—since I woke up and can't seem to stop, not even now that I'm in Roberto's arms. If I go on like this, I'll turn into a fountain like the naiad Pirene of my school years, and maybe become part of Argentinean mythology. And to think that I've always held *i piagnoni*—those crybabies who find refuge and release in floods of tears—in great contempt.

"Francesca, don't go! Stay with me. You're scared at the idea of George and New York. Stay with me," he pleads, holding my hand, scanning for signs that I want to be with him, too.

I'm terrified of my own desires, scared by my reaction to his love and passion. My inclination to run away from my life in New York frightens me. I want to stay here, I need to continue to feel alive, to feel like a *real* woman capable of living a passionate life. But how could I do that at my age? I have to grow up and bite the bullet. Either I save my marriage—if it's still possible—or I figure out what options I have for the future. I'm an emotional wreck right now, and poor Roberto is trying in vain to pick up the pieces.

The car proceeds smoothly, running over the highway, leaving Buenos Aires and its million lights behind. In a way it seems as if I've been living in a dream during these past weeks. Days and hours have melted into each other: tango, dramas, new friends, sex . . .

Only a few hours ago I woke up on a sofa! I yawned and realized that I was in my *milonga* clothes: black silk trousers and an embroidered top. In this country I'm either busy making love like I've never done it before, or I'm trading secrets for hours, just like I did in high school! I'm as irresponsible as a teenager. Luis and I had come back at four a.m. and decided to have a *trago,* a drink. Well, one thing led to another and we started sharing even more secrets, opening our hearts. It was a feeling I hadn't experienced since my college days: up until dawn, talking, trying to analyze and solve our problems. Then, just like that, we fell asleep, next to each other on the couch, sharing the warmth of our new friendship.

I slowly got up, leaving Luis asleep, and crept to the bathroom. My conversation with him weighed heavily on my mind and I looked at the mirror expecting to see the gloomy shadow that strangled my soul: Luis's past, my future with George, my brief, intense affair with Roberto.

I yearned for him, I wished he was there. Would he remember to call me before I left? I suddenly realized that I had never given

him my New York numbers. I combed my hair and looked criti-
cally at my reflection. Did I really care about Roberto? Had it been
a dream? I was still there, and I looked the same as always . . .

The CD Luis gave me two weeks ago, *Demoliendo tangos,* must
have been a premonition, as in the past days I've actually demol-
ished my entire life. Tango has awakened my body through its
notes and *letras,* and now I have to feed this new hunger. It's not
easy to start from scratch, and I have no idea what I'm going to do
once I'm back in New York.

"*Buenos días,* Francesca!" Luis peeped in the doorway. We had
to laugh at the improbable couple reflected in the mirror: his hair
stood up as high as an eighteenth-century French wig. An Argentinean *Roi Soleil!*

"Do you think Analia will forgive me? Will we stay friends?
Will we continue to dance together?"

"My dear, it takes two—not just to tango, right? I think that
everyone has acted irresponsibly here. Including me."

Luis lowered his head, looking down. He twisted his hands
and remained silent. "You're right," he whispered, without looking at me.

I took him by the arm and made him sit down at the kitchen
table. A good coffee would help both of us to think straight. I
opened the freezer, and sure enough, Ellie had saved all the *medialunas* I'd bought before embarking on my excellent adventure
with Roberto.

"I'm never going to touch a woman again in my life. Not even
with a ten-foot pole! Why would I bother?" But his demeanor
belied his words; his eyes—always the mirror of his soul—had
darkened, and his jaw set on a hard line.

"Luis, *quel che è fatto è fatto.* What's done is done. Stop thinking about the past and concentrate on the present. Analia should
remain an important person in your life, but from now on, you

should keep your hands off her. Your sexual hunger was simply libido, and not a real attachment."

On the other hand, I know that for Analia it's different and she's translated all that Luis told her to suit her own wishes, continuously hoping that he will change. If he holds her hand, Analia imagines that his stomach does a little flip just as hers does. When he closes his eyes—dancing a tango—she hopes that his heart leaps inside his chest and that he feels the same *boom* that echoes inside hers.

In order to understand Analia, he has only to think of his own affair with his Italian lover and how much it still hurts. I'd touched a raw nerve; I saw it in his eyes, the way he looked at me while I was talking. I could almost see his tail tucked between his legs.

Luis shifted uneasily under my direct stare. I was harsh, but his delight in being loved, in being the chosen one, could bring tragedy in this situation.

My cell rang and we looked at each other, surprised. It seemed as if we'd slipped into another time and that, while talking, reality had disappeared.

"Let's see: you just woke up and are thinking about your last night at the *milonga*." Ellie's voice reached my soul.

"Ciao!" I squeaked with happiness. "Luis! Come here, it's Ellie! Ellie, I am *dying* to see you tomorrow, in New York. I'll come to your place as soon as I land. I need an injection of courage before I meet George." I picked up the two books I'd brought from the States—untouched—and moved to my bedroom to start packing. Later, on the plane, I would read. Over the past weeks, though, even the pleasure of a book eluded me. That, too, was completely atypical.

After a brief conversation with Ellie, I sat on the bed looking in horror at all the extra clothes—and shoes, of course!—I had accumulated over the course of fifteen days. You'd never suspect that I hate to travel overloaded with too much stuff. It's obvious that Roberto loves a sophisticated woman next to him—but would he accept me and still love me in my baggy work clothes? When I'm cooking or writing, I can't even *think* of dressing up.

"Stop worrying now. Go, I must finish packing. Nothing you can do at this point. Just talk to Analia and ask her for forgiveness." I gently showed Luis to the door. "You owe it to her." He had behaved none too well from the very beginning. Such a doomed love affair. What a pity.

"I'm okay, don't worry. I'll see you in New York a week from now." Luis held me like he didn't want to leave me. "Meeting you was special. I know our friendship will be important. Thank you."

Ellie, Luis, Analia, Roberto—all gone and scattered around. So much has happened in such a short time. It's as if the normal cycles of life were suddenly put on fast-forward, and I've been propelled into a different world.

I went to my computer to check my e-mail. Was I expecting something from George? What could I possibly think—or hope—he'd write? But my in-box was dry: a desert of communication, not even a note from the kids. Immediate guilt washed over me. I cringed. I was the one who had neglected my family, absorbed as I was with my passions, my disasters. Everything I'd built during all those disciplined years of wifehood and motherhood was upside down.

Dear all,

I bit my fingernails, staring at the screen.

But how could I write about the joys of learning tango and getting to know B.A., when inside I was slowly dying? Rereading some of my mail made me realize how different I was only two weeks ago. If my parents and kids only knew.

I was halfway through my description of the difficulty of *walk-ing*—the way a tango teacher expects you to—when the doorbell rang.

"Francesca, *querida!*" Roberto bounced into the apartment carrying with him the happiness I thought I'd left behind in Men-doza. Suddenly I felt as light as a spring leaf. Forget the e-mail, forget the family. All of it could wait.

"What are you doing here? You're supposed to be in Córdoba!" But deep inside I wasn't too surprised. I'd hoped against hope to see him again before leaving.

"I managed to get out of my polo game and the plane took me straight to Baires. We still have the entire afternoon ahead of us." Roberto took me in his arms and covered me with kisses, all over my nose, my lips, and my chin. I laughed, wiggling in his arms to get a look at him—to touch his lips, his nose, to make sure that he was really with me.

"You've got to try this before you leave." He carried a bottle of Escorihuela Gascón, a wonderful red wine from the Mendoza region. "And I even brought you homemade *dulce de leche.* Your favorite." He took a large plastic container from a shopping bag and placed it on the kitchen table. Mmm! I nearly swooned at the intoxicating smell of the perfect golden confection.

But as soon as I tried to steal another look at his edible loot, Roberto's feverish hands were all over me. It was impossible to remain indifferent: I answered his frenzy, abandoning my body to his with the avidity of a starving woman. When I see him, he takes hold of my entire being with a force I've never experienced in my life. Only a day, and we couldn't keep off each other. Thank God Luis was already gone!

I realized that I'd ached for him for all the hours that had sepa-rated us. The moment he touched me, all pain was gone and that mad craving instantly calmed down—like the sullen, heavy quiet before a storm—in anticipation of what was to come. Roberto slowed down and took my face in his hands, and then continued his crazy kissing, stopping only to look at me.

"I'll miss you so much." His words were simple whispers that pierced me like arrows. I didn't want to be reminded that I had to leave him.

"Take me, please. I want to make love to you until it's time for me to go. Shush! Just love me." I took his arm and guided him to my bedroom. I undressed slowly and helped him take off his shirt. I made him lie down on the bed, kicking away all the shirts and sweaters I had stacked in neat piles. Packing could wait.

I love his body: those muscles sculpted over his chest, his powerful arms, his long, strong legs. I pushed down his trousers and then bent to kiss his chest, his navel, down to his pubes, where I could see his hunger for me. I held his penis in my hands and stroked it, kissing it, taking him in my mouth, until I saw that he couldn't contain his ardor anymore. At that point I straddled him and lowered my body onto his. I watched my lover intently, happy to see the thirst in his eyes, his joy in being the recipient of my desire. I exulted in his obvious pleasure as I encased him in me. I gave him a few seconds to fill me, accommodating my body to fit, and then, rhythmically, I started to ride him, bending over to reach his lips with mine. I needed us to become one.

Roberto moaned as my hair brushed his chest. His hands took hold of my breasts and started pulling my nipples, twisting them gently. As the rhythm changed and we both started moving more slowly—tenderness taking over from frenzy—a kind of sadness turned our lovemaking into an even more meaningful moment. Every inch of our bodies longed for each other, and powerful feelings ran through us like heavy raindrops sucked up by needy soil. By then we had reached a totally different plateau of sensation.

"Wait . . ." Roberto clasped my shoulders, pushing me away. He closed his eyes and placed my fingers over his heart. "Feel it . . ." It pounded inside like waves of an infuriated ocean, reverberated through his chest like thunder.

I stopped and kissed him again, softly, at the corner of his mouth. I licked his eyes and brushed his cheeks with my lips, as if I could swallow his entire being and make it mine forever.

"Roberto, I'm coming. I'm sorry . . ." An enormous wave of excitement took over and, without any warning, it over-whelmed me. I cried with anguish and joy, passion and fear. "I am yours, yours, *yours* . . ." I looked at Roberto's eyes and saw them dilate with passion. His body arched and he filled me with his love.

The pale winter sun had washed the room with a bright lemony light which was reflected in the half-broken mirror. Even the old paint, peeling off the walls, took on an improbable metallic shade. The solitary green plant in the corner—a palm as shabby as a boa in a small-town burlesque—had assumed a new beauty. When the music of his desire invaded me, the drab buildings outside disappeared; and then there were only notes to be pursued, achieved, reached, interpreted. Yes, I would miss my modest Abasto apartment.

The sweetness of our final lovemaking was different from all the lust we had experienced in the previous days and it filled us with something as primordial and as surprising as first love. We stayed silent, holding each other, listening to our bodies until we fell asleep, nursing our physicality, content to have been together.

I woke up a few minutes later to find his eyes wet with tears, and he hugged me again, silently. I had no need for words either, and took shelter in his arms as if he were my last refuge. I started crying.

"Mi corazón una mentira pide
para esperar tu imposible llamado.
Yo no quiero que nadie se imagine
cómo es de amarga y honda mi eterna soledad . . ."

Roberto sang sotto voce the old *letras* of an even older tango.

"Stay with me. Marry me. I can't be wrong; you must feel the way I do. I can hear it in your voice; I read it in your body and the way you have surrendered to me. I recognize it in your eyes when they look at mine." Roberto took me in his arms and rocked me like a child, whispering sweet words, passing his hand through my hair, brushing my forehead, my cheeks, tracing the lines of my nose, my chin.

"I can't, Roberto. I just can't. I must go back to New York, I have to sort out my life." I lifted up to kiss him all over his hazel eyes. Had any man ever been so tender with me? And yet I was afraid of dropping my resistance and feared what could happen in the future. This entire situation was only an interlude: real life is not like this and I don't believe in abandoning all self-imposed constraints and letting go in the name of just a dream. Not at my age, anyway.

"Francesca, think about it. What will you do in the States? At least stay here a little longer. Move in with me!" Roberto pleaded. His soft lips played with my lobes, stroking them, kissing them.

"I can't." I'd frozen up. My usual fear of being dominated, of not being in control, had suddenly resurfaced. "No, Roberto, I have to go."

I tenderly pushed him away from me. "I'll be back. Buenos Aires is not that far from New York. Let me go and see with my own eyes what's happened. I have to confront George and find out about Isabel."

"But you *know* what happened between them! You know that they were together for the last few years, right? When I met Isabel she hinted that she had an ongoing love affair and her reaction when she met you was clear proof that something was wrong, wasn't it?"

"How can you be sure?" I stubbornly wanted to hide behind the truth.

"I know her and by now we both have the facts. How can you accept George's behavior? He practically kept you as his glorified personal cook." Roberto shook me, frowning. "You weren't a woman anymore to him. How could he?"

"Roberto, you have to admit that you barely know me. We've had a few days of pure bliss; let's not ruin it with fake hopes of a future together. You're much younger than me. You deserve a woman who can give you children, somebody who can be a credit to you socially. You're just coming out of a bad marriage yourself. How can you plunge, headfirst, into another relationship with no chance for success?" A ten-year difference; a decade older: I can't lose sight of these facts. A heavy curtain of fear slowly lowered itself between us while a portentous Greek chorus intoned, Danger, danger! I lifted my chin and looked straight into his eyes.

"How do you define success? And what do you think are those parameters that a woman has to meet? Who decides these things? You're being unfair. Why are you so afraid? Of what? Of suffering? Are you a coward?" Roberto let go of me, angrily, and wrapped a towel around his hips. He walked to the living room and poured himself a glass of wine.

"Please, *amore mio,* please, don't be angry with me. Let's not ruin our last afternoon together. You're right—I *am* a coward. I'm afraid of suffering and I am only too aware of my age and both our positions. I'm a married woman with children and you are an important player in the Argentinean business world. Whatever we do is bound to affect a lot of lives. How can we decide anything in the space of just a few days?"

I know I'm right. I know that I've got to rely on my smarts. If only there wasn't that powerful thing pulsing away in my chest, gnawing at me, pulling my guts . . .

"Don't say anything. This is not the moment. You must be patient."

Automatically I latched on to the spoon and opened the jar in front of me. *Dulce de leche,* my panacea.

I reach up and feel for my eyes, in order to ensure that I haven't already metamorphosed into the naiad I imagined I've become. What an ending to my trip to Buenos Aires. And yet I wouldn't have given it up for all the gold in the world. In the past days here, I have finally lived. I've discovered that I'm still in full possession of my sexuality, that I'm still desirable—a woman with all the same wishes and needs of a long time ago, before I married and turned into a wife, a mother. Roberto and tango have brought the old Francesca back and I've never felt so young.

Will it last? What will happen to me, to *us*?

I lie quietly in Roberto's arms. He doesn't move and I can feel his calm breathing. My nose in his jacket, I enjoy his scent and just let myself be. I can feel the driver's eyes checking us out from time to time in the mirror. He must have seen a lot in all his years of working for him. I wish I could feel carefree, but I must still suffer from some outmoded sense of shame. I'll admit—but only to myself—that I would like to officially belong to Roberto. And yet I'm perfectly aware that it just can't be. I'll have to file our relationship away as what it really is: an impossible dream.

"I want you to call me the moment you land at JFK. Will you?" His words startle me. "And I'll see what I can do to come and visit you soon in New York."

"What are the plans as far as you and Isabel are concerned? Will all of this interfere with the international launch of the clinics?" I'm worried that my presence has changed the balance in his relationship with my nemesis.

"Still unclear. I have a conference call later on with the CEO. You do realize that I don't give a damn? I wouldn't have given up a second of our days and nights together. Do you believe me? You probably don't understand what you represent for me."

I sigh and snuggle deeper into his arms. I wish I could believe not just his words but also in the possibility of a future together. I want to memorize him. I'll get his cologne, Bulgari Blue, at the airport and take it with me on the plane. I'll close my eyes and think about him.

"You've changed my life. Just being allowed to see you is a joy that fills my entire being. But I understand that you don't want to hear what I have to say. Who hurt you so much that you refuse to accept my promises? Are you afraid of romance? Don't you believe in love at first sight?" Roberto's voice rises high in the silence of the car. José, the driver, looks ahead, seemingly concentrating on driving.

At the sight of Ezeiza airport, my heart sinks. In seconds my suitcases are piled on a luggage cart and José pushes it to the check-in counter.

Passport, ticket. No, I haven't allowed anyone to touch my luggage and no, I have nothing inside that resembles a weapon. Only my heart: it looks and sounds like a grenade and it's about to explode. I smile automatically at the security agent; he is only doing his job. I am the one who's dying inside.

"I love you . . ." Roberto takes me into his arms and—for the last time—his lips touch mine. He kisses me with a passion that spills over the two of us, like a river in flood.

"I'm sorry," I whisper. I have to leave him. Now! Immediately! It will only get more difficult, the longer I wait. I can't allow myself to believe in this dream, as quixotic as any cheesy romance novel I've ever read. I'm a hardened adult, and I know what's best for me. ·

I can't even make myself confess that I love him.

He looks at me, his eyes full of tears. I reach for him. "Roberto." And I leave him behind, walking straight through passport control. I show my documents to the airline staff, pulling my hand luggage behind me. I don't want to turn around to see him; it's too painful. But then I give up and wave. He stands there, not moving, like the biblical statue of salt.

The first-class lounge is quiet. Very few travelers tonight, and all the ground hostesses fret around me. I ask myself if it's just their natural kindness—one of the best traits in this country—or if they've all read *Gente* recently.

Those looks that try to be unobtrusive are actually as distracting as direct stares and intrusive demands. But nothing really matters now. I commandeer an entire group of chairs around a table, scattering my belongings everywhere to suggest that a large group of travelers has appropriated the space. I don't want anyone to sit next to me. I just want to cry.

I lie back, my head against the chair. I close my eyes and wait for those tears to come. But I'm empty now. Empty of everything: of thoughts, of fears, the ability to worry or decide a thing.

From my ears to my heart, my iPod delivers words and music, even more emotion. Exhausted, I barely register the words of Pink Martini's "La Soledad."

. . .While I, ignorant of the meaning of love,
Protected my heart.

Slowly, slowly I drift away.

"We will be boarding in a few minutes, *señora*."The hostess's voice brings me back from the depths, like a pump inside a still pond creasing the limpid surface with rippling waves of emotion. I jump in my chair and look up at her.

"What did you say? Which flight?" I can't quite see straight.

"Flight 956 to New York. Your flight, madam," she repeats slowly, like a teacher talking to a student.

"New York?" I parrot, astonished.

Suddenly I know. I realize what I couldn't before. And yet it was all so clear from the very beginning! Why am I giving up happiness? I can't allow it to pass me by: *I, ignorant of the meaning of love, protected my heart.*

Why do I have to follow this rigid discipline I've inflicted on myself? My children are grown up—they've already begun their adult lives—and George doesn't want me. He's made that clear for years now. Why did I impose this ridiculous self-flagellation on myself? Is it my Catholic upbringing?

I jump up and almost collide with the hostess. I gather my bags and jacket, sweater and magazines.

"There's no rush; I'll accompany you to the plane personally. Don't worry!" The woman is horrified and tries to calm me down.

She doesn't understand.

"Forget about the plane. I'm not leaving. Get my bags off it. I'll call the airline and tell them where to send my things. Don't worry. I'll pay!" I rush out of the lounge and start running, my heart beating furiously in my chest. I trail my luggage behind, my coat sleeves dusting the floor as I stride through the corridors.

No way back from this point on! A big sign warns me that I might regret my decision later on.

But I don't care.

I push past the other passengers in the departure hall. I feverishly search for the sign for ground transportation. I'll take the first car I can find: A taxi? A *remise*? I don't care. I run. I cannot find my happiness fast enough. I will not allow cowardice to dictate my behavior, to impose on my feelings, to silence my heart.

And then I see him. I stop.

Roberto sits on a bench, doubled over. He doesn't move, his elbows on his knees, his head inside his hands.

"Buenas tardes!" I tap him on the shoulder.

Acknowledgments

I must begin with Walter Perez, a great tango teacher and friend, whose invaluable support allowed me to chronicle the wonders of the tango world. Because of him I was able to have a unique insight into the Buenos Aires days and nights. To many more dances together!

And then Assia, who made me write the novel that was bubbling up inside me with such urgency. She *knew* I had to do it. She pushed me, and, as always, I listened.

My eternal gratitude to Jane Kramer, who first read it when I was *stuck*. She's responsible for the first person choice. Afterward it all flowed out of the keyboard, easily.

Maria Campbell, who's always believed in me and always pushed me even when presented with those crude first pages. And my über-agent, Michael, who took me on just on the basis of an idea: a tango novel. *And why not? I know you can do it,* he said, and I did it.

Jill Foulston, friend and editor who helped me so much through the first drafts, encouraging me and rooting for Francesca. Yana Blinova who had to endure hours of chapters read aloud via Skype, from Todi to New York, from Shanghai to Manhattan.

Nan Graham, who once again surprised me by buying the unfinished manuscript. Yes, Nan, mighty Nan, whose vision I trust. Her corrections are always infuriatingly right.

Francesca Campbell, who found the perfect title, in between a *börek* and a *köfte*. (Never mind Alexander who wanted to call it "Tango and Roast Beef")

Thanks to Lynn Goldberg and Camille McDuffie, who will promote *It Takes Two* as if it were their own child. All my gratitude to Andrea Tese for lending me her lenses and to Dardo Galletto for lending me his legs.

And as usual I have to thank my husband Kimball who always supports all I do, who never asks and patiently waits to read my books until we have galleys. (Thank God he's not George!) And Saverio, who probably will never read this novel, but I know he believes in it.

And then last, but certainly not least, my wonderful Whitney Frick. Beautiful Whit who accompanied me throughout the past year, editing me, helping me, pushing me with a vision far above her age and experience. We've become friends, forgetting about the difference in years.